MY EX'S BABY

CRESCENT COVE BOOK 8

TARYN QUINN

RAINBOW rage
PUBLISHING

My Ex's Baby
© 2020 Taryn Quinn
Rainbow Rage Publishing

Cover by LateNite Designs
Photograph by Lindee Robinson Photography
Models: Travis Bendall & Kelly Kirstein

First print edition: February 2021
ISBN Print edition: 978-1-940346-67-0

ACKNOWLEDGMENTS

A special shout out to one of our favorite Wenches, Stephanie Scrivens, for always being so supportive to us and our books. You've been here since the beginning, girl!

We love you!

Sometimes we make up fictional places that end up having the same names as actual places. These are our fictional interpretations only. Please grant us leeway if our creative vision isn't true to reality.

For anyone who thinks they aren't enough.
Know that you are.

KINLEIGH

PROLOGUE

Fall - morning after Rhiannon's birth

I needed some air. Just a few minutes alone.

I wasn't used to all this peopling.

Ivy Beck, my bestest friend in all the world, had decided to have the most dramatic birth in the history of Crescent Cove—at least I was pretty sure it was. Right in the middle of Brewed Awakening's library and craft corner. Luckily, the café had been closed for an impromptu ladies' night. No alcohol for the ladies I hung out with lately, but we'd definitely been covered in glitter from our pumpkin decorating party.

I glanced down at my hands. I'd scrubbed most of the purple and pink paint and galaxy spray glitter off with the industrial strength soap at the hospital so I could hold Rhiannon for precisely seven minutes before Ivy demanded her back. I'd been there for her entry into the world—heck, my hand was still sore from Ivy's freakishly strong hold. Then again, she did create vats of ice cream for a living, so I guess it wasn't surprising.

Regardless, I'd been in the hospital all night. And I'd only gotten a precious few minutes with the little pink bundle of perfection. No one had wanted to leave Ivy alone until her husband arrived. Instead, we all took turns going in to sit with her, rotating through the waiting room like an actual princess had been born.

Rory, the princess's father and song doctor-slash-producer, had officially arrived an hour ago, thanks to a private flight. Ivy didn't even give him shit about using his status and money this time. Then again, there had been many tears since he'd missed the actual birth.

I'd agreed to be a coach with her brother, August, as a backup. I'd never truly believed I'd be tapped for the actual shindig. Especially with her overprotective husband trying to control every aspect of the last trimester.

"Kinleigh?"

I looked up.

"Could you help me post to Facebook again?"

"Didn't you just post some pictures?"

"Well, yes. But these are prettier. Rhiannon's all pinked up and sweet-looking. Isn't she?" The older woman turned her phone toward me to show off one of the photos she'd snapped from the nursery. As Rhi's grandmother and a queen bee herself, Annie Beck had been holding court in the waiting room between visits.

"Sure." I stood and took her phone. She was entitled to her excitement, of course. I was just so tired I could barely see straight.

"Oh my God. Can we see her?"

"We heard what happened as soon as we got to the diner. Even Mitch let us go without bitching."

Gina Ramos and her sister Gabby rushed in. They'd become quite tight with Ivy and I over the last few months. Of course the diner being right next door, as well as my usage of Hannah and Gabby's food service—which I might or might not have used a freaking lot—could've had something to do with that.

But this was my chance.

I escaped down the hall while Annie showed them photos of the newest addition to the Beck-Ferguson clan. I got to use clan now because we had Irish people who'd actually been born in Ireland in

2

the building. Rory's parents were on the way and that would be another whole bag of crazy.

I followed the signs for the four seasons atrium on the swanky maternity floor. The hospital had been a revolving door of people at this point. Ivy was very popular in Crescent Cove.

And while all of them were amazing, the level of love, conversation, and merriment was exhausting. I'd been riding on adrenaline for... I looked at my Apple watch.

God, was that really the time? No wonder I was exhausted.

I picked up the pace when I spotted the glass door. It was chilly due to the endless panes of lightly tinted windows, but it was so much better than the waiting room decked out in pink and blue. Seriously, were those the only colors we could come up with in the myriad rainbow colors available to us?

A handful of nurses were clustered by the door. Some mindlessly scrolling on their phones, others quietly chatting. I took a left to find a quiet corner and slumped onto a bench. I lifted my face to the early morning sunlight struggling through the dense copse of trees, giving a lovely bit of privacy to the back of the building. We were in a new medical center just outside of town that catered to maternity and rehabilitation.

Huge, leafy plants were clustered around tables and weathered barrels were jammed with mums in half a dozen colors. I grinned at one of the trees decked out in flirty little bat lights. Macy, our resident Halloween obsessed café owner, would approve. I got up and pulled out my phone to take a photo of the lights so I could find them. They would be a perfect addition to my own shop.

A pair of battered boots stuck out just beyond the large white pot. I quickly backed up so I wouldn't have to engage in any more polite chitchat, but I needn't have bothered.

A light snore would be the only conversation.

August Beck had his ancient red hoodie pulled up to shade his eyes and his arms crossed as if he was chilled. Of course that only emphasized his ridiculous arms.

The ones I shouldn't have been looking at.

Lately, he'd been the bane of my existence. His sister Ivy wasn't only my best friend, she was also pretty much the sole member of my family. That phrase *don't shit where you eat* had practically been created with me in mind.

And yet because we were alone, he was sleeping, and no one would know... I indulged a little.

His usually clean-shaven jaw was dark with stubble, which only made his stupidly perfect full lips seem even more tantalizing. No one knew how hard it was for me to ignore those lips. Especially since I shared an address with said lips—and they were attached to a distractingly attractive face. Even his lashes were long and lush. Where was the fairness? Add in the huge, mouth-watering body and my hormones had been on hyperdrive for well over a year.

I'd known him for far longer. I wasn't going to lie to anyone, including myself, and say I'd never had improper thoughts about Ivy's older brother. However, they'd been the fleeting kind that any woman had about an attractive guy.

Healthy.

Not obsessive in the least.

Until last year.

And it was all his fault. We shared the rent on a storefront on Main Street. Neither one of us could afford it on our own, but he took the bottom half and I took the top—Kinleigh's Attic. I mean, c'mon, it couldn't have been more perfect.

Except for the part where he was forever intruding on my space to fix things and making excuses to increase my security. Like it was any of his concern how I ran my business. He just kept showing up and taking over.

Now the scent of rain and sawdust made my girl parts get all tingly.

August's scent.

And no amount of essential oils and incense got rid of it.

That part about his sister being my bestie? Yeah, that made things sticky. Well, actually, didn't allow me to get sticky. Okay, *ew*...but relevant. Lately, all I could think about was mounting him on a pair of sawhorses at the back of his workshop.

The worst part was the little devil on my shoulder who kept whispering for me to just get him out of my system. Because most men never hung around long enough for me to get attached. Actually, no one had ever hung around except Ivy.

And that was exactly why I kept stuffing down these lusty daydreams. Even if facing my empty bed every damn night was getting harder and harder to do.

The door to the atrium slammed and August jerked awake.

Shit.

His sleepy eyes drifted down my body to where I clutched my phone before he arched an eyebrow at me. "You wouldn't be taking pictures of me drooling or something, right?"

I laughed. "Bat lights beside you, actually. But it would make a good Instagram story. Drooling baby Rhiannon and Uncle Auggie are a matching pair."

He sat up, stretched, and yawned so huge I could hear his jaw pop. "I'm so tired I don't even care if you do."

I dropped onto the bench beside him. "Same."

He tucked his hands under his arms again and scrunched down beside me to my height.

I gave him a wary side-eye. "What?"

"Nothing. I'm assuming the revolving door is still going strong?"

"Only way I escaped." I mirrored his crossed arms situation. It was better than curling against him like my traitorous body wanted to. Partially so I could sleep, but the other half of me wanted to breathe in his rain-scented cologne or soap and find out just how blessed he was behind those Carhartt work pants.

I needed an intervention.

Or to soak my head.

"Hey, maybe we can go home then?" He straightened and shoved his hood down. "Coaching is done now that Lucky Charms finally showed up."

When Ivy called her husband that, it was usually with affection.

5

Not so much when it came to August with his brother-in-law. "Don't sound so bitchy. Rory feels guilty enough."

August stood up with a grunt. "He shouldn't have left her alone."

"Don't go in there and make him feel bad."

He held his hand out to me. "No problem. I just won't talk to him."

I rolled my eyes. I paused for a moment before putting my hand in his.

The rolling low frequency hum started at my fingertips and sent shockwaves through my bones. Thankfully, I was alone in this problem.

What he did not know would not embarrass me.

I took my hand back and shoved them both into my pockets. "I can get a ride back with Gina."

"No, I'll take you home."

"Your house is the other direction."

"So?"

"You've been up all night. Obviously, you're tired."

"So are you. At least I got a twenty-minute nap." He slid an arm around my shoulders and hauled me against him. "Ivy would never forgive me."

"Can't have that." I curled my arm around his back automatically and got a full-frontal attack of his scent. Damn him. Most dudes would smell like gym socks after a night of stress-sweating through coaching a birth then spending the night in a hospital.

Life just wasn't fair.

We managed to only get waylaid for a few minutes with his parents. Gina and Gabby had already gone down to the nursery to see the baby with Ivy. Part of me wanted to join them and see her again, but the other half of me was so done.

Watching Ivy and Rory with their heads together, whispering and crying, made my chest hurt for reasons I did not want to analyze.

I let August lead me out to find the sun had already disappeared. Living in a lake town gave us a front row seat to rolling clouds on a semi-daily basis. It just made the sunny days seem all the sweeter. Fall was crisp in the air, and I burrowed into my lightweight jacket.

Suddenly, he draped a hoodie over my shoulders, and I was literally shrouded in August's scent.

Was swooning allowed if it was only in my brain?

When he opened the passenger side door to his truck, I finally snapped him into focus.

"You all right?"

"Just tired."

Still studying me, he blocked the open truck door. His stupid shoulders were so wide and distracting.

"You want to get this show on the road?" My tone was sharper than it should have been, but he was crowding me and dammit, my resistance was low.

I was supposed to be the bigger person.

The smarter one.

Not that he probably noticed my heart rate skyrocketing and my need for a new pair of panties. Because goddess, it was ridiculous how twisted I was getting.

Breathe.

To steady myself, I grabbed the small nest of fluorite and amethyst I kept in an Art Deco glass locket I'd found last summer. I'd bought it to resell, but something about it had called to me. And I would've done just about anything to calm the hell down during Ivy's pregnancy. As it was, I had a new person in my life with Rory, and my niece Rhiannon. Things had been changing at a rapid rate, and no amount of chill vibrations from crystals were helping right now.

"You're being weird." He laid both his bear paws on my shoulders, his thumb skimming over the chain of my necklace.

I shut my eyes and counted to five. I knew he was just trying to be the sweet August I knew he was under the gruff and grumbles. He liked his space, same as I did. It was why we understood each other and had leaned hard on one another during Ivy's whirlwind romance and pregnancy.

Maybe that was why I was having such a hard time.

Things would go back to—

My eyes shot open.

7

Dear goddess.

Warm, firm lips brushed along mine. His hands slid higher on my shoulders and up to frame my face. His eyes were closed so he couldn't see my panic.

I couldn't decide if I wanted to haul him closer or shove him away.

My heartbeat roared in my ears as he swiped his tongue ever so gently along the seam of my lips and panic got beat over the head by my rampaging lust. I went onto my toes and there was nothing but the scent of wood-soaked rain and Diet Coke-flavored August.

The best taste in the world.

I twisted my fingers into the front of his T-shirt and took everything. My mouth raced over his, and my fingers snaked under the hem of his shirt to his rock-hard belly. The just-right level of chest hair over rippling muscles made me want more. His skin was so warm and smooth that I wanted to spend all day finding every place that would make him shiver under my touch.

He groaned into my mouth when my nail scraped over a nipple.

Sweet August left the building.

He turned me into the frame of the door, bracing one arm on the roof of the truck and the other around my waist as he obliterated my brain. There was a fine art to kissing. I'd kissed plenty of males in my years on the planet. Most never got past that because if you couldn't kiss then my interest level hit the skids.

August had fourteen freaking medals—all gold.

The scruff on his face abraded my flesh, but it only ramped up the buzzing under my skin. My heartbeat thundered, and my breath caught in my chest. He opened me up, demanding participation, and I gave it. I twined my arms around his back, my nails digging into his muscles and smooth skin.

I plastered myself to him until there was no air between us.

My back arched as he nearly bent me backward to get closer. His teeth scraped over my lower lip and chin to my neck. His lips and tongue made quick and thorough trails along each side to nip at my ear before going back to my mouth once more.

I couldn't catch up.

I couldn't control it.

I couldn't breathe.

Too much.

Too hot.

Too perfect.

I pushed him back. "Stop."

Dazed, he clutched the back of my neck and went for my throat again.

"August."

No.

Everything inside me railed against the word, but I knew this was a mistake. I'd hurt him. I'd steep myself in the taste of him, in the utter pleasure, but then I'd ruin everything.

I always did.

I couldn't chance it.

Not with him. Not Ivy's brother.

I shoved him back. "What are you doing?"

He smiled into my mouth and nipped my lower lip. "Kissing you."

"Why?"

He frowned, the heat and playfulness draining from his eyes. "Didn't you want me to?"

I swallowed down the need to scream *yes.* I wanted it so much it terrified me. "Are you crazy? Ivy would kill us."

He took a step back. "Why would she care?"

"We're family. It's weird." I grasped at anything. "It's just the adrenaline from the baby. I don't want to ruin..." *Everything.* "Our friendship."

"It wouldn't."

"It would." I ducked under his arm. "It's not real."

"It tasted real. I like kissing you, Kinleigh." He rubbed the back of his neck. "We can be adults. If it didn't work out, we'd be fine."

See, he knew. I wasn't the one that men took home to mom. I was the weird orphan girl his mom put up with because Ivy loved me. I shook my head. "I work upstairs. We'd have to see each other every day." The laugh that came out of my chest was rusty and too high-pitched. "Imagine us getting naked? It's just crazy." So crazy that I couldn't stop thinking about it. I touched my lips. "Crazy."

His face went stony. "Sorry kissing me was so abhorrent."

"No, it was fine."

"Fine? Thanks." He raked his fingers through his hair. "Let me just drop you off."

I looked around the parking lot and spotted Gina. "No, it's okay. I'll just go with the girls." I shouted Gina's name.

She twisted around, her dark hair in a ponytail and half of her diner uniform already on.

"Can I grab a ride?" I shouted.

She nodded and made a *come on* gesture.

"See?" My voice was more than a little panicky as I gazed at August. His forehead was lined, and his jaw was like granite. He looked perplexed…and pissed. "You can go home, and we'll just forget this happened. Okay?"

"Right." He slammed the door. "Sure."

I could go to work. Crash on the couch in my office for a few hours then open up the store.

Working was smart. It was the one thing I'd always been good at.

Not marriage material, Kin. You're good with the biz side. Not so much the personal.

I started to take off his hoodie, but he shook his head. "Keep it."

"Thanks."

What was I going to do with this? Not wear it to bed when I was cold, that was for sure.

I definitely wasn't going to sniff it to remember how it had been to kiss him—and for him to kiss me back. He'd even started it.

Why had he started it?

"Yeah. See ya whenever." Then he disappeared around the front of his truck and got in.

I watched him pull out of the space and drive toward the exit without a backward glance. My throat was on fire, and I was pretty sure I was going to keel over from an adrenaline crash. Two of them in the span of twelve hours.

"You okay, Kinleigh?" Gina crossed the parking lot to me. "Was August all right?" Her gaze dropped to my mouth.

Did it look he'd just kissed the hell out of me? My stupid Irish skin showed everything. I pushed my hair out of my face. I probably looked like a train wreck. "Yeah, just tired. I didn't want to make him go all the way to my house then to his. Opposite directions."

"Oh." She smiled brightly, just like Gina always did. Thankfully, she didn't call me out on my obvious bullshit response. I must've looked really bad. "Yeah, that makes total sense."

Of course it did.

See? I could be smart. I hadn't ruined anything.

I'd prevented a colossal mistake just in time.

ONE

KINLEIGH

New Year's Eve

I GAZED OUT THE WINDOW OF MY SHOP. KINLEIGH'S ATTIC WAS currently closed. Heck, most of Crescent Cove was currently closed, and not just because it was the biggest night to party. Nope, the place had practically shut down because we were all going to witness the very chilly nuptials of two of the central figures of our town.

Macy Devereaux and John Gideon were getting hitched in a very impromptu New Year's Eve wedding at the gazebo. Their fast-forwarded timeline was occurring mostly because Macy was knocked up. Not really a shocker in this town, but they were one of the few couples who'd actually gotten engaged before implantation.

However, the real kicker was that Macy had given the green light to starting a family. Then the water in the Cove had struck again. It was almost research-worthy. Actually, I'd seen more than one article pop up on Reddit about our little town's baby boom.

If we had to be famous for something, I guess the baby thing wasn't a bad deal. But for once, today wasn't about babies. It was about love.

For a thrown together wedding, the view was breathtaking. Personally, I'd figured a Halloween wedding was totally going to be their thing. However, the baby's due date was going to make that a big ol' *no.*

I leaned against the windowsill, tapping my short blue nails against the frosty panes of my window. The sun had set, dropping the temperature quite a bit from what it had been earlier this afternoon. The rare sunshine had been a bonus for decorating the pier and surrounding trees. I could see just enough of the park from the back of my shop to get a peek at what the guys in Gideon's crew had been up to.

Mason jars danced from the branches, thanks to the brisk wind off the water. I knew they were lit up with battery-powered tealights since the guys had raided my shop and all the nearby ones for any and all they could find. Amazon Prime didn't have enough tiny candles to handle the look Vee—Veronica Masterson, the co-matron of honor and the bakery wiz over at Brewed Awakening—was determined to pull off.

She and Rylee Kramer were part of Macy's very small inner circle and were prepared to move heaven and earth to make this wedding as special as possible.

Vee was also heavily pregnant and had taken on some Macy personality traits over the last few days. Yikes. Her husband, Murphy, was one of Gideon's closest friends, so they were all fired up to make this wedding as perfect as possible given the abbreviated timetable.

The gazebo itself was still lit up from Christmas, but they'd swapped out the fat vintage colored lights along the overhang with sassy orange ones. Bats hung between each bulb. The rest was a wash of white twinkle lights everywhere with a Macy flavor.

Meaning more bats. I was surprised there were no floating horror movie masks or creepy severed heads, but maybe they were going for subtlety.

I turned back to the dress form standing in the center of my dressing area. I'd pushed all the comfy chairs and oversized bean bag chairs aside to make room for the women who would be coming in to get ready for the wedding. The wedding party was small, but I wanted to make them as comfortable as possible.

I'd been in charge of altering a vintage cream dress we'd found on a shopping trip into one of the big bridal boutiques in Syracuse. I'd used all the tricks in my arsenal to make the dress as Macy as possible. Including a little surprise I'd found at one of my favorite online vendors.

Kristy always had the perfect gothic one of a kind—or in this case, a dozen—items.

I fluffed out the short train I'd added to the dress. I'd held onto the extra yard of almond-colored silk for something special, and this was about as perfect as it got. I'd spent all night cutting out spaces for the appliqués I'd bought and had hand sewn in each one.

If you didn't have a discerning eye, you'd totally miss it.

I smiled at the lace eyelets. "Damn good job, Kin."

"Love when I walk in to hear a strong woman patting herself on the back. You deserve it."

I spun around with a snort. "Shut up, Ivy."

"What? I'm totally being serious." She crossed the room to stand next to me with Rhiannon snuggled up tight inside her baby wrap, which matched her dress, thanks to moi. She started swaying, which caused me to sway too because I was terribly susceptible to the baby-comforting stance.

I really wished there was time for me to unwrap Rhiannon and get a snuggle, but Macy would be here any second. I made do with brushing a finger over her pink chubby cheeks. "She's getting so big."

"Tell me about it. She looks for the boob almost as much as my husband."

I wrinkled my nose. "Okay, thanks for ruining a sweet moment."

"Just you wait. You'll understand what I'm talking about someday."

The familiar tightening in my chest seemed to be happening more and more these days. You couldn't turn a corner without finding a stroller out, or toddlers taking over the park. Holding out the hopes for my own happily ever after was getting more difficult by the day.

Except for that one moment...

Shove that crap down, girl.

I was *not* going there with the perpetrator's sister—and my best friend—standing right next to me. That unforgettable moment with August the day Rhiannon was born had been nine levels of wrong. Or was that sixty-nine?

It had been so long since I'd even had missionary sex, I wasn't going to start getting ambitious.

"You feeling okay?"

I blinked out of that dangerous memory lane. "Why?"

"You're all flushed." Ivy swayed her way in front of the mannequin. "Or is it because you're exhausted? You must have been up all night with this, Kin." She smoothed her hand down a long, lacy sleeve. "It's beautiful."

I lifted a hand to my burning cheek. "Yeah, you know me. No sleep and ruddy cheeks all day. Thank goodness I'm not going to be in the pictures, huh?"

She absently patted the baby's back. "You're sure that's all it is?"

"Yeah. I'm just nervous for Macy to see it. I hope she likes it."

"What did you do to it?" Macy's husky Demi Moore-esque voice came from the doorway.

I rushed over to her. "I did some alterations like we talked about." I nibbled on the corner of my thumbnail. "And something else."

"You aren't going to make me look stupid, right? That's all I really care about. God, I knew I should have just gone with the orange dress."

I clutched Macy's hands. "While you definitely could have pulled off that orange dress," and probably would have scandalized half the town council, although she would've looked awesome, "I think you'll like the addition to the dress. It's very you."

Macy squeezed my hands back quickly before dropping them. She wasn't exactly the touchy-feely type and I could feel the nerves radiating off her. Good thing I'd upped my essential oils in the shop for this last fitting. I was pumping lavender and lemon into the air as well as wearing my tree of life wrapped amethyst crystal against my heart.

You know, the one currently racing like it was my first time, for goddess's sake.

I'd altered every kind of clothing since I was fourteen. When you didn't have any money, you got creative with Salvation Army finds. But this dress was the first one I'd actually adjusted with a single person in mind. Usually, I created in just my own funky style that I hoped would resonate with someone out there in the universe.

Macy slowly walked toward Rosalie. Okay, yeah, it was weird that my dress form had a name. She had been with me since I'd opened my shop. She was actually the first thing I'd bought with money made under my business's name.

I had half a dozen dress forms and twenty mannequins all around the store, but this one was special. I didn't care if my appreciation of her was strange. It wasn't as if I was kissing her like in that movie from the eighties or anything. That and she didn't have a head.

Whatever.

"Did you add a train?" Macy shot a look at me over her shoulder. "You know I'm not into that girly shit."

"I know." My throat was dust dry as I swallowed. "Hear me out. This is a very special train."

Macy folded her arms. Her striking features were accentuated by her new short haircut, and Rylee's deft hand with makeup. At least that was my guess, since I'd never seen Macy wear more than a little mascara at the café. "Do I look like the type who goes for the princess stuff?"

"First of all, everyone wants to be a princess on their special day."

"True story," Ivy piped up.

I shot her a grateful smile. "Exactly." I tucked one of my wild curls behind my ear. I should have straightened it today, but I hadn't had time. Heck, I'd been impressed I managed a shower with my lack of sleep.

I spun Rosalie around to show off the lace and silk panel I'd added to the back. I'd ripped out the boring ruffles and went with simple silk then used the largest appliqué of the bunch to stretch between her shoulder blades. The rest floated down the skirt of the dress as if they were flying.

"Bats." Macy's whisper was a little watery.

I pressed my lips together, afraid to look up at her. "Yeah. A friend of mine has a really cool online shop, and I hope you don't mind—*oof.*"

Macy grabbed me into a tight, crushing hug. "It's fucking awesome. I can't believe you did this for me."

I patted her lightly—mostly because I couldn't move from her grip. Holy cats.

She pushed me away to go back to the dress. "You found lacy bats. I didn't even know that was a thing." She dabbed at her eyes. "Dammit, if you make me cry, I'm going to punch you."

Ivy and I laughed.

"I'm so glad you like it."

"I love it." She ran a trembling hand over the shoulder then stepped back. "I'm afraid to touch it."

"You can't hurt it." I unzipped the side zipper I'd hidden. "You're going to look amazing. Do you want me to help you?"

She chewed on the inside of her cheek. "Yeah. Is that cool? I mean, I know you've seen plenty of chicks naked, but...weird."

I draped the dress gently over my arm and led her to the dressing room. "Tell you what. I set out the foundation stuff we bought you. See how you do with that, and then I'll help you with the dress."

"Yeah. I can do that. Cool." She blew out a breath, stopping in the doorway. "Thanks, Kin. Seriously. I didn't think this ceremony would be me at all. And that's okay. I just want to marry him, and in the grand scheme, it doesn't matter."

"You're only getting married once. At least that's the plan for all of us."

"I'm definitely only doing this once. Besides, if he screws it up, there won't be a divorce, just a murder trial."

"And there's the Macy we all know and love."

She shrugged. "Vee's got me listening to all those murder podcasts she's into. Gives a girl ideas."

"Pretty sure Gideon would rather cut off a leg than let you down."

Macy's eyes reddened again. "Yeah. Kind of amazing." She blew out a breath and smoothed a hand down her still flat middle. "Now let's make sure I still fit in all this stuff."

I closed the door behind her and hung the dress on the silk hanger attached to the intricately carved door I'd found in an estate sale in Salem. It had been the inspiration for the entire dressing room area. I'd seen photos of the original black stain that had now faded to a soft beachy gray. Each door had a black cat carved into the lower corner doing something different. One sleeping, another playing with yarn, and the last arched in a stretch.

I'd painted the rooms hot pink with a different tone on tone stripe. One horizontal, one vertical, and the last one pinstriped, which Macy was in now.

I settled on the huge round hassock that served as a parking spot for friends who were shopping together or for an armload of clothes. It was a dark lush pink that complemented the lighter pink dressing rooms.

A particular scruffy guy with his perpetual backwards ball cap covered in pink fuzz had been the highlight of that week last fall, pre-Rhiannon's birth. August had built the base for me and had helped me stretch the material over the massive centerpiece. He'd come through in the clutch, so who could blame me for occasionally wondering what it would be like if he spread me out on it and…

Nope. I could not think about that right now.

Especially couldn't let myself remember the late night full of sweat and rare laughter we'd spent putting it together. We were usually sniping at each other because everything he created was dense, manly man furniture. He had such a fine eye for detail and whenever I managed to rope him into a refinishing project, they were the ones that flew out of my shop.

Except this one. I smoothed my hand over the velvet. This one was all mine.

I nibbled on my thumbnail. I missed seeing those rare smiles. Now he just glowered at me.

All because I couldn't control my-damn-self. So freaking stupid. If I'd just pushed him back faster, if I'd just bitten his tongue...

Perhaps that was a good move to have skipped.

The dressing room door opened, saving me from my runaway thoughts. "Wow."

Macy put her hands on her hips then covered her middle before finally lowering her arms to her sides with a huff. "Are you sure about this? They feel like granny panties."

I laughed. "They're high-waisted shapers, and you're rocking them. Goddess, your legs are miles long." The champagne-colored lingerie was striking on her. While the look was a throwback to the days of pinups, it made her angular body seem softer.

"Handily, my guy is tall."

I popped up and went right to the dress. "Well, I'm not, so this should be interesting." I laughed. "Let's start with you sitting there."

Macy fluttered fingers through her hair. "I don't know why I'm nervous."

"Well, we know that gorgeous man is going to be waiting at the gazebo for you, so that's not a concern."

"Yeah. He knows I'd hunt him down if he wasn't."

"Drag him by the hair?"

She laughed. "Tempting. And I probably could. Might have to knock him out first, but I have my ways."

I gathered the dress up so I could get it over her head. "Arms up."

It took a few strings of inventive swear words, but we finally got her long arms into the lacy sleeves and over her head.

"Okay, stand up." I guided her to her feet, and the dress simply floated down her to swish around her ankles.

She was breathtaking.

I was used to the café proprietress who wore an endless parade of denim and black pants with rude, colorful Halloween-themed shirts. *This* woman was striking with a surprising elegance.

"Oh, Macy." Vee's astonished voice had both of us turning around.

"I think that about covers it. You look amazing, Mace." I held her in place. "Wait a second. Let me get the zipper so you can see the full effect." I fussed with the hidden button and twisted the fabric so it fell in perfect lines. It didn't quite go to the floor since it was an outdoor wedding. But the train had a special extra layer of material to support the elements and protect the lacy bats. I'd even sewn some citrine chips in with the appliqués for some sparkle and to boost her energy to get through the day.

Support from a few special crystals never hurt anyone.

I turned Macy around and ushered her toward the raised dais with the trio of antique mirrors so she could get a 360° view of herself.

Vee chased after her, followed by Ivy and the newly arrived Rylee.

"Holy shit." Rylee rushed over to stand behind her and peeked around the dress to look at Macy in the mirror. "You're a girl."

"So I've heard."

Rylee's peal of laughter filled the room. "Yeah, but like *really* a girl. You're gonna kill Gideon. Oh my God, are those bats?"

Macy's lips twitched as she did a little sway in her dress to see the back. "I really am, huh?" She sniffed and tipped back her head. "You people are not going to make me cry."

"It's probably the hormones." Vee was full-on sniffles with the waterworks on high.

Macy hugged her and patted her shoulder awkwardly. "Right. Hormones. You doing okay?" She glanced down at Vee's mammoth belly. She had twins cooking in there. "Not going to go into labor at my wedding, are you?"

Vee laughed and dabbed at her eyes with a colorful handkerchief she pulled out of a magic pocket on her dress. "Would I do that?"

"Yes."

We all laughed.

"Well, I'm going to try not to. We still have some cooking time, don't we, babies?" Vee patted her belly under the blue and orange layers of tulle that didn't do a thing to hide her very pregnant self.

"Why don't you sit down? You've been running around all day." Gently, Macy led her to the high-backed chair crammed in the corner.

"I could sit."

I hurried to the drink station I'd set up. Mostly non-alcoholic for those in the baby way. Except for the punch. That was for Rylee and me, and maybe a little for Ivy now that she wasn't a total slave to the breastfeeding deal.

I filled one tumbler with the punch and went for the sparkling fruity waters for Macy and Vee. "Here you go." One cup said *Bride* in scrolling wedding lettering with a bat for the I in the word. I handed that to Macy who took a grateful sip.

"Not coffee, but pretty tasty, Cinnamon."

I grinned at Macy's nickname for me. She liked to hand out nicknames to give us a tiny clue of our specialty coffees she created for us. Not everyone got one, but we were all secretly happy when we did.

I gave the pink MOH tumbler to Rylee. "Spiked."

"Yesss." She accepted it and took a quick drink.

"Not spiked." I handed the rainbow one to Vee.

I rushed back for my own and a smaller one for Ivy. After I was done passing out the drinks, I took a fortifying sip. "Now let's get everyone else ready."

Next time, I was buying much larger cups.

TWO

"Shouldn't this have been done earlier?"

"This is a public area. We had to wait until our scheduled time." I grabbed half of the arbor. "Look, weakling, if you can't handle your share of the load, let me deal with it."

"Shut up and shove over." Jared—known as Sheriff Brooks to most, but not to me since I'd been busting his balls for years—hefted one half of the freestanding arbor I'd created from pressure-treated wood, sweat, and a few not so metaphorical drops of blood when I'd hammered my own thumb.

"Hang on. I got it." Murphy Masterson, otherwise known as Moose, hustled forward to grab the opposite end of the arbor. It wasn't that heavy, but all we needed to do was to step into a hole and drop the thing an hour before showtime.

Carefully, we set the arbor into position. I adjusted the last minute addition of purple gauzy fabric with tiny silver stars, a Kinleigh suggestion. I'd figured white might be nice, but she'd said it looked as if it belonged in a church and didn't match Macy's Halloween aesthetic in any case.

I glanced at the orange lights and decorative bats fluttering from the trees. Couldn't argue there.

"Damn nice piece of work, Aug." Moose cocked his head, studying it. "Wish we'd had something like that at ours. Vee would've loved it."

"Sign is sweet too." Jared scratched his stubbed jaw. "Minus the add-on, but hey, if the bootie fits."

I grinned. "That was a last minute fix."

The ornate hand-tooled sign that hung from the top had been carved from cherry wood and bore the names of the bride and groom.

Mr. Jonathan Gideon and Mrs. Macy Devereaux Gideon.

Between them was a small emblem of sorts of a ladder and a coffee cup. It had been a bitch to etch into the wood, but the finished result was charming. I hoped. Then beneath that I'd etched two more names with a heart between them.

Danielle Alicia Gideon. Hell Baby Gideon.

The hell was just a post-it note that could be pulled off. Gideon was always joking how Macy was sure their kid was going to come out with horns and a tail because of her all-day sickness situation.

If everyone was in a good mood, they should both laugh. And if they weren't in a good mood at their wedding, well, I couldn't help them.

The idea was they could remove the sign from the arbor and set it somewhere in their home, perhaps over a mantle.

"Wonder if you'd be willing to build us one of those things?"

Jared arched a brow and adjusted the badge on his pressed gray shirt. "If you're looking to use that for possibly sordid means, Aug just might have time to finish it before Vee is ambulatory again after those twins."

Only Moose, now a father of one with two on the way, would flush at a sex joke. I wasn't quite sure what kind of sexual activities my arbor could be used for, but anything was possible with Jared's filthy mind. "No, I was thinking for Vee's roses."

"How did you ever have trouble getting dates?" Jared shook his head. "I'd think women would eat you up with a spoon."

Since a joke of my own came all too quickly to mind, I moved to the arbor and tugged at Kinleigh's airy fabric. It draped perfectly down the sides, shifting in the growing breeze. Late December in Crescent Cove wasn't pleasant to say the least, but we'd gotten lucky with a day without snow. I glanced up at the swiftly darkening sky with its sliver of moon and sprinkle of stars and hoped any flakes held off until the ceremony was over. Then again…

"Is snow considered romantic?"

Moose frowned. "Like in the context of a wedding?"

"Yeah."

Jared reached up to take off his hat to smooth out his hair before putting it back on. God forbid if anyone forgot for even an instant he was sheriff. "Most people I know consider it a pain in the ass, including me. Do you have any idea how many MVAs I have to deal with from November to April?"

"We all have our crosses to bear."

"Then again, didn't your sister get snowed in with her Irish husband? Not that he was her husband then."

I shut my eyes. I knew what was coming. Jared only razzed me a few times a month about asking Ivy "to cease and desist" while she was in the backseat of her car with Lucky Charms.

"I ticketed him once for double parking, and then there was the time I caught them in their vehicle at the lookout point—"

I held up a hand. "Haven't I asked you repeatedly not to go there?"

"Too late." Moose tugged on his tie.

I could tell he felt about as comfortable in his penguin suit as I did, though I'd gone with dark jeans and a shirt, tie, and jacket. I spent my days in T-shirts and jeans. I didn't even own a full suit. The Ireland contingent at my sister's fall wedding had been attired as if they were attending a royal event, while I'd worn much the same as I had on now. Lucky Charms' mother had even worn a hat with feathers.

So far, their over the top style wasn't rubbing off on my sister, who'd worn a simple white backless gown. I didn't doubt some of her fashion sense was due to Kinleigh, who'd worn a long floaty dress that had only accented her willowy figure.

"What do you call that color?"

Her witchy blue eyes narrowed on mine as if she was looking for the punchline. "Soft peach."

Peach, a color I couldn't have precisely identified before that day yet had now been burned into my memory. She'd stood so proudly beside Ivy as my sister said her vows, her dress vivid against the flames of her hair—

I rubbed my temple. I really needed to stop working so damn late in the shop.

"Earth to Beck." Jared snapped his fingers in my face. "I asked if you'd managed to con some poor hapless woman into attending tonight's wedding with you."

"Do I look like I have a woman with me?" There was no helping my cross response. Not hot on the heels of my most recent remembrance.

Talk about dumping a salt truck on the wound. Kinleigh and I weren't anything beyond friends, but that didn't mean I didn't sometimes wish we could be.

Jared smirked. "No, but from the sounds of things, you should work on it."

"What about you, smart ass? I don't see you with anyone on your arm."

He bristled. "Gina will be here."

"So? Unless you two have finally stopped dancing around each other, she doesn't count as a date." I propped my fingers under my chin. "Or does she?"

"Gina is my best friend. It isn't like that with us."

"That doesn't mean it can't be." At Jared's sharp look, Moose cleared his throat. "If you want to change your status, you just have to alter your approach so you step out of the friend zone."

Jared crossed his arms. "Now you're an expert?"

"Well, he's happily married," I reminded him.

"Very happily," Moose agreed. "Stupidly happily. So happy that—"

"That if you could, you'd knock her up again while she's already pregnant." Jared tapped his gloves against his thigh. "Yeah, yeah, we get it. Don't be smug."

Moose grinned and tucked his thumbs in the pockets of his suit pants.

Smug bastard was right. That expression he was wearing said it all.

His life was marital bliss. Jared was locked in the friend zone, whether he would admit it or not. And I…

I looked up and glimpsed Kinleigh gliding across the grass in her mile-high purple boots. Her sunset-colored hair streamed behind her in the wind, and she had on another one of her long dresses. This one was purple to match her boots with some kind of secondary lacy layer in dark blue that swished around her ankles.

I was thoroughly fucked.

"Oh, shit, look who it is. The man of the hour. John Gideon, ready to get hitched?" Jared slapped Gideon on the back as he joined us. He was already dressed in his tux and looking more than a little harried. And slightly green.

He nodded rapidly, his eyes wheeling in that panicked manner I'd seen at my sister's wedding. Not from her. Nope, that expression had belonged to Lucky Charms, which I'd found ridiculous. He'd married up with my sister, no doubt about it.

Gideon pushed a hand through his hair and blew out a breath. "Yeah. I'm good. But I keep checking my phone."

Moose, Jared, and I exchanged glances.

"In case Macy decides to bail?" Moose finally guessed.

Of course. He was the sensitive one among us. Jared and I had the combined emotional barometer of a rock encased in seaweed at least half the time.

Gideon nodded, swallowing hard.

"She's not going anywhere. At least not until she sees all this." I gestured to the wedding wonderland around us. I didn't have a thing for Halloween like Macy did, but even I had to admit it was pretty cool with the mason jars hanging from the tree branches and the twinkling lights draped all over the place.

"Wow. You did this, Aug?" Gideon zeroed in on the arbor that we'd put at the beginning of the aisle where Macy and her ladies would proceed to the gazebo. A length of purple carpet led right up to the gazebo's steps where the actual ceremony would take place, like many of Crescent Cove's fine townspeople before them.

Minus the bats.

And the orange lights.

And the—

"Hell Baby Gideon?" Gideon glanced my way with a grin. "She's going to roast your nuts for dinner tonight, brother."

I held up my hands. "Blame yourself for that one. You're the one who said she's been cursing at you and threatening to Bobbetize you whenever she's sick."

Moose's eyebrows lifted. "Really? Vee has never—"

Then we all spoke in unison, including Gideon.

"Macy, remember?"

Macy definitely made her own rules and had her own very unique personality. I was sure she wasn't the first pregnant woman to threaten her man's member while pregnant but she was doing it colorfully, that was sure.

Eh, his problem, not mine. I wasn't going to have to deal with anything like that anytime soon.

Or maybe ever.

"It's a very tumultuous time in a woman's life."

Gideon glanced at Moose. "You'd know better than any of us. Those twins almost cooked?"

"Soon." Moose ran a finger along the inside of his collar. "She's getting induced in a couple of weeks."

"So you can knock her up again pronto?"

"It doesn't work like that. You have to wait a certain amount of time."

"Right, so you *have* been thinking about it."

Moose just laughed and shook his head at Jared. "Three little kids are a lot, man. You don't have any yet. Just wait."

"And best of all, they grow up and become teenagers." Gideon gave a not so mock shudder. "Not that Dani's there yet, but she's buying makeup now. She's not even quite nine. Macy said it was better we let her use a little so she doesn't decide to lift some while she's with her friends."

Jared angled his head. "Is your girl going wild? Do I have to keep an eye on her?"

Gideon snorted. "She's an A and B student who's obsessed with Macy's cat's kittens. Hardly wild. She's just a kid. You were probably one once too, unless you were born wearing starched CCPD shorts."

Jared pretended to pull back the waistband of his dress pants to check. "Oh, look at that, don't have any shorts on period."

At that, Moose dispersed to meet up with his wife, and Jared quickly followed suit, claiming he'd spotted a "ruckus" across the way he needed to check out.

More likely, he was headed over to the diner to see what was keeping Gina. Those two were always attached at the hip. And possibly at other things as well, if town scuttlebutt was to be believed. It usually wasn't, but every now and then, the gossip was spot-on.

"This is really incredible, thank you. Macy will love it as much as I do." Gideon stroked a hand over the arbor, smiling up at the sign with his family's names inscribed. "I would've said more sooner, but the Sheriff turns anything into snark."

"He was dropped on his head as a boy. Don't hold it against him."

Gideon grinned. "I don't. I've learned to appreciate snark more myself in recent months."

"Surprise, surprise there." I reached up to remove the post-it note that said Hell and handed it to Gideon. "You can show your wife that later if you'd like. Don't want her to decide to make a meal of me on her special day."

"Oh, she'll laugh her ass off, don't worry. But I have to say I enjoy when she gets mushy. This will definitely do it. Mainly because I take pictures for later bribery."

"That so?"

He shrugged and pocketed the note. "Gotta do what you can to get a leg up on her, man."

"Since we're on the topic anyway…" I cleared my throat and

glanced around to make sure no one was close enough to overhear our conversation. The guests were all starting to arrive, talking and walking in small groups and admiring the decorations. But time was running short, so I couldn't belabor this point. "How exactly did you bag Macy?" At Gideon's slow blink, I pushed back my knit hat and tried again. "What worked with her to, you know, soften her up?"

"You see Macy practically every day when you stop by Brewed Awakening. Does she seem any softer to you?"

"Not particularly, although she did get a little misty when I told her my black pekoe was particularly strong the other day." I was trying to cut back on the caffeine so I wouldn't be up all night as often, but all I'd managed so far was to add tea to my daily coffee regimen.

I didn't think caffeine had much to do with my wakefulness anyway. I tended to stay in my store working until a certain redhead went down to her car. Most of the time, I planned my exit just right so we could walk together.

Of course that had all changed since we'd kissed. We'd fucking *kissed,* and she'd acted as if I'd tripped and slid my tongue into her mouth.

Whoops, sorry, no big deal.

She'd moaned when I had her in my arms. Yet since then, she'd been as cool to me as a stranger. Sometimes the ice chipped and the real Kinleigh peeked out, but just as swiftly, she disappeared again behind careful politeness.

"Well, Macy takes her business very seriously. But that was probably hormones. I caught her sobbing over Garfield the other day."

"The cartoon cat?"

"None other. She reads the strips online and something about Odie taking Garfield's candy set her off. Beats me, man." Gideon sighed. "We hugged it out and she didn't offer to give me a vasectomy herself, so it was a good day."

I didn't even crack a smile. This was serious business and the clock was running down. It wasn't as if he had time to counsel me on his damn wedding night.

At least the ceremony hadn't occurred yet.

"So, c'mon, Gideon, tell me how you managed it." I sounded more than a little desperate but it couldn't be helped.

"Managed what?"

"Winning over Macy." It sounded like a Lifetime movie of the week. "Surely you have some...tips."

"Tips?"

"Is there a damn echo? Look, you're getting married. She let you knock her up."

His lips twisted. "She did. I don't even think she regrets it most of the time."

"She wasn't the sort of woman who wanted any of that, at least on the surface, so how'd you break the ice?"

"Sex," he said seriously.

It was my turn to be a parrot. "Sex? That's it?"

"That's everything. You have good chemistry in bed—or on the bar," he didn't even smirk when he said it, "and suddenly, a lot of objections fly out the window." Before I could process that, he angled his head. "Who's the lucky lady?"

"No one."

He shrugged. "I get it. Don't show your cards too soon. But if it's a certain redhead—"

I shook my head. "Absolutely not."

This freaking town knew everything about everybody. Sometimes it was a comfort, sometimes it pissed me right off.

Damn, had someone seen us kiss at the hospital? Maybe even Gina. She'd been right there, and she was a notorious gossip.

If Jared knew, I'd never hear the end of it. Which actually gave me a measure of relief. If he knew already, he would've struck while the embarrassment was fresh.

So, Miss Scott turned you down, hmm? Pity. But that means she's still on the market, right?

Not that he would've intended to do anything about it. He just liked to amuse himself at his friends' expense when he wasn't being Mr. Straight-Laced while on duty.

The guy needed a hobby, and for that matter, so did I. One that didn't include obsessing about a woman I couldn't have.

Gideon ignored my denial and continued on. "You're probably thinking too hard. Just get in the same space with her and let it happen naturally."

"Yoohoo, John Gideon, tonight's the night you bang your woman!"

Gideon groaned and turned his head as the quite literally larger than life Lucky Roberts from his crew—and another one of our friends—stampeded across the grass. He had on a bright turquoise suit with a ruffled shirt that looked as if he'd borrowed it from Elvis, circa 1975.

"He realizes Macy is already pregnant, right?" I asked in an undertone.

"He knows. He's just an asshole."

That was the last thing he got out before Lucky lifted him off the ground in a ribs-cracking bear hug.

"Congratulations, man. Don't know how you did it, but good fucking luck!"

Gideon was a big guy himself, but Lucky was a battering ram. And he sounded as if he'd already had some liquid lubrication to get his night started.

Since Gideon was now being swarmed by the rest of his crew, I turned to leave, but he called my name before I'd taken a step.

"Here, man." He whipped out his wallet and opened it to withdraw a small square item. He pressed it into my hand and lifted his brows. "I don't need this anymore, so just in case." He gave me a quick one-armed hug. "Thanks again for the arbor."

Gideon and his band of merry men turned to go on their way, and I was left staring down at the foil packet cupped in my palm.

John Gideon had given me a condom.

One side had the picture of a metallic swirled lollipop. The other contained a prophetic bit of advice.

If you lick, be quick. If you stick, take this.

I couldn't imagine where he'd gotten this. For all I knew, it was a joke rubber, not meant to be used. But it wasn't as if I carried any with me on the regular, and it wasn't smart to be too hasty.

Sexy feminine laugher carried on the wind, and I caught sight of a swish of familiar red hair in the growing crowd.

Swallowing hard, I slipped it into my jacket pocket.

Just in fucking case.

THREE

KINLEIGH

WHAT A NIGHT.

Music blared from a pair of fancy speakers that had to have been provided by Rory, my bestie's husband. No one else had access to that kind of equipment in this town. I got passed around a few times as spontaneous dancing started as soon as the groom kissed the bride.

A navy star-strewn sky chased the raspberry and purple sunset, leaving the park and the pier in fiery orange, purple, and white lights. Everything swayed due to the wind off the water. Mason jars lit up the trees and flickered like fireflies in the summer.

Only it wasn't summer.

No, it was the dead of winter in Central New York, and we were hardy people. In fact, I dared to say this was a delightfully balmy evening in our little lake town. Children ran around with sparklers, laughing and clapping in what was probably their Christmas finery— miniature peacoats, snowsuits, and mini-me adult-style jackets.

The townspeople were also dressed to impress. Brilliantly colored dresses peeked from long jackets and winter coats as coffee, hot chocolate, and ice cream were passed around. Because of course there was ice cream. I was pretty sure some of it had actually been dumped into various mugs to boot.

It was chaos and perfection.

Crescent Cove wasn't the usual town. Getting married here was a big deal. Even strangers stopped to watch the New Year's Eve wedding in the gazebo. Most of the town had turned up to see Macy take the plunge. Not just because Brewed Awakening had become Crescent Cove's hub, but because she'd been so anti-marriage, kids, and love.

Joke was on her.

This was one of the most romantic weddings I'd ever seen in all my twenty-six years. Granted, I hadn't attended too many of them, but living here was certainly changing that.

Gideon had a mug in his hand as he climbed up on one of the big speakers. "Hey, everyone. We're having an open reception at The Haunt. Join us there so we can warm up, huh?" He looked down at Macy. "My gorgeous bride and I aren't ready for the night to be over." He quickly grabbed for his daughter, who was climbing up after him.

He drew her into his arms, handing her the hot chocolate. "My family would really love for everyone to come. Bring in the New Year with us. We have a huge box of sparklers near that gorgeous arbor if you'd like to do it up stroll-style along Main Street."

The crowd clapped and more sparklers fired into the night.

A little girl with red braids and a purple jacket came up to me. "You can haff mine, so I can have a new one."

I laughed at her pronunciation and took the sparkler from her. "Thanks, sweetie."

A woman in a sharp crimson jacket held her hand out for the little girl. Gold flashed in her ears and her fingers. She was hella put together. All class.

She smiled at me and then tugged her daughter away.

With my free hand, I clutched the antique wire of my large pendant and glanced down at my navy dress. The purple lacy edge along the hem fluttered in the breeze and tickled the back of my matching suede boots. The ones I'd spent weeks dying to match.

I might never look as classy as that woman, but at least I had a one of a kind dress. And my gray long jacket had been rescued on a trip into the city. I always got the best stuff down there to repair and resell. It was what I did. Repurposed and made things shine again.

"Careful, Kin." A large, warm hand curled around mine.

My breath hitched as August pulled me in, taking the dying sparkler from my fingers. It gave one last flash and died between us.

"Guess you got a defective one." He waved it quickly to get the last of the heat out of the burned out stick.

I shivered. Because it was cold, of course. Not because I hadn't been *this* close to him since...well, since that day at the hospital.

I'd done my damndest to keep out of his way—as much as one could when one worked in the same damn building as the guy she was avoiding. Oh, and couldn't forget the whole helping with the wedding thing. But I managed well enough most of the time. Unfortunately, my stupid body hadn't gotten the memo that he was off-limits.

His gaze drifted to my mouth then back up to my eyes. "You look amazing, Kin."

I pulled my hand from his. "Can't compete with the bride and her party, but I clean up all right."

He frowned. "Why would you need to compete? You're one of the most beautiful women in the Cove."

My mouth went dry. "Wow."

"You know you're gorgeous."

I looked down at my feet and jammed my hands into my coat pockets. "That's sweet of you to say."

"Get over here, Beck!"

We both looked up at the barked orders from Sheriff Brooks. It just felt weird to call him Jared, even in my head. He was as much the badge as a man in my mind. And I'd learned long ago to be wary of the badge even when I hadn't done anything wrong.

Badge equaled social services and social services meant being trapped. I'd learned to avoid any and all of that when I was a kid.

I shook my head. Where had that come from?

It had to be all the crazy emotions of the day. It had been a damn long time since I'd thought of my teen years. I preferred to be firmly rooted in the now.

Now was where it was safe. That safety did not include the very tall and pleasantly wood-scented August Beck.

He'd even put on his good, dark-washed jeans for the occasion. The ones he wore to go to the bank or to meet with important clients. His baseball cap was gone. Instead, he wore a heavy green knit hat that made his green eyes glow. His dress coat—well, dressy for August —was open to show the crisp white Oxford shirt and tie that Ivy had to have picked out.

I didn't think he knew to buy that shade of forest green and celadon plaid mix.

I tugged on his tie. "You look pretty good yourself, Aug."

He flushed and reached back to tug his hat down. "Ivy threatened me with a month of diaper duty if I didn't at least wear a tie."

"Did she tie it for you too?"

"No." He jerked at the knot. "I know how to tie a damn tie."

I pressed my lips together against a laugh.

"I'll see you at The Haunt?"

I nodded. "Sure. Of course. I'll be there with the girls." I looked over my shoulder and spotted Rylee and Ivy with their heads together. "I should go over there with them anyway. See if I can help too."

"Beck!" Sheriff Brooks called. "Before I freeze my goddamn nuts off."

August walked backward. "See ya."

I waved.

Jeez. What the heck was all that about?

I picked my way through the carnage of footprints packing last week's snow down to ice. Rylee was hopping up and down in front of a cooler.

"To starting the night right. I have a babysitter and plan on seducing my husband, thanks to Jose and Cabo Wabo. What's your poison?"

"Two different tequilas?"

"Margies in this one." She flipped her dark braid over her shoulder and did her best Vanna White impression, indicating the red and white Coleman thermos we generally used for lemonade. "And this one..." She stepped aside to show a matching blue one. "Tequila Sunrises."

"Oh, hello."

Rylee tossed me my cup. "Have at it."

I looked over my shoulder at Sheriff Brooks. He wasn't paying attention—yet.

"Closed container, who's gonna know?"

"Ever the troublemaker, that's my sister." Kelsey tucked a wildly fluttering lock of strawberry hair behind her ear. "However, I recommend the Sunrise." She licked her lips. "Yummy."

"You too?" But I went right to the blue thermos and opened the spigot. I definitely needed a little bit of liquid courage to get through this night.

We sipped from our covered tumblers as we gathered the small amount of trash that had been left behind. As cups and wrappers were dumped into bags, we laughed and cupped our hands over our mouths to keep in the warmth.

While we cleaned up, I finished off two rounds of Rylee's dangerous Tequila Sunrise concoction that I had a feeling was heavy on the Cabo. Whoa.

The guys finished taking down the arbor and packing it away in August's truck. He came back and took the two big bags of garbage from us and ushered us out of the park.

"Get inside, ladies. It's fu—freaking freezing."

Ivy patted his cheek. "Such a good guy." She giggled and bumped his hip.

"Just what have you guys been drinking?"

I swung the blue Coleman, my new best friend, and patted his chest. "Don't you worry about it. Just our go-juice for the evening."

Ivy, Rylee, Kelsey, and I danced our way around him and over to Jared before Rylee stole his hat.

"Mrs. Kramer," he warned.

Rylee tossed it to Kelsey, who fumbled it and picked it up off the snow with a laugh. "Whoops."

The sheriff shook his head. "Don't make me arrest you today."

"Aww, come on. Have a little fun, Jared." Rylee saved his hat from her sister and jumped up to plunk it on his head. "We're gonna go right across the street to The Haunt and be good little girls." She tapped her chin. "*Ish*. But no one will be driving, so don't you worry." Rylee shook her booty and headed for the sidewalk.

I rushed after them, the thermos and its icy contents slushing the whole way. I laughed and hooked my arm through Ivy's. "She's crazy, but I really kinda love her."

"She's so happy for Macy. And relieved that this is all over like the rest of us. We need a little break from all the planning. Even my planner is tired."

"I hear that." I hugged her arm. My bestie and her perpetual planner. She and Kelsey had tried to convert all of us. I'd actually been enjoying the traveler's notebook she'd gotten me for Christmas. I liked the feel of paper over the endless spreadsheets I had to deal with for the shop.

I'd even found some cool vintage papers to use in one of the estate sales I'd sneaked away to yesterday. When I was overwhelmed, I went shopping. It calmed my crazy and streamlined it into about a truck bed's worth of new stuff for the shop.

Including a beat to hell Art Deco chair and stand I'd be working on as soon as all the wedding festivities were over.

Ivy clasped my hand and we danced our way around the line of cars that had been parked in front of The Haunt. People were loitering out front and down near the café where the tables were being used even on this cold night.

Plates of finger food were being passed around by a few of Macy's waiters and waitresses, as well as some other people I didn't know. Probably temps for the occasion.

I grabbed a crescent roll wrapped something or other from a tall guy who might've been out of his teens. Maybe. I suddenly felt very old, but I enjoyed the fluffy, salty buttery treat.

In fact, I'd waved Ivy ahead and gone to chase him down for another when I bumped into August.

"Hey, watch it."

"You keep saving me from my clumsiness today." I laughed up at him and slipped my hand into the warmth of his jacket. "Gonna wonder if you're following me."

His fingers curled around my elbow to tug me more into his heat. "You're freezing." He peered down at me. "Or are you not feeling the cold?"

I shrugged. "Maybe not." I swayed toward him. "Rylee was pretty heavy-handed with her Sunrise of tequila."

"Tequila Sunrise?" he asked with a laugh.

"Right. That. She used that Cabo Wabo tequila, and whew, that Sammy Hagar dude is no joke with that stuff."

"Evidently." His eyebrow rose.

"Is that judgement? It's a party, you know. Everyone is having some." I waved my hand toward the couple at the table near us. "Okay, maybe not her. Another baby on board," I sang out. "Congrats."

The woman laughed. "Thanks."

He steered me over to one of the covered tables full of food. "Let's get some of this into you."

"No fun."

"Better than you not having any fun because you pass out in the corner."

I sighed. "Fair point. I really didn't eat today. I was too busy sewing things. I love to sew, did you know that?"

"Is that a fact?"

I narrowed my gaze at him as another flood of people came out of the restaurant. I had no choice but to crowd into him. "Sarcasm isn't a good color on you. Green is though. Really nice." I flipped the end of his tie up.

He gave me a half smile, then went back to building me a plate heavy on the carbs. Really heavy. How much did he think I could pack away? Then again, all I wanted to do was eat when I had alcohol in me. Did he know that?

Probably did. Ivy was always blathering about everyone's secrets. At least the secrets she knew about me anyway.

He reached back and took my hand, leading me to the quieter part of the sidewalk and across the pavement between the buildings to the café. He held out a chair for me. "Here you go."

I looked down at our joined hands and gently twisted out of his hold. "Thanks. You don't have to take care of me though. I'm a big girl." I dug into the pile of stuff and found pepperoni and cheese bread. "So good."

"I know. I like it."

He kicked out a chair next to me and and dropped into it with a groan. "I swear I haven't sat down since noon."

"I hear you." I held out a spinach roll. "Want?"

He leaned in and took it from my fingers with his teeth.

I slowed my chewing, my gaze locked on the way he licked his lips.

He sat back and laced his fingers over his rock hard, very flat belly. Dear goddess, why did he have to be so damn delicious? It was usually way easier for me to ignore such things.

But I knew firsthand just how tight that middle was. And how amazing that lower lip tasted. I still dreamed about it some nights. He had the perfect level of wet and dry in his kisses. Was there anything worse than a guy who used too much tongue?

Not as far as I was concerned.

Not that I had a huge number in that knowledge category, but I'd kissed my fair share of nope-never-again guys in my life. August was definitely in the repeat offender column. At least in my dreams. Repeat again and again with oh, yes, please, one more time.

"Do I have something on my mouth?" He flicked his thumb over the corner of his lip.

I shook my head and looked back down at my plate. "Nope. All good."

He reached for my plate, and I moved it to the right. "Get your own."

"You are a hard woman. And after I made that whole plate for you."

I sighed and slid it back. "Not fair."

"Who said I have to be fair?" He leaned forward and unearthed a breadstick. He glanced at me and sighed, handing it to me. Then took another spinach roll.

I smiled and broke it apart to nibble on one end. "You're always fair. That's who you are. The good guy, can't change that."

"Is that so?"

I flicked away a tempura-covered pepper to get to another piece of the pepperoni bread. "Yep. You, Becks, are super kind and safe." I handed him the pepper. He must like them if he picked it. *Ick.*

He wrapped his long fingers around my wrist and lifted it to his mouth to chomp off the end.

I swallowed. "You can take it, you know."

He finished it and took the other half, licking the tip of my finger. "No napkins." He sat back. "Go on, keep telling me how much of a nice guy I am."

I tapped my finger against the side of the plate and frowned down at it. That wasn't an insult. "Your whole family is. Your mom keeps trying to fix me up with some guy named Brent. I mean, why? Do I look like a girl who's going to go out with a Brent?"

Been there, done that. I didn't need any more Brents in my tool chest, thanks.

"Brent Spielman?"

I popped the last bit of pepperoni in my mouth. "Yes." I shuddered. "No thanks."

"Definitely not."

I pushed the near empty plate away. "Oh?" The hurt made me pull my hands together under the table. Of course I wouldn't be good enough.

"Brent is a douche. He's slick and talks a good game around people like my mom. In reality, he's been banging his receptionist for the last three months and is always trolling at the Spinning Wheel." He jerked my chair by the arm and twisted it toward him. "Don't go fucking near him."

I balanced myself with a hand to his knee. "Why do you care?"

"How blind are you, Kin?"

FOUR

August

HER BLUE EYES WIDENED.

She couldn't really be that fucking surprised, could she? I hadn't been alone with that kiss in the fall. At least I didn't think so.

I eased back and she grabbed my hand. "What do you mean?"

"You know what I mean." I propped my elbows on my thighs until our gazes were even. I licked my lips and stared at her mouth.

She sucked in her bottom lip, her teeth denting the pale skin. Her lipstick had rubbed off, thanks to her drinks and food. Would she taste like tequila? Or maybe the sharper spice of her food?

Would I find out? That was the real question.

Gideon's words rang in my head.

You have good chemistry, and suddenly, a lot of objections fly out the window.

Okay, there had been a bit more than that to it for him and Macy, but maybe I needed to actually take the plunge. The kiss by the truck had been weird. Hot, but weird. She'd been right there, with her eyes closed, practically begging me to lean in.

I didn't even think about it.

Now?

All I'd been doing was thinking about it. And I knew I'd screwed up after we kissed. I'd been just as surprised how incredible it had been. I should have dragged her back in and gone for part two.

But then she'd bailed on me. That wasn't happening a second time.

I cupped the back of her neck. The realization lit her depthless blue eyes. They always told me exactly what was going on in her brain. She'd probably hate that I knew it.

I knew when she was pissed, when she was tired, when she was hurting.

This Kinleigh was new.

Sexy.

Aware.

Wary.

I leaned in. Maybe I could get rid of the wariness. Our eyes were still open as I closed the gap, and then she was mine. Those long lashes fluttered down and she breathed into me. And I took.

No holding back.

This wasn't a game for me. She never had been, but maybe I'd have to convince her of that.

I brushed my lips with hers, lightly tasting the corner of her mouth, the fullest part of her lower lip, then the sharp divot along the top of her bow-like shape. I was rewarded with spice.

I *loved* spice.

Her fingers twisted around my tie, and the little groan nearly brought me out of my seat. I wanted to hear more of that. Taste it on my tongue.

The sounds of the crowd around us invaded my lust brain.

I pulled back, looking around. No one was paying us any mind. People were moving inside, probably for speeches or something. Someone bumped my chair, and Kinleigh jerked back.

Nope. Not this time.

I stood and took her hand, drawing her with me as I wound my way around the chairs and to the back gate of the fenced-in area of the café.

"What are you doing?"

I looked down at her. "Finding somewhere a little less conspicuous."

Her gaze narrowed before she looked over her shoulder.

I dragged her down the alleyway beside the café and the stretch of pavement that led to the parking lot.

"August, this is—"

I swung around and hauled her up against me. The flare of her skirt gave me enough room to get my knee between her legs. "You really going to say this isn't what you want?"

She swallowed and wouldn't look above my mouth. "I don't know."

My need to protect her, to make sure she was okay, warred with the instinct to not let her think right now. I didn't want to be a mistake, but I didn't want her to slot our kiss—kisses, plural now—as a regret before she saw how good we were together either.

One taste and I knew. Maybe I'd always known, even if I didn't want to own up to it.

I crowded her into the brick wall beside the side door. I lowered my mouth to hers. I didn't hesitate. I dived in to show her exactly what I meant.

Her arm went up around my neck, and she flattened her chest against mine. Her heart was hammering, and God, she tasted like everything I'd ever wanted.

I didn't put myself out there very much. I preferred the quiet of my shop and the wood that I understood. I could touch a stack of lumber and know exactly what it needed to be.

Women weren't as easy to figure out.

But this woman, I knew. Years of having her around had taught me a few things about Kinleigh Scott. And I needed to tap into that wild girl who sang with her music upstairs. The one who laughed with her whole body. The one who was more excited for a truck bed full of junk than the sparkliest gemstones.

I drew her up onto her tiptoes. Even her heeled boots weren't quite enough to line us up. But I'd help with that. I cupped my hands around her firm ass and set her tighter against me to let her feel just how serious I was.

She moaned into my mouth as I went deeper. Sought more of those sweet sounds. I rocked her tighter against my leg and groaned at the heat of her blasting through the filmy dress into my shirt and jeans.

Her coat shrouded us from any prying eyes, so I was a bit bolder than I usually would've been. I inched up the skirt of her dress while I got very acquainted with her mouth. Jesus, she could kiss.

I thought I'd had the steering wheel firmly in hand, but I was drowning in her taste. Instead of hose or tights or whatever women usually had under these things, I only found a scrap of silk.

"Fuck, Kin," I muttered against her lips.

"Don't stop now, dammit."

I laughed into her mouth. My fingers curved around her soft, slightly chilled skin. I lifted her thigh up to hook over my hip to get closer to her. A barely there thong was the only thing keeping me from her sweet softness.

I hoped the friction was enough for now because I needed a minute to get my head around this. The logistics of it. I was not going to take this woman against the side of a building with people tromping through.

As much as I wanted her and for her to see just how awesome we could be together, I couldn't disrespect her like that.

My elbow rapped the doorknob and I swore, the pain giving me a second for my brain to engage.

Upstairs.

I knew the code to get into the apartments since I'd helped with some of the work up there. Gideon and his crew were forever rehabbing one of the apartments and where Gideon went, I was usually dragged in to help.

I let her dress fall and cursed.

"What?" She was undulating against me so sweetly. Those big blue eyes were hooded with desire and a bit of hazy confusion.

I lifted her off of me. I didn't realize just how much she'd crawled up on me. "I want you all over me, in like three seconds. Okay, maybe three minutes."

"What?" She moved back, her heels clicking on the pavement.

I grabbed her hand. "Nope. Inside."

"Where? There?" She glanced over her shoulder, her expression frantic. "We can't go in there."

I wiggled my fingers to get the blood flowing. Okay, brain bring back that code. It was in my head somewhere. Too bad most of my brain cells were located in my very unhappy dick, currently banging on my zipper to come out and play.

"Shit."

She crowded into my back. "What?" She was looking around. "Do you know the code or not?"

"Give me a second."

"This isn't a good idea. Someone is going to come down—"

"2-3-1-8. Got it." The panel turned green and the locks disengaged. I swung the door open and dragged her inside. "Up the stairs."

I stopped at the huge stack of lumber left in the stairwell. Well, that was a fire hazard. Whatever, a problem for tomorrow. I vaulted over the stack and held my hands out for her.

"August, this is crazy." But she reached for me.

I lifted her up against me and slowly let her slide down my body. "It is crazy, but I like it."

She stared into my eyes, her gaze uncertain and yet there was a spark of the wild there. Exactly what I'd been looking for all night.

"Don't think. Let me show you just how amazing we can be together."

She opened her mouth. I could see the questions and the second-guesses behind her eyes, but I covered her mouth again and kissed her until she was sagging against me, the little purr in her throat back.

I locked my fingers with hers and headed up the stairs, dragging her behind me. The second floor was a hot mess, but the third floor was almost done.

A woman with more money than sense had decided she liked having a whole floor to herself. Gideon had been rehabbing it to make the space into a huge loft apartment. I'd just delivered one of my bed frames last week.

"I'm not built for sprinting, Aug."

"Just a few more steps." I shouldered my way into the half finished door. It was just a frame, but the door hadn't been plumbed yet so it was just a piece of particle board closing it off. The nails creaked under the weight of my body and finally let free. I stepped over the threshold and caught her around the waist, dragging her inside.

"Holy Goddess." She twirled around, her heels clicking on the endless stretch of beachy gray hardwood. There was light coming in from the street. No blinds were up on the windows yet.

But thank God there were actual windows in so we wouldn't freeze. A huge bay window slashed moonlight and lamplight over the room. It hit on the gorgeous island countertop and L-shaped kitchen. The living room was wide open and her steps echoed in the space.

I followed her slowly, watching the wonder and curiosity chase across her face. Then she slowly let her coat slide down her arms and she tossed it on a stack of flooring that needed to be finished.

She turned and her curls glowed in the moonlight. Her pale skin was gilded in silver and one of the crystal necklaces she always wore glinted between her breasts.

I hadn't gotten a look at her without her jacket before. Her dress was a floaty bunch of layers that draped along her willowy form. The edges of it floated around her knees and hung a little lower in the back. The neckline curved along the gentle swell of her breasts in some complicated layer of material.

So many layers. And I wanted to strip her out of each one of them.

I crossed to her, my soft-soled shoes silent in comparison to the quiet click of her stilts. I steered her gently to the right and sure enough, there was my large four poster bed made out of ash.

We weren't in my bed this first time we were together, but at least I'd be able to spread her out on something I made.

Our fingers twisted together and her chest rose and fell with… excitement, I hoped.

I couldn't read her eyes in the dim light, but maybe the darkness was best for now. Maybe she wouldn't see how nervous I was. How much I wanted her.

I reached up to the little ties between her breasts and tugged one free. The layer of dark material slipped open, showing her milky skin. I lowered my mouth to her chest, teasing my tongue around the chain of her heavy pendant and up to her neck.

I buried my face in the sultry scent of her. Crisp winter with a layer of lemons. Not the summery fresh kind though. Something darker, spicier layered over it. And the scent of wood and sawdust swirled around us.

The walls were framed out, but they hadn't put drywall up yet for the bedroom. I inched her back, her heels making tracks in the dust to the bed. A plastic-wrapped mattress was tucked into the frame.

Not exactly the Hilton.

Hell, not exactly my own four poster bed either, but it would do for now. I tossed my jacket on the bed as I dragged her closer and covered her mouth again, thirsting for that little sound she made.

There it was.

I chased it, my rough fingers catching on the flowy material, but then she was helping me. She stripped off a layer to leave her in a slip of dark material. Her breasts beaded up at the tips and I lowered my mouth to take one through the fabric.

Her fingers slid into my hair as she arched her back. I curled my arms around her, pressing her tighter against my jeans. I nosed my way into the layers of her dress to find the lacy thing she called a bra.

It was see-through.

"Christ, you're beautiful."

I twirled my tongue around the little pink tip until it was taut and the tiny moans she gave me heightened into groans. Her nails scraped along my scalp, holding me there against her.

There was no doubt she was with me.

Thank fuck.

I lifted her up and wrapped her legs around me, dragging her skirt up so I could fill my hands with her perfect ass. She held on tight, her arms around my shoulders as I positioned her to get to those breasts again. Her curls curtained around me, drowning me in her scent.

I dragged my teeth up over her chest to nip at her throat. She arched against me, her breath catching and her heart racing. I backed up until my thighs hit the mattress before turning and rolling her under me.

I didn't quite hit my jacket, but considering the way she was arching up under me, I didn't think she cared. I settled her across the middle of the bed, her hair fanning out as she reached up for me.

Her knee hooked around my hip as she dragged me down by my tie. "Can we get rid of this?"

"Yes, please. I hate ties." I leaned back enough so I could jerk the tail through the knot. She made a gimme fingers gesture as I got it off.

I handed it to her as I went for my belt. She trailed the end of the tie down the middle of her breasts. "It smells like you in here. Sawdust, like your shop."

I swallowed at the thought of her stretched out over my workbench. "You're going to kill me."

She grinned in the dark, her heeled foot dragging up the back of my jeans. "I don't think I've ever killed a guy with lust before."

I shoved her skirt up and hooked her knee over my shoulder. "Let's see if I can do some of the same." I kissed my way down her inner thigh.

"August, wait... Holy—" Her voice cut off as I tucked my tongue under the little scrap of silk she was wearing.

She was wet for me. So wet. I learned her sighs and her intimate taste. The salty seascape that would forever be Kinleigh in my mind. Her thighs quivered and my name rumbled through her throaty sighs.

I found her tight little clit and circled it ruthlessly. She writhed under me and I had to hold her down from bucking me off of her. Her moans turned into cries, and she twisted to get away from me at the same time she gripped my hair to make me stay.

I grinned against her thigh and drank her down as she vibrated under me. I couldn't take it anymore.

Tugging at my jacket underneath her, I prayed my hands were steady enough to get on the condom. Thank God for Gideon.

I hooked her legs around my hips and leaned back to get to my belt again. She reached for me, helping me until we were laughing and fumbling with the buckle and zipper and then her cool, long fingers were around me.

Her huge blue eyes glimmered in the low light. "Well, hello there."

My face went hot, but luckily, I was pretty sure I was hidden in the shadows. She tightened her hold and licked her lips.

"No way. I won't make it."

She tried to sit up. "It's only right to return the favor."

"Next time." She tightened her hold and I grunted. "Definitely next time."

She went quiet, but I didn't want to let her think. I couldn't do this only once with her. Not after knowing just how perfect she was for me. But I wouldn't push now. I'd wait her out just like I'd been doing for months.

Surely I had more patience inside me. Just not right now.

I lifted the foil packet between us and she snatched it from me. "Dear Goddess, thank you." She tore it open as I freed myself fully.

Before I could ask for the condom back, she rolled it down on me.

"Shit."

She dragged me down over her and I had to get inside her. I nudged aside her panties and hissed as I slid inside to the root, as if we'd done this a million times instead of this being the first. She fisted around me with so much warmth and softness my vision hazed. I threw my head back at the perfection of it and then she was vining her way around me, surrounding me in her heat and wetness.

Her arms slipped around my neck and her legs curled around me until there was no air. Just Kinleigh finally wrapped around me.

I braced myself on either side of her and drove into her. Her boots were probably leaving marks on my ass, but I didn't care. I was so far gone, pain and pleasure were a rioting mass of colors inside me.

Like an imprint I'd never get off.

All too soon, I knew the end was coming for me like a freight train. I tried to hold it off, but she felt too good.

There was no way I was going alone.

Not this time.

I reached between us, searching for where she was flushed and swollen. She cried out my name, clamping down on me. Wrenching my release from me no matter how much I tried to stave it off.

God, I was so fucking gone for her.

I threw my head back and locked my gaze with hers as she shuddered, her fingers digging into my shoulders as we matched each other in every way. I lowered my mouth to hers and swallowed her cries, giving her back a heated groan of my own.

"Kinleigh." Her name burned my tongue. "Fuck, Kinleigh."

Losing myself inside her was the sweetest pain I'd ever known.

FIVE

KINLEIGH

WARMTH AND BULKY MUSCLE WRAPPED IN THE SCENT OF EUCALYPTUS draped over me. I didn't want to let him go.

August Beck had just been inside me. Dear Goddess, he still was. He'd left me battered like a shell along the shore, but I'd never felt more delicious.

How was he still hard?

He pressed his face into my neck, nibbling a little until I wiggled under him with a laugh.

He rose up to look down at me, his hips rocking slightly. Reminding me all over again how good we'd been together.

I groaned and dug my nails into his shoulders. He was an oak wrapped in skin. Not a single part of him was soft. And I could verify that. Whoa.

"How?"

His lips quirked. "Incentive." He lowered his mouth to my neck again, rubbing his scruff against my skin until I shrieked out a giggle.

"*Shh*. Do you want to broadcast we're up here?"

"I'm a passionate woman."

"No truer words, Kin." He hovered over me, his lips gentle on mine. "I never want to leave this room."

I rubbed the upper part of my heel down his thigh. He still had his jeans on. I still had my panties on for that matter. He'd just shoved them aside and slid in. And yet I still felt like purring like a contented cat. In fact, I could curl up right now and take a nap.

My arms slid away from his shoulders to flop on the plastic-wrapped mattress.

He laughed. "Is that—oh, man, you rocked my world? Or thank God today is over?"

I opened one eye. "Need a little ego stroke." I tightened myself around him still inside me.

He groaned as he dropped his chin to his chest with a hiss. "Oh, I don't need that. I felt how hard you came. And how hard I'm going to make you come again."

"Is that a fact?" I hooked my knee around his waist, holding him tighter. "Round two so soon?"

"I'm good until sunrise." He curled his arm under me and lifted me like I was no more than a blanket.

I yelped as he shifted to sit on the mattress and sat me astride him. I tipped my head back at the fullness and his recovery time. I mean, he'd finished, right?

My dress was half off my shoulder and my nipple was caught on the edge of my slip. Which August was fully taking advantage of. Jeez, he was good at that. He sucked harder, making everything in me clench.

He scraped his teeth up over the middle of my chest to my throat. "If only I had a second condom."

I laced my fingers at the back of his neck as he drew me up straight. "I thought you were a Boy Scout?"

"Fuck no. I suck at being a joiner. Really good at building shit for people though."

"Exceptional." I tightened my knees along his hips to hold him where I wanted him. I so shouldn't be. But I couldn't remember feeling so deliciously sated and on edge at the same time. I counted myself lucky if an orgasm was included with some form of friction.

Especially something like this. Under the cover of night in a place we shouldn't be. Or maybe that was what had made it so good? I wasn't exactly the illicit sex kind of girl. Heck, I wasn't a booty call kind of girl, period.

Not that he was a booty call.

Nope, he was even worse. A wedding reception hookup. Not that I'd actually made it into the reception. Oh, and couldn't forget the fact that he was my best friend's brother.

"Where did you go?" He dug his fingers into my ass.

"I was just thinking how unusual this is for me."

"Me too." He tipped his forehead to touch mine. "I've wanted this for—"

My phone started vibrating. Dammit.

"How do you have a pocket in this thing?" August tugged at the flowy layer pooling between us.

"Yes, because I can sew. And every woman should have pockets in her dress for just these times."

He wrapped his arm around my back. "Ignore it."

I wanted to. What had he been saying? Had he really wanted me before tonight?

Then he was kissing me again. And he really deserved a few gold medals in that arena. He cupped my jaw and his flavor and scent just seeped into my bones.

My phone pulsed against my belly twice more.

"Ignore it," he said against my mouth and dragged me back under.

The ice cream truck chime had me scrambling off him, almost tripping in my haste to get off.

Ivy. Dear goddess.

I fumbled for my phone.

August hissed and cupped himself. Hopefully, I hadn't injured anything important in my hurry.

Sorry, Mr. Wonderful. Seemed like the best name for August's number one tool right now.

I didn't want to answer the still chiming phone. Nope, I couldn't answer it. No way.

I silenced the ring and pulled my dress up over my shoulder. My ankle buckled and August shot out a hand to steady me.

"Sorry. Just scared me."

He shoved his hair back from his face. I wasn't used to seeing it without his backwards cap. Then again, I only usually saw him in work mode. He was kind of like me, always working. We both pulled late nights at our respective shops.

What had I been thinking?

My thighs still throbbed from twining myself around his thick middle. So much muscle and layers of strength. And he'd felt so darn good.

Focus. My phone started ringing in my hand again. This time, it was a text chime. I flicked it open and found a barrage of text messages waiting for me.

Rylee: How much tequila did you drink? Do we have to fish you out of one of the bathrooms around town?

Ivy: Where are you? You're missing cake.

Ivy: Seriously, where are you?

Kelsey: You're missing all the dancing. Where you be?

LuckyCharms: Don't make me get sober. Where are you?

Rylee: You ok? You're harassing my buzz, girl.

Rylee: Oops. Harshing. Stupid AC.

Ivy: Don't make me turn on the friend finder app.

I quickly typed back a message that I was coming. And I hadn't been able to answer the phone because I was in the bathroom. Seemed safest. I kind of needed to find one of those, to be honest.

"Is there somewhere I can, you know..." I gestured at my disheveled self.

He nodded toward the left. "I think the main bathroom is actually done."

"Great." I snatched my coat off the bed.

"Kin?"

I stopped, turning toward him in the shadows. His ultra white shirt practically glowed in the moonlight. That and the endless bit of tanned skin underneath there were riveting. I couldn't see him clearly, but the memories of him at the lake were burned in my brain already.

Now I could add this shadowy, hot, ridiculously decadent encounter to my memory banks.

Oh, sleepless nights, here I come.

"You're not gonna get weird about this, right? We're good?"

"Of course. Why would I get weird?" I'd just freak out instead. That wasn't weird. Because I'd totally screwed up for the sake of an orgasm and maybe almost another. Okay, so there were definitely two, on the way to three. But I wasn't counting. Mostly.

I escaped to the bathroom. He was right that it was mostly done, except for the whole no paper of any sort in there issue. Or towels. But I did what I could to get my clothes back to semi-presentable. One of the ties was frayed.

I shivered.

I remembered when it happened. His impatient hands on me had driven me crazy. I'd never had a guy that wild to get into my pants. Or lack of pants. To rip at my tie to get closer to my skin—well, that would live with me for a long time.

Good thing, because this definitely couldn't happen again.

I shrugged into my jacket. My hair was beyond help at this point. So that was what sex hair looked like. My finger in a socket. Wonderful.

"Kin?"

"Yeah, coming." I stuffed my hands into my jacket pockets and met August in the moonlit room. He'd cleaned up our wreckage. Funny how it was just a high-end mattress in the middle of a pile of sawdust when it had felt like so much more.

He moved in front of me, smoothing his hands along my arms. "You okay?"

"Sure. Why wouldn't I be?" I was glad he couldn't see my face or the fact that I was freaking out. How many times had I done this sort of thing?

Oh, right. Never.

The rare handful of guys I'd been with in my life were always after careful consideration and perfectly pleasant sex. It hadn't been boring or anything, but it was never like...*that.*

I couldn't even look at that mattress.

"Let's get back to the wedding before someone comes looking for us."

I tried to move around him, but he caught my arm. "Kin?"

I stared at the floor. I could barely see anything, and I hoped to the goddess that was the same for him.

"No regrets?"

"No," I whispered.

"I don't believe you."

I forced my voice to even out. "It was just...intense."

"I can work with intense. And repeat it."

"I'm sure you could."

"Would it be so wrong?"

My phone started ringing again. Ivy. Like I needed a reminder of my epic stupidity. "That's your sister."

"Who cares?"

"I care." Finally, I stared up at him. His eyes were barely a gleam in the room, but his scent and warmth were right there, overwhelming me. I wanted to lean into it. Into him. I couldn't remember wanting anything more in my life.

I pulled away. "We've got to get back before a search party comes looking for us."

He sighed and let my arm free.

The trip down the stairs was decidedly less exciting this time. Now it seemed full of debris and hazards that should have stopped us.

Before I could try to climb over the stack of lumber, August was behind me. "Careful."

His breath caressed my ear as he lifted me over and gently lowered me down two stairs before hooking one of his long legs over it all and meeting me at the bottom of the stairs.

I blasted through the door and had never been so happy for the brisk wind coming off the water, whipping down the alleyway. A good ol' slap of reality.

Music and laughter chased the wind as whoops and catcalls came from The Haunt. I followed the sounds like a beacon. Anything to get away from the tumultuous feelings from next door.

I'd totally lied to him. I regretted every second right now.

It had been way easier when I'd had no idea how good we were together. It had been so much easier to live in the denial I'd been steeped in for all these years.

Yeah, years. There was no sense lying to myself now.

"Kin, wait."

But I didn't wait. I practically ran down the alley to the sidewalk and lost myself in the street traffic flowing in and out of the restaurant. I followed a river of people into the usually dimly lit horror fan's wet dream.

Except this time The Haunt was lit up with wild purple and orange lights strung around all the scary replicas. Michael Myers had a bat perched on his shoulder wearing a veil. Jason Voorhees and Freddy Krueger were dressed like a bride and groom and had been moved behind the cake. Obviously, Rylee's handiwork. No one else would have the balls to touch them.

Macy had lost her veil—now on Jason's hockey mask—and her train was hitched up on her hip with a rainbow-colored scrunchie. Her shoes were gone and she was getting dipped by John Gideon in front of everyone.

My heart squeezed as I came to a halt just outside the circle gathered around them.

I'd never seen Macy so at ease with public affection in my life. But she was kissing him in front of all of our friends. Rylee and Vee were whooping it up, and the war cry Ivy let out reminded me of the crazy blond from the end of *Dirty Dancing*.

There was no doubt as to why Macy had ended up pregnant as quick as humanly possible when Gideon put that ring on her finger. The whole restaurant was flooded with their sex pheromones.

Looked like the honeymoon would be just as hot.

My chest was tight.

Suddenly, I wanted to leave. To go to my safe little shop where I knew every corner, every piece of clothing and trunk, every couch and chair, every crystal and jewel. Not stay here where it was so full of laughter and love.

All the things I couldn't have. Probably would never have.

"Kin, there you are." Ivy snagged my arm and pulled me forward. "Where have you been?"

"I—"

"Never mind. You're here now and it's time for all the single ladies to line up."

"No. I really don't need—"

"Oh, but you do. All us married mamas have to live vicariously through you and Gina and Gabby. Even Macy's girls from the café are here." She pushed me forward. "Go."

Instead of a garter and bouquet, there was a stuffed bat and cat sitting in a place of honor on a small table beside the remaining cake shrapnel. Evidently, they'd fed the entire town with the huge gothic haunted house cake that Vee had designed with Tabitha over at Sugar Rush, the town bakery.

And I hadn't gotten a single piece.

Clapping sounded in time with the song being pumped into the room. Macy climbed up on the chair someone had dragged over to her and Gideon.

"All right, people. I'm ready for my damn honeymoon, so let's get this crap over with."

The room booed when she held up the black stuffed bat.

"What? You think I'm letting you animals watch my husband feel me up for a garter? Get real."

More booing.

I couldn't help but laugh even as I was getting herded into a group of women. Gina hooked her arm through mine and dragged me in closer.

"I say we escape."

Gina grinned. "No way. I'm looking for my luck to change from this eternal single status."

"And a stuffed cat is going to be the answer?" I snorted.

"A kitty is always the answer." Tabitha Monaghan blew a curl out of her face, giggling as she bumped into Gabby who fell into Gina, bumping me back a step.

Oh, this was going to be a cluster for sure.

A waiter buzzed along the edges of the pen of desperate women. I reached out for a cup and took a long drink. It was the only way I was getting through this.

My eyes watered. Holy spiked version of the punch.

"Oh, I need one." Gina wiggled by and chased the guy, dragging him back to pass out drinks to all of us.

She clapped to Adam Lambert's "Stranger You Are" and wiggled her little butt before bumping Gabby and Chloe, one of the servers at the café.

"How much of the punch did you get into?" I asked Tabitha.

"Not enough." She took another off the tray. "Thank you!" She winked at the waiter and then it was bottoms up.

When in Rome. I lifted mine. "Sláinte."

"That's more like it." Gina also tossed back her cup of dangerous orange punch.

The men were whooping it up from the other side of the room, Lucky being the instigator of the most noise. His suit really was something to behold.

"Okay. Here we go!" Macy held Gideon's shoulder as she stood beside him. She handed him the bat.

He sighed and turned around. "All right, let's do this."

Macy whacked him. "Hurry up."

Gideon dragged her down for another kiss. "Don't rush me, woman."

"I can if I want. Bride's prerogative."

Jealousy crawled up my throat as I reached for another one of the full cups of punch. The waiter just sighed and held out the tray for us all to take another.

Lucky was moving his hips in ways I hadn't seen since *Magic Mike.* Wow.

Gideon threw the cat like a damn softball and hit Lucky square in the forehead. It bounced up and August immediately shot his hand up, catching it like a pop fly.

Oohhhs and *ahhhs* filled the room.

He met my gaze across the room and my cheeks flushed. I was hoping most people thought it was from the booze. *Please, goddess.*

"All right, enough! My turn." Macy steadied herself on Gideon's shoulder. He turned around and slung his arm around her hip.

"All right up there?"

"I'm good." She licked her lips then turned her head, momentarily breaking whatever spell was between them.

My throat tightened. To have that kind of connection with anyone seemed so out of reach.

The music went up another few notches and Gina and Tabitha held their hands up. I tried to shuffle behind them. I didn't want any part of cat-catching, thanks.

I sidestepped to the edge of the crush of single ladies and Chloe dragged me back. "Where are you going?"

"Here we go," Macy shouted.

The black, gray, and white stuffed cat went flying. Gina snagged the tip of the paw and it bounced off Tabitha's head and right into my waiting hands.

"Dammit."

Gina grabbed me into a hug and twirled me around. "You're next!"

"No way."

"Yes way." She pushed me out of the crowd of people and into August's arms.

He slung an arm around my shoulder. "Helluva thing, huh?" He smiled down at me. The crinkles beside his crazy beautiful green eyes made the breath back up in my lungs.

"Crazy is one word for it."

He curled me closer into his side. "Picture time." He twisted the cat until it was upright and tucked it into the crook of my arm. His fingers brushed the side of my breast and I shivered.

"Killing me, Kin."

I pasted a smile on my lips, then it turned into a real one when August made the bat kiss the kitten. He was such a sweet dork.

"Kiss her!" Lucky yelled from the back.

I didn't know if I wanted to dropkick Lucky or thank him. Possibly both.

And then August lowered his mouth to mine. It was chaste compared to before, but it brought up every memory. Reminding me exactly what I had to walk away from.

I hugged the kitten closer and hoped my lurking wistfulness didn't bleed into the photos. Then thankfully, August was dragged away by his sister for a dance.

Rylee and Kelsey cornered me to dance to a song by One Direction we all loved.

I laughed when I was supposed to and endured all the ribbing for catching the kitten. But the only thing I could focus on was escape.

Finally, I got to the door and took deep gulps of cool air.

Too much excitement, orange punch, and...well, just too much of everything was slamming into me. I wasn't exactly in driving shape, but my shop was close. It wouldn't be the first time I'd crashed on the couch.

I got to the sidewalk and thought I'd be home free.

Wrong.

"Leaving?"

I folded my arms around the kitten, but I didn't turn around. I really wasn't sure I could face him right now. "I'm beat."

"Are you sure that's all it is?"

I glanced over my shoulder. The bat was sticking out of August's jeans pocket and his dark hair was disheveled around his angular face. I wanted nothing more than to fly right into his arms.

Why not set yourself up for more heartbreak, Kin?

I forced myself to take a step back. "Of course. I'm just tired. I didn't sleep most of the night because I was finishing up Macy's dress."

"Right." He took a step forward and I immediately took another one back. He stopped. "Let me take you home."

I shook my head. "I'm just going to crash at the shop."

"Kin, your locks are crap over there."

"No, you put new ones on, remember?"

"They aren't the kind to keep you safe."

"If they can keep my shop safe, good enough for me."

He jammed his hands into his hair. "Not really. Let me take you home. It's not that far."

Then he'd want to come in. And I wasn't entirely sure I would say no. I shook my head. "I'll see you tomorrow."

"Kin, it's not even midnight. You're going to miss the ball drop."

Well, that wasn't unusual for me. A few times I'd been able to party with my friends, but there had been a lot of lonely New Year's Eve's in my life.

What was one more?

I booked it across the street before he could change my mind. Right now with a bridal kitten in my arms and memories of just how good he felt around me, I really didn't have any strength to say no.

And that was dangerous as hell.

I turned at the door to my shop and took a look over my shoulder to see him watching me. Then I closed the door behind me, throwing both the deadbolt and the regular locks. The familiar scent of lemons and spice immediately put me at ease.

The shop was what mattered. That and making sure I didn't screw things up with Ivy.

She was my family. The closest person to me in the world. She was the important thing. Not this weird connection with August Beck that couldn't ever go anywhere.

SIX

I'D GIVEN HER LONG ENOUGH. AT LEAST I WAS PRETTY SURE.

I twisted my Crescent Cove softball hat around backwards for the third time in an hour. Then again, the sun was bouncing off the snow like a damn spotlight to the eyeballs today. We'd gotten a good dumping the day before, and I'd spent the better part of my early morning plowing.

It was nice side money in a lake town because we surely didn't lack for the white stuff.

Unfortunately, my pickup and I were loaned out for a lot of moving too. A nice couple had hired me to plow them out on moving day—bad idea in mid-January—but it had actually given me a reason to bug Kinleigh.

I smoothed my hand down the Art Deco-style sideboard. It needed a little Kin TLC, but it was exactly the kind of thing she loved. Usually, she would drag me upstairs to help her refinish something like this. She was determined to show me the finer side of rehabbing furniture.

I was usually more interested in creating from scratch, but I had to admit this was a beautiful piece. The cutouts in the front needed a few sections replaced. I traced my thumb over the maze design. I could make an easy template to match that up.

Knowing Kin, she'd have some crazy material stretched behind it to give it...what did she call it? Visual interest. Everything about Kinleigh was visual interest.

She'd probably put some weird pattern behind it and sell it for seven hundred dollars on her website.

Whatever she did would be amazing, but my goal was to actually see her and not watch her perfect backside escaping up the stairs before I could get out of my shop to talk to her. Not that I minded the view, but she was driving me crazy.

Ever since I'd gotten my hands on her New Year's Eve, I couldn't get my mind off her. The sounds she made, the way she kissed, even the way she dug her heeled boots into my ass. I wanted all of it again. And fucking again.

I raked my fingers through my hair then shoved my hat back on my head. Enough stalling.

I grabbed the smaller sack of goodies I'd gotten from the moving couple. Evidently, they liked Art Deco everything. And I knew that was Kinleigh's catnip.

I tucked a larger box under my arm. I'd landed a few cool switch plate covers and three pendant lights that she'd love.

"Pathetic," I muttered to myself. But I headed up the stairs to her shop anyway.

She'd added new photos to the stairwell. That was Kin—forever finding ways to sell stuff. Tiny price tag stickers in matching designs were artfully tucked in the corners. Obvious but not intrusive to those who wanted to just enjoy her style.

I knew plenty of people took day trips into Crescent Cove to look around our endless little shops, mine included. A lot of us store owners—at least the younger owners who were determined to make our shops successful—did most of our sales online. We had plenty of foot traffic in the summer months, thanks to the lake and the vacation cabins dotted all around Crescent Cove. But the winter was a little rougher. Especially now that Christmas was over.

At least I had enough special orders to keep me busy until April, thank God.

The closer I got to her door at the top of the stairs, the louder her music became. Evidently, it was a grunge rock kind of day. Gavin Rossdale and the heavy guitars of Bush met me when I opened the door. As usual, the spicy lemon scent of whatever it was Kinleigh always had in her various diffusers was the first thing I noticed.

The bell over the door tinkled and Kinleigh's voice came from the back.

"Feel free to look around. I'm back here if you need anything."

The shop had been mostly de-Christmassed though there always seemed to be an abundance of twinkle lights wrapped around dress forms, furniture, or shelves. Her Christmas tree had been stripped of all the interesting ornaments she always seemed to have.

Instead, they were artfully arranged on a table beside the tree with a chalkboard sign stating they were at a reduced price. Now the tree was full of pink, red, and white Valentine's Day type items.

I shook my head. Only Kinleigh would make a Valentine's tree.

I spotted a sweet little harp that would be a good gift for my mom though. Shifting the box to my other hip, I set the bag down as I plucked two more things off. One for Ivy and Rhiannon.

Shopping done.

Add some flowers and I'd be a hero for about three minutes. Then again, that was all it took some days to make the women in my life happy.

Except the one I wanted more and more as the days went by.

I tucked the fluffy baby rattle attached to a flamingo, the dainty harp, and the sparkly ice cream cone into the crook of my arm.

Then nearly lost it all when Patches tried to trip me.

"Really?"

The cat purred and wound her way around my ankles. She sat and curled her tail around her feet, the white tipped end twitching.

I set everything down on the huge old table Kinleigh used for her checkout station. I'd been about to bend down to give Patches a little loving when she sashayed her way under a table. Unshockingly, another female in this building had decided I wasn't worth their time.

I headed to the second level of her store. It was the pointed part of the place that had given her spot the name Kinleigh's Attic.

The beams were decked out in fairy lights—I knew since I'd helped her and Ivy staple them up there when she opened a few years ago. Back then, all the little chores I'd been dragged into from my sister had seemed more like a pain in the ass than anything else.

But looking at it now with fresh eyes, thanks to Kinleigh blasting into my brain with that kiss back in October... Yeah, everything seemed even more important. My stamp had been all over her life for years and I'd never opened my damn eyes to it.

The closer I got to the woman herself, the more disorganization I encountered. Things were always a little chaotic when it came to Kinleigh's place. At least compared to my orderly space downstairs. She had doodads and bright colored trinkets tucked into corners, on tables, and stacked on shelves. Mysterious racks of clothing were arranged all over the place.

Her filming lights were up, and her tripod stood off to the side. The box lights gave off a diffused glow. Right now, they flanked a pair of jeans hanging by painted clothespins across a wire. Half a dozen pairs were draped over as many chairs.

And in the middle on the floor, Kinleigh was surrounded by threads in every color of the rainbow. Swatches of fabric stuck out of a quilted bag that reminded me of something my grandmother had in her craft room. An array of patterns made my eyes hurt. Some neon, some floral, and still others that were probably older than both of us put together.

She was sitting in the center of it all, patiently stitching some design into the back pocket of the shredded pair of jeans. Each former hole in the denim had a scrap of colorful fabric patched with amazingly detailed stitches.

Her hair was gathered on top of her head with a bandana trapping her curls away from her face, save for one stubborn lock that floated forward to catch the light streaming in from the hexagon window.

She hadn't bothered with makeup—or, more likely, she'd been working all through the night and day.

Kinleigh on a creative tear always put a hum in the air.

"Hey."

She jolted and hissed, bringing her finger up to her mouth. Her huge blue eyes darted to mine, and then down again. "Ouch."

"Sorry. Didn't mean to startle you."

"You didn't. Well, you did, but the needle..." She shrugged then set the jeans she was working on aside. "What are you doing here?"

I stuffed my hands into my pockets. "Had something you might be interested in."

"Oh. For the shop?"

"Yeah. Want to check it out? It's in the truck."

She pressed her lips together. "I'm kinda..." She fluttered her hands to encompass the chaos. "Can it wait?"

"Yeah, of course."

Disappointment slapped hard.

"I'm just kinda in the zone, you know?"

"Yeah, totally get it. How many times have I done an all-nighter?"

"Right?" She gave me a half smile and blew the curl out of her face.

The phone rang and she popped up. She was wearing a pair of the artfully stitched jeans. This one was bright pink thread on dark washed denim. A matching bright pink tank peeked from underneath the oversized dark sweater she was wearing.

I wanted to step forward and kiss the slash of skin showing.

But that definitely wasn't happening. Not when she practically sprinted to get to the phone when just a second earlier, she'd practically told me to buzz off.

"Stupid," I muttered to myself. The call was business, but still, it felt as if she didn't want to be in the same space with me.

I shifted to see her at the ancient avocado-green wall phone. The cord was stretched to the limit as she ducked in the back.

Private conversation?

"You are seriously losing it over this chick." I twisted my hat around. "And talking to yourself."

I backed up. My big boots would probably crush something up there if I got any closer anyway. Her low voice floated out of the back storeroom. Seemed like a customer call.

I sighed and took the box with the large pendant lights to a rare naked corner in her place. I'd outfitted the ceiling with various hooks for just this kind of thing. I pulled the little stepladder out from behind a heavy curtain. She'd wanted to soften the brick and cut down on some of the echo of the large room.

Yet another thing I'd helped her with. Just how blind had I been about this woman?

I pulled my multi-tool out of my pocket and quickly hung the lights. I'd already checked the guts of the unit to make sure the lightbulb wouldn't start a damn fire. Just what this place needed, another fire hazard.

The brass patterned box around it was pretty cool, all things considered. Maybe she'd notice it.

I stepped down and tucked the ladder back on its hidden hook. Kin was still in the back. Today was definitely not my day—again.

Just as I got to the door, I noticed her peeking around.

Looking for a customer? Or to see if I'd left?

I slammed the door behind me and headed back down to my shop where shit still made sense.

Three days later, I was staring at the Art Deco console in the corner of my shop again. Part of me wanted to do the rehab on it and then bring it up, the other half wanted to see Kinleigh's reaction first. She got such a kick out of old, broken pieces that she could make new again.

My heart kicked under my ribs. That side of her used to annoy me.

"Think it's going to talk or something? Does the wood do that for you?" Jared whispered out of the side of his mouth.

I couldn't fight back my grin. "Where'd you come from?"

"St. Marie's Ave."

"Smart ass." I straightened and tossed my rag at his stupid large brimmed hat.

He caught it and threw it back at me. "Is that any way to talk to your favorite public official?"

"I like Christian better."

"You wound me."

I snorted. Christian was Moose's brother—though he was almost his polar opposite—and Jared's lone deputy. "Since you're here, you can make yourself useful."

"You know asking favors after insulting me isn't advised."

I nodded to the console. "Just take the other end. We're bringing it upstairs."

"Up Kinleigh's stairs? Are you high?"

"If I was, I wouldn't tell you."

Jared attempted to lift one side and grunted. "Why are we doing this?"

"Because Kin loves projects. Especially if they're Art Deco."

"Art what?"

"Never mind. Just lift."

"Would you just ask the girl out and put us all out of our misery?"

My side of the console thudded to the floor.

"What? Like this is a shocking revelation?" He stacked his arms on his side. "You've been into her forever."

"Would you keep it down?"

"She doesn't know? Or is your river of denial deep enough to swim in?"

"Look, it's a new thing. And not going too well."

"Couldn't seal the deal?"

"Jesus, Jared." I collapsed against the sawhorse behind me. "Like I'd give you details."

He tipped his hat back. "Oh, so it *is* serious. Huh. Well, I suppose we all have to do it sometime."

"It's not like that." I didn't think. How could I know for sure? She was too busy avoiding me as if I smelled rotten.

Sure, I got a little ripe somedays with the heat of the shop. I took a hesitant sniff and luckily, just smelled sawdust and laundry detergent.

When I looked up again, Jared was grinning at me.

"Shut up. Just help me bring this upstairs and maybe—"

"Maybe you'll get rewarded for your present?"

"No. Well, that would be nice, but it isn't why I got it for her. I just saw it and knew she'd want it. And it's not like I want favors or whatever."

"You don't?"

"I mean—Jesus, just help me. I can't talk about it. I'm not going to talk about it."

He gave me a narrow-eyed look, one eyebrow disappearing into the shadow from his ridiculously big hat.

"It's private."

"It's the Cove. There is no private here."

Was that why she didn't want to date me? Beyond her favorite excuse of Ivy, that is.

"I'm sick of looking at this thing."

"Handily, I'm sick of looking at your mug too."

I straightened and grabbed my end of the surprisingly heavy piece of furniture. Then again, it was all solid wood. None of the particle board crap that newer furniture was made out of. Nope, this was solid and would definitely stand the test of time.

Then again, so did my pieces.

We shuffled our way out the front of my shop and onto the sidewalk. Our two businesses didn't share an entrance. The wind was howling and the sky was churning. So much for that sunny January day we were enjoying.

Then again, lake effect was often cruel and capricious. Most likely, I'd be doing some more plowing by tonight.

Jared grunted. "Is there a body in here?"

"Need some help, old man?"

"Who are you calling old?" The wind gusted and Sheriff Brooks' hat went soaring.

I sighed.

Lucky hustled after it. I winced at he stomped his size fifteen on it to halt its progress.

"Dammit," Jared muttered.

Lucky lumbered back to us. He was a big dude and while not exactly clumsy, he definitely didn't excel in the grace or tact department. He glanced down at the khaki-colored hat now wearing said size fifteen boot mark and crushed it back on Jared's head. "Want me to take that?"

"I got it."

I pressed my lips together at Jared's rapidly reddening face. It was damn heavy. I'd had to use my dolly to get it off my truck and into the workshop. And okay, maybe I should have waited to unwrap it fully before I took it up to Kinleigh. But she'd pissed me off and I'd actually contemplated refinishing it myself.

Ugh, this woman was going to make me insane. I never overthought stuff. Plan, act, sell or gift merchandise and move on. Period.

"Can we put it down for a second?" Jared's vein was going to pop out of his freaking neck.

Lucky slid one big paw under it and lifted it easily. "Got it."

Just then, Jared's radio chirped on his shoulder. "Sheriff, we've got a 10-54 on Elm Street."

Jared frowned and tapped on his mic to reply. "A what? Gina? Is that you? Where's Bonnie?"

"Mom had an emergency."

He gave Lucky a disgusted grunt as he effortlessly helped me maneuver the console toward Kinleigh's doorway.

"We got this." I nodded to Jared. "Oh, what's a 10-54?" I called after him.

"You don't want to know." He slapped his hat against his thigh then tossed it into his SUV with a grumble of words that were snatched by the wind.

"Sure we have to do those stairs?"

"I'm sure."

Lucky waggled his eyebrows. "Think Kin would want to go out with me sometime? She's hot."

My fingers ached from my hold. Or maybe from the harder grip I'd suddenly taken.

Lucky shouldered his way through the door and up the stairs. He barely needed my help. Damn battering ram that he was. "Is that a no?"

"You do what you want."

He shook his long hair back. "I don't poach if that's the deal. I thought you guys were just friends." Lucky grunted as I climbed the stairs faster. "Hey, ease up."

"Gravity, Lucky."

"Right." He backed his way into Kinleigh's shop.

The chimes above the door gave a friendly hello. She'd changed out the jangling bells she'd used for Christmas. She was always changing things.

"I'll be right with you," she called.

I jerked my chin to the semi-empty spot under the windows.

Lucky steered that way and set it down gently. I honestly hadn't believed he had a gentle bone in his body. He collapsed into the bean bag chair and stretched his back. "I need this thing."

I left him to his weird bowed situation. I didn't want to know or watch.

"Kin?"

She popped her head out from the back room. "Hey."

"I brought you something for the shop."

"You did?" Her huge eyes danced even as her attention strayed back to her storeroom. "I'll check in a second. There are ducks crossing Elm Street. Well, not exactly crossing. They've stopped traffic. They keep walking in drunken circles. It's riveting."

"Well, I guess that's what a 10-54 is."

"A what?"

"Did I hear ducks?" Lucky's voice boomed from behind me.

Kinleigh squeaked out a yes and waved him over. "You gotta see this."

Why didn't she invite *me* back there?

I tried to shove down the little annoyance. "I'll just be out here."

"Okay. I'll be out soon." Her gorgeous fiery hair was piled up in a weird turquoise wrap that matched the embroidered jeans she was wearing. An oversized rust-colored sweater slipped off her shoulder, showing off creamy skin and a smattering of freckles.

Lucky's interest matched mine and then some. He moved in behind her to look down at whatever she was watching on.

"Man, they look drunk." Lucky laughed and loomed over her.

"Right? Tabby's been chasing the brown one with the white tail up and down the street. She can't get her delivery truck out."

"How am I supposed to get my afternoon cupcakes?"

Kinleigh's magical laughter floated out to the store followed by Lucky's lower chuckle.

My fists clenched at my sides. It wasn't as if it was any of my business if she flirted with him. Except I was going to rip his hair out by the roots and strangle him with it.

No big deal.

I re-directed my attention on the honey-toned wood of the console and moved it farther in so it didn't block any foot traffic.

Maybe I should have refinished it. It looked pretty shabby next to all of her carefully curated pieces.

Patches wound her way around my ankles and hopped up on the console, and then sprawled out and started licking her paws. "At least you like it." I rubbed my thumb under her ginger and white chin. The top half of her was almost black fur, making her big green eyes stand out. She blinked at me then resumed licking.

"Just like your master. Only interested in me for a second."

I glanced around the room and found the lights I'd brought up a few days ago. She'd added a few things to that spot and highlighted the lamps with her Kinleigh ways.

At least she seemed to like them. Maybe she'd feel the same about the console.

Her giggles rolled out again and I blew out a breath. Yeah, I couldn't listen to that right now. Especially since I hadn't heard that particular laugh since before…

Well, just before.

Maybe I just needed to take the hint. Obviously, she wasn't that into me.

I could probably come to terms with that in a lifetime or two.

SEVEN

KINLEIGH

Mid-February

HAVING A BABY WAS SCARY BUSINESS.

Not even just the physical act of pushing one out, which I had to admit had traumatized me when I'd watched Ivy go through it. I still felt the occasional phantom pain in my hand, and I wouldn't have been surprised if Ivy had broken a bone with her mega-ton squeeze during labor.

But the whole thing. Having to care for a tiny person who relied on you for everything. One who couldn't even hold up her head on her own for long if you let your arm droop.

"There you go. That's a love." I adjusted my hold on the baby and barely resisted burying my nose in her russet curls. She didn't have a ton of them yet. Just enough for Ivy to wrap her head in a festive red headband with hearts all over it and a big floppy bow. "Who's a pretty girl? Who's a sweet munchkin?"

Rhiannon didn't so much as blink. She seemed fascinated by me. My face was must-see TV for the six-months-old-and-under set.

She wasn't the only one. Her eyes were so stunningly blue I was transfixed.

Ivy and Rory had made such a beautiful child. What must it be like to look down at the precious baby you'd made from your love?

Or from extreme fondness on a plastic-wrapped mattress set in a frame on a floor covered with sawdust.

I shifted on Ivy's sofa and bit my lower lip at the slight pressure in my lower belly. Maybe that was a good sign.

Anything else wasn't possible. It just could not be.

"Ivy, I gotta pee," I called out. "Too much tea."

A total lie, but I needed to check my underwear for the sixteenth time today. On top of another twenty times yesterday and the day before that. For the first time in my life, I was hoping for an accident. I'd even worn one of my nicest pairs to tempt the karmic gods.

Please, please, please.

"Kin, just hang on a sec," Ivy called back from the kitchen. "My food purifier isn't working. She can't have her bananas if they aren't properly—oh, fuck balls!"

I scooped up the baby and raced into the kitchen, half expecting Rhiannon to start wailing. But nope, she just kept looking at me, her chubby fist in her mouth. Then she turned her head to look at her mother just as I did, following Ivy's gaze to the congealed dripping lump of yellow on the ceiling.

"Fuck balls," I echoed.

I wasn't even much of a swearer. But today I was ready to unleash all the curse words until I got my damn period.

"Thank God she can't understand that yet." Ivy blew out a breath that ruffled the auburn hair that had come free from her topknot. "I intended to use this stupid food processor to make dinner tonight. Rory's on his way back from LA and it was supposed to be perfect. I'd put the baby down and while dinner cooked, I'd slip on a sexy nightie and turn on the music and chill a bottle of wine. Then we'd fuck like rabbits before the dinner timer went off." She sighed. "Now I have to go to the store and get a new processor."

Rhiannon fussed in my arms, so I juggled her and cooed softly to get her to settle again. When it actually worked, I smiled. Hey, maybe I could do this after all.

Good thing, since that test in your purse in a ticking baby time bomb.

I didn't even need that test. Nope. I'd just grabbed it on a lark. My period was late, big deal. It had been late before, multiple times. In fact, it wasn't even that odd for me to have inconsistent periods. But I hadn't had sex in a very long time.

Until Macy's wedding night.

Until tequila had made not only my clothes come off but had caused my sense of self-preservation to take a hike.

Until August and I had made—sex. We'd made very good sex.

And that was that.

Even so, I was always pragmatic. I'd bought a test and visited my best friend to try to get her to spill the beans on her preggo symptoms before she knew she was knocked up. I had no intention of telling her about my situation. Or if I did, I certainly wasn't going to name who the daddy was.

Could be. Emphasis on probably not.

Instead, Ivy had whipped up mashed bananas for the baby, and I'd cuddled with her adorable child while hoping fervently I was ruining my favorite panties.

How was this my life?

I shifted restlessly. Now I really did have to pee. "Ivy, speaking of fucking—"

Ivy whipped off her apron. "God, you don't know how pent-up I've been. I mean, we just got off probation, and for the first few months after having this one," she nodded at Rhiannon, who appeared unrepentant, "I couldn't even think about his dick. But now? I just need it. You know?"

I bit my lip and resisted the urge to cover the baby's ears. "Yeah."

Regular sex wasn't a part of my world, but I could imagine. Doing the deed basically stirred a dangerous bloodlust. It wasn't sex with August per se I was craving. It was just—

Okay, it was completely August's fault. I couldn't even look at his broad, competent hands without imagining them wrapped around my breasts.

I swallowed hard. "Maybe you should try a hobby? That's what I'm doing. I'm taking classes on how to knit."

And knotting yarn more than I was actually completing a pattern, but still. At least I was making an effort not to become a sex toy junkie.

Or an August Beck junkie, which was even worse.

"*Pfft,* forget knitting, I want sex."

I couldn't argue with such sound logic.

"He's been so busy with work we haven't even been doing the Zoom naked thing." Ivy sighed again and moved forward to take Rhiannon, who continued to stare at me even once she was ensconced in her mother's arms.

I'd never realized I was so interesting.

"Zoom naked thing?" I repeated, clutching my stomach.

There, that was a cramp. Totally. I was almost certain.

"Yeah, you know. Get on the webcam, take off your clothes, and—"

"Seriously, Ive? This is what I have to hear when I stop by to see my baby sister?"

Goddess, no. This could not be happening.

I shut my eyes and hoped I could make myself vanish just from the power of my mind. There was no way I could face August while I was potentially carrying his child.

Planning to just hide yourself away for the better part of a year, are you?

No, I wouldn't have to. Because I was *not* pregnant.

My back was even starting to ache. So there.

Ivy just rolled her eyes as her brother's heavy boots thumped up the hallway. "Do you ever knock?"

"We share this duplex, remember?"

"Not for much longer."

"Yeah, yeah, when your house is finished being built, you'll be gone. I know the spiel. Maybe I enjoy just being able to pop in on you from time to time." He moved forward to tug on one of Rhiannon's naked baby toes, making her giggle and hold out her hands to him.

He immediately took her into his arms without bobbling her head. I would've sworn my ovaries stood up and did a cheer.

Ivy heaved out a sigh, but she was smiling now. It was hard to watch August making gooey eyes at his niece and not curl your toes.

At least if you were me.

"Yes, but you have your own side, remember? I'm a married woman now, and I need privacy."

"Not when Lucky Charms isn't present and accounted for. Where is he anyway? Thought he was bringing his fancy a—" He glanced down at Rhiannon and cleared his throat. "Butt back from LA today."

"He'll be back tonight. Do you always have to give him such a hard time?"

"He isn't here right now, so I'm not giving him anything. But yes." August turned his head and gave me a smile dripping with sexual promise. "Hey, Kin."

I fumbled for my amethyst cluster necklace. I had a feeling I'd be clutching my crystals a lot today. "Hi. Wasn't sure you even saw me."

Oh, lovely. Sounding needy was the last thing I needed to do right now.

His green eyes heated as he cupped Rhiannon's head in his big hand. "I always see you."

Pleasure bloomed inside me, but I squelched it as I noticed Ivy's pinched brows as she studied us. "Look who's trying to be charming. Even a broken clock is right twice a day."

No one laughed. Or even smiled. The quip landed as many of my attempts at jokes did.

Much like the banana that had just splatted on the newly mopped kitchen floor.

August frowned and tilted his head back, toting his niece with him to get a better look at the ceiling. "You have a leak? What the—it's yellow."

"It's banana. The food processor exploded. I need to get a new one. You can't have a romantic dinner without the dinner."

"Haven't you two had enough romance?" August swiped a finger through the mixture coating the plastic container on the food processor and licked it.

I didn't whimper. I hoped.

"Hmm. Pretty good. Banana? You like those, princess?"

Rhiannon yanked her fist out of her mouth and started to cry.

"You're eating her lunch, jerk. Here, sweetness. Let mama get you a bottle until we get this banana mess sorted." Ivy grabbed a prepared one off the counter and handed it to her fussy daughter, who started sucking on the nipple like it was her job.

It basically was.

"I've got to run to the store. Do you have a few to watch her?" Ivy patted the pockets of her jeans as if she was trying to remember something. "I'd started a grocery list for the rest of the week, so if you can manage, I'll stop by the Piggly too while I'm out. Shopping is so much easier when I don't have to bring the baby in with me."

"If your husband ever stayed home, he could watch his daughter."

"He's working."

"Right. While gallivanting around LA. Wasn't he on some magazine last week?"

"Meeting with rockstars is part of his actual work, Aug. Not sure why this concept is so difficult for you to grasp." Ivy made a face. "So can you watch her or not? Actually, never mind. I know you're on lunch, Kin, but maybe you can—"

"I've got her," we said in unison.

Then we stared at each other.

"We'll figure it out," August said after a moment, his voice low and rough. "Go."

"You're sure?" Ivy grabbed her purse off the counter and stuffed her phone inside. "I'll try to be quick."

"Don't forget the whipped cream," I said over my shoulder.

August's sour expression made me giggle even in the center of my own personal chaos. Which was not helped by the idea of alone time with Ivy's brother with a rosy-cheeked baby between us.

Not in the slightest.

"You know it, sister." Although the phrase was one Ivy had said a million times before, somehow it hit different. "Thank you both! Back soon. Bye, baby girl!" The door closed behind her as Rhiannon kept right on sucking in baby contentment.

"She's pretty much the perfect child." I reached out to stroke her cheek. "They're so lucky."

"Uh-oh," August teased. "You're not getting baby fever, are you?"

"Goddess, no." I jerked back as if the baby had become radioactive.

She hadn't, but August and his possibly too talented penis might as well have been.

"Happens to the best of us when confronted with an absolutely perfect kid. Right, Rhi-Rhi?"

The baby blinked up at him and kept right on drinking.

"Do *you* have baby fever?"

He didn't laugh as I'd expected him to, just shrugged. "Kids are cool."

"Oh, sure, you think they're cool because you have the easy part."

His eyes zeroed in on my face, and my nipples did a double-barrel salute through my raspberry-colored sweater. His gaze dropped and he licked his lips. "Not so easy from where I'm standing, Kin."

I didn't know what he meant, and I was too wiped out right now to analyze it. "Not a picnic on this side of the kitchen either." All at once, my bladder reminded me I had other things to take care of. As did my racing heart. "Excuse me a second."

"Sure. Is everything okay?"

"Fine. Perfect." I hurried out of the kitchen before he could be sweet and make me cry. I wasn't normally that sloppy, but right now, nothing was normal.

As soon as I closed myself in the bathroom, I checked my underwear. I already knew what I wouldn't find.

Nope, no easy outs for me today.

Or hard ones, since I couldn't decide what the hell I wanted.

Closing my eyes, I leaned my head against the wall beside the toilet. Tears hovered far too close. Except now I wasn't even sure why I was about to cry.

I'd always wanted kids. The husband part had gone out of focus a few years ago, but the kids portion of the equation had never quite managed to fade no matter how often I shoved the idea into the background. Juggling business and motherhood wasn't easy. I was practical enough to realize it would be hard to do both well alone.

And of course I would be alone, because when had I been anything but? Once or twice, I'd thought I might have met someone special who would stick around.

I'd been wrong. Ivy and her family were the only people I could count on besides myself.

August is part of her family. You can count on him too.

For normal stuff, sure. When a kid had kicked the bottom of my shop door and messed up the wood, August had brought over a new kickplate without me even asking—and he'd matched it perfectly to my wood. He never hesitated to help if I needed something special for the store that I couldn't find. He'd even offered to build me a tall, narrow dresser to fit in a space I wanted to outfit with accessories to go with some of my vintage finds.

But this was different. How did you tell a guy a hookup at a wedding might end up in forever?

I didn't know how long I sat there, swallowing over the lump in my throat. After a few minutes, August knocked on the door. "Kin?"

I forced myself to rise and wash my hands. "Sorry, did you need to use it? Just a sec." I dried off my hands and opened the door.

August was leaning against the jamb, his hands tucked in his pockets. I stopped short, unprepared for him to be that close—and lifted a hand to his chest when he leaned in.

"Wait." There was no keeping the panic from my voice.

"It feels like I've been doing is waiting." His gaze lingered on my mouth as I flexed my fingers over the shirt warm from his body. "You make me crazy, you know that?"

"I do?"

"Oh, yeah. You can't be that oblivious."

When I dropped my hand and tucked my hair behind my ear, he let out a rough chuckle. "Or maybe you can be." He lifted my chin with his thumb and forefinger. "I can't stop thinking about you."

"With or without clothes?"

The corner of his mouth twisted upward. "Both. But I'm not going to lie I can't forget the wedding. And not because you caught the cat."

The plush cat that currently lived in my closet, hidden under a pile of scrap material. I didn't need any reminders—not of the amazing time I'd spent with August or of the ridiculous possibility I could ever get married, never mind any time soon.

"I can't forget it either, but it's not that simple."

"Sure it is." He drew a finger down the side of my face before moving back the same curl I'd just tucked behind my ear. It wouldn't stay put. Just like my jumping belly as August's bottle green eyes searched mine. "We don't have any rules. We'll just do what feels good." He dipped his head, and this time, I fisted a hand in his shirt.

To hold him off or hold on, I wasn't sure.

"I might be pregnant."

EIGHT

My head kept moving toward hers, the white noise in my head fuzzing out her words.

We could talk later. Right now, I was focused on her pursed glossy pink lips and the way she was clutching my shirt—

Wait, she wasn't tugging me closer. She was holding me off while still gripping me tight.

I forced myself to suck in oxygen as my all too active dick surged against my zipper without any concern for manners. I'd just had to wear my tightest pair of jeans today. They might as well have been a tourniquet, for fuck's sake.

"Okay, try again." I shut my eyes to get myself under control. "I'm listening. And I'm ignoring my cock."

Her quick burst of laughter edged on maniacal. "If I'd ignored your cock, we wouldn't be here. I'm not actually sure we *are* here yet, but if we are, your cock is to blame. How old was that condom anyway?"

"What are you talking about?"

She shook her head then pulled a box out of the purse she wore cross-body and slapped it against my chest.

I stared down at it. "Clear Blue—what the hell?"

"Yeah." Kinleigh blew out a sigh. "I haven't gotten my period."

"What?"

She surprised me by smiling. "You know how babies are born, right?"

I almost said *what* again then decided I'd just sag against the wall and hope this dick-deflating conversation would help the blood flow reroute north again.

"Okay, catch me up. Slowly."

Her lips twitched. "We had sex."

"Amazing, life-changing sex, yes."

Her smile grew, lighting up the fire behind her blue eyes. I was addicted to her expression. Intoxicated by it. So much so that I almost forgot what we were talking about.

Until she spoke again.

"Might really be life-changing." She gripped the box. "I should probably take this."

"It hasn't been that long, right? So maybe you're just late."

"Maybe. Sometimes I am." She frowned. "Where's the baby?"

"I sold her for some extra wood. Figured Ivy wouldn't mind, since she's always on the hunt for romance." Which I wasn't thinking about, especially not now.

Kinleigh's cheeks turned pink. "Seems like you have plenty right now."

"Smart ass. And that's even when you scared half a decade off my life."

Her humor vanished as she turned away.

"Kin, c'mon. I'm just kidding." I touched her shoulder. "Let's take the test before we panic."

"You think you're scared? What about me? I'm the one who has to do this alone."

I hated being repetitive, but in this case, it couldn't be helped. "What? Why would you be alone?"

"August, be real. We had sex."

"Yeah, I was there."

"It was just—"

"Don't." I cupped her shoulder and shifted her toward me again, but she held her ground and stubbornly remained facing the other direction. "It wasn't 'just' anything. I care about you. You care about me. Right?"

When she didn't answer, I let my hand fall away. I'd been chasing this woman around both of our stores for weeks. I'd thought it was just because she was weirded out about Ivy and would get over it. "Hell of a way to tell me, Kin."

"I'm not trying to tell you anything. We burned off some steam, and we're friends."

"Good friends. Friends who got naked once. I would love it if we got naked again, assuming you want the same thing."

She didn't respond.

I pushed a hand through my hair. Why did I keep trying to beat my head—and other parts of my anatomy—against the brick wall of this woman? She was sweet and creative and sexy as hell, but there were other women who rang those bells. Other ones who wouldn't make me feel as clumsy as an outcast high school kid trying to win a date with the homecoming queen.

I wasn't that guy. I had a great business. Supportive family and friends. A full life with, yes, women who would've been happy to go out with me. Or stay in.

I'd even come close to wondering what life would be like with someone more permanent. The only problem was none of them were Kinleigh Scott. And now there could be a baby.

Fuck, we might've made a *baby*.

Us. Her and me, together. The idea was scary as fuck, but somehow it was still…good.

Crazy but good.

Even if she didn't think I needed to be a part of it. I was just the sperm donor, after all. We'd let off steam, so now I was supposed to get gone. That was the role she expected me to play.

Her plot was just about to twist.

"You can think of us being together as casually as if we'd met for lunch, but I'm not like that." I struggled to keep my voice steady. "Just because I'm male doesn't mean I treat sex as if it's meaningless. If I go there, it's important to me. *You're* important to me."

She pivoted to face me. "You're important to me too. But what about Ivy?"

"What about her?"

"I don't know. Isn't this weird for her?" She lifted her hands and dropped them. "I mean, one time, she never has to know. But if there's repeats...if there's a—" She pressed her lips together and shook her head.

I clasped both of her hands in mine. "She loves you. I'm pretty sure she loves me. I'm going to guess she'd be okay with it. My sister only wants us to be happy." I rubbed my thumbs over the backs of her hands, so pale and cool in mine. "Let's take it one step at a time, okay?"

"Yeah. I suppose I should take this." She stepped away from me and drew the test from her purse. "Before Ivy comes back. I mean, I could go home and take it."

"No. Do it here. Now. I can't wait to find out."

A wrinkle formed between her brows. "I thought you weren't freaking."

"Of course I'm freaking. But until we know there's something to worry about, let's just...not."

"Right. That's logical."

Rhiannon started to cry from her room just down the hall. "I'll get her," I said quickly. I'd known I probably wouldn't be able to put her down for long, but I'd wanted to see what was going on with Kinleigh. "You take the test."

"You're sure?"

"Yes."

She moved toward the bathroom, suddenly seeming so fragile although I know she wasn't. She was anything but. Even so, everyone needed reassurance sometimes.

Including me.

"Kin?"

She glanced back.

"We'll be okay, no matter what. I promise."

Nodding, she stepped inside and shut the door.

After rolling out the tension in my neck, I went to check on my niece. Rhiannon had worked herself into a good head of mad. Cheeks red, big blue eyes streaming.

Probably a Ferguson family trait.

I scooped her up and rocked her gently, walking to the big window that looked out on the street. I sang a lullaby to her, one that usually worked, while Rhiannon sobbed.

Good God, did I really think I could do this? Being an uncle was one thing. I was still finding my way there, but I also got to give her back if she fussed or made too much of a mess. I'd changed a couple of diapers when I had no choice. Still, my sister was in charge.

What would it be like if *I* was in charge? Well, Kinleigh and I. We would be a team, no matter what she believed.

That concept didn't bother me nearly as much as I would've thought, huge freaking surprise aside.

I smiled down at Rhiannon as she reached up to tug on my whiskers. I'd been involved in a special order project for a customer until the wee hours of the morning, and shaving had been the last item on my list today.

Ow. My niece had a grip on her.

As the minutes passed, my heart throbbed in my ears. What was going on in there? Was she all right? Maybe I should make sure she hadn't passed out or something.

I turned with Rhiannon in my arms as the door opened.

Kinleigh's eyes were shadowed and heavy, her mouth drawn tight. Neither diminished her beauty, but there was no missing her pervasive sadness.

Momentarily forgetting the baby in my arms, I crossed the room to her and wrapped my arm around her to draw her close. I brushed a kiss over her forehead. "It's okay, Kin. We'll figure it all out, I swear." Even as I spoke softly, my mind was whirling and my pulse was racing. I couldn't take in enough air.

This was really happening. We were having—

Kinleigh combed her fingers through Rhiannon's baby fine curls and looked up at me, her chin trembling. "I'm not pregnant."

Her words struck me mute. No delay in my brain this time. I understood exactly what she'd said, and I didn't know how to compute it.

Rhiannon looked up between us and grabbed for one of Kinleigh's curls, tugging hard enough that she broke our eye contact and squeezed Rhi's chubby little fist.

I didn't know what to say. So many emotions were tangling inside me that I couldn't verbalize them.

As if Kinleigh understood—or maybe she just needed to hold onto the baby right now—she eased Rhi out of my arms so I could walk to the window. I braced my palm against the glass and tried to come up with something rational.

This was a good thing. It was. We weren't even in a relationship. Not from lack of trying on my part but still. We definitely weren't in the space to have a baby.

"August?"

Kinleigh's soft voice just about killed me. I forced myself to smile as I turned back toward her, noticing my niece had quieted in her arms and fallen asleep again. Soothed by her easy rocking and how she cuddled her against her just right.

"You have a way." I nodded at the baby and she glanced down, smiling faintly before her chin trembled again.

She lifted it defiantly and met my gaze. "Glad I have my niece."

So much was unsaid in that statement, and none of it made sense. A few minutes ago, she'd been worried about being pregnant. We both had been. So why did it feel like now we were...disappointed?

I tucked my hands in my pockets. "This is what you wanted," I said carefully.

"What *we* wanted."

"You're sure?"

"About what?"

"The test...you did it right?"

94

"It's not rocket science, Becks. You pee on a stick and it tells you your future."

"Maybe it didn't work? Isn't that a thing? Like sometimes it says you aren't and you are?"

She shifted the baby, seeming as if she couldn't figure out how she wanted to hold her. Rhiannon was currently unconscious, so she didn't mind. "Do you want me to be?"

"I didn't say that. The timing isn't good. We aren't—hell, what are we?"

Kinleigh shifted her gaze somewhere over my shoulder. "We're important to Ivy."

"Right. We are. But as for us, you and me, what are we?"

"We're friends."

"Yeah. And? Because gotta say, Kin, I don't usually fuck my friends."

"August," she gasped, tilting the baby precariously so she could cover her ears. Very belatedly.

The baby who didn't bat one silky eyelash.

"She's too little to care. Also, I guarantee Lucky Charms swears plenty around her. When he even bothers to be home."

"You really don't like him, do you?"

I pulled off my ball cap and finger-combed my hair before putting it back on. "I don't hate the guy. He loves my sister."

"And this baby."

"Yeah, he does," I agreed reluctantly as Kinleigh started circling the room, humming softly to a sleeping Rhiannon. "He's a decent guy. It just feels like my job to bust his balls."

"You know, you could start practicing now to moderate your language. In a few months, she'll understand what you're saying."

"Probably more than a few months until she knows about balls."

Kinleigh shook her head. "You're a contrary sort. I never realized."

"Could be because you run out on me whenever we're alone for more than five minutes." I crossed my arms. "Why is that?"

"I do not."

"Right. So you'd go out with me then. On an actual date."

"Why, so we could have sex again?"

"Little ears," I mocked. "And we don't need to go on a date to do that."

"Maybe we dodged a bullet." She wouldn't look at me. Instead, she stared down at the happily snoozing baby, now sucking on her fingers in her sleep.

"Because I didn't knock you up? Maybe. Depending on if that test was old or something."

"You mean like your condom?"

"I never said it was old. John gave it to me. I'm sure it was perfectly satisfactory." At least I assumed it was. I had no clue how long he'd been toting it around. Macy had gotten pregnant right away. For all I knew, maybe they'd free-bagged it from day one.

"You got a condom from *John?* Like a high school boy? Can't you buy your own?"

"I could, if I had a reason to use one. But I haven't been on the hookup circuit for a while, so I was unprepared. Sorry to disappoint you."

She narrowed her eyes. "So you got the feeling you'd be getting lucky and asked the newly married guy to spot you some latex?"

"No. I asked him for advice about one specific lady—whom I didn't name—and apparently, he enjoys action more than talking."

"What specific lady?"

"Take a wild guess that ends with you looking in the mirror."

She huffed out a breath and the baby just curled more fully into her cleavage. Couldn't say I blamed the kid. I enjoyed that particular spot myself, though I'd barely had time to get familiar with it. "I can't believe you mentioned me to John."

"I didn't say your name. He guessed."

She flushed right up to her hairline, making her freckles pop like cinnamon on her fair skin. "He gave you a condom so you could slip it to me?"

"Pretty much." I shrugged. "Not sure how long it's been since you've dated, but that's usually the way of the world. You like someone, you get to know them, you kiss, you fuc—"

"August," she snapped. "You don't have to draw me a picture."

"Oh, I think I do. I think you need a roadmap complete with little stick figures and timelines and projected materials, just so we speak in the language we're familiar with." I stepped closer, bumping the toes of her sexy suede boots with my much heavier work ones. "You might not agree, but in mine, we use condoms. A lot."

Her lashes fluttered before she closed her eyes and shut me out. Still clutching the baby as if she was drowning and my sister's child was her only chance of keeping her head above water. "It's all going so fast."

"Fast? You've barely talked to me in six weeks. I didn't put a ring on it, Kin, I just want to spend some time with you. If that leads to the bedroom, awesome. If it doesn't, fine. We can play it by ear, as long as we play it."

She smiled briefly enough I wondered if I'd imagined it. "I'm not really good at dating. It's been years."

"Same."

"We didn't exactly start with first date material."

"Nope. But we can rewind, hit some of the steps again. Or speed up and go at our own pace. We make the rules. We can do whatever we want."

She wetted her lips and carried the baby to her bed before oh so carefully setting her down. Rhiannon didn't stir. Thank God. I didn't think I had it in me to soothe another temper tantrum today.

I definitely had no reason to be disappointed Kinleigh wasn't pregnant.

Absolutely none at all. Because seriously, what would we do with a baby? We didn't have a damn clue. Rhiannon had given us both a bit of an education, but it wasn't the same as being the ones responsible. There was so much more to it than giving her a bottle and playing with her and her plastic frog in the bath and dressing her in those snuggly onesies that were so ridiculously cute they were almost capable of making a guy wonder.

And maybe even wish.

"You could always take another test."

Kinleigh's back stiffened. She didn't fully stand from where she'd leaned over the crib to fuss with Rhiannon's...something. But when I moved closer, she was just stroking her fingers over Rhi's fine ginger curls.

My heart kicked hard.

"It's going to be the same answer. I just panicked when my period was late. I'll probably get it tomorrow."

"Yeah." I slid my hands in the back pockets of my jeans. "But if you don't, you could take another. Just in case."

"We'll see," she said, her voice distant. She was already closing me out as effectively as a slammed door.

I knew she would never take another test. She probably wouldn't go out with me either.

What we'd had was probably going to be the extent of what occurred between us, and I would just have to learn to live with that.

Somehow.

NINE

KINLEIGH

I TOOK ANOTHER TEST A COUPLE OF DAYS LATER, AFTER DRIVING TO THE drugstore outside of town and getting another one, this time a different brand. It wasn't as if I'd never been this late before, but it was rare.

I didn't know if I wanted the proof conclusively that I wasn't pregnant or if I was still hanging on to hope I could be carrying that piece of August inside me.

It didn't make sense. We weren't a couple. We'd started…whatever the heck we were with a hookup. Even if he claimed he wanted to date me, as if we'd gone back in time to a much simpler way of life.

We hadn't. The reality was I didn't want to risk my relationship with Ivy—and Ivy's family. They meant far too much to me to cause a potential ripple in our relationship just because I was horny.

Right, that's all you are. Which is why you're two steps from tears staring at the test on your bathroom counter.

But I didn't cry. Not even when the test came back negative yet again.

Then the next day, I got my period. A super light, super short version, but good enough.

It was a relief. My life wasn't set up for a baby in any shape or form. And goddess knows, I wasn't mother material any more than I was meant to be a wife.

What example had I grown up with for either? I hadn't known my father. Not his name or anything else about him. My mom had been a partier who had lost interest in being a parent when I was still a kid. Actually, she'd never had any interest. But she'd stuck around for a while, mooching off the state, doing the bare minimum so that I didn't go to school with holes in my shoes or knots in my hair. When I did, sometimes there was a teacher who cared. Sometimes there wasn't.

Even so, I didn't understand that last day when she dropped me off at a church in Syracuse. She went up to the first priest she saw, tugging me by the hand, telling me to shush as I started to cry. The next thing I knew, she was gone.

She didn't even say goodbye.

I cleared my throat and rubbed my thumbs under my eyes just in case before sweeping the test into the garbage. Nope, no tears. I might want to cry, but my eyes were dust dry. I was far too used to shifting dreams aside to get lost in my emotions now. Once before, I'd thought marriage and a child or two might be possible for me.

Now I knew if I didn't make it happen for myself, it never would.

Frowning, I braced my hands on the sink and faced myself in the bathroom mirror. It was probably where I was heading this evening that had me out of sorts. Vee was having a little get-together with her friends so everyone could meet her twins, Theodore and Elijah.

The boys had been born early right after the wedding, so after spending a bit of time in the preemie ward, they were finally home and healthy. Understandably, Vee and Murphy had wanted to make sure the twins were doing well before they had friends over to meet them, and even so, this would be a relatively small gathering. Vee was doing shifts with her friends. She had a ton of them, and let's face it, Crescent Cove was baby central. Everyone wanted in on the sweet talcum smell action.

I did too, although today wasn't the best for me for obvious reasons. I couldn't make a baby appear just from sheer want, no matter how insane it was to even wish in these circumstances.

The bright side was no one knew what was going on in my head. I'd just fix my makeup, toss on a heavier sweater over my winter-inappropriate dress, swap my killer boots for some ballet flats, and put on my game face. Tonight would be fun. And these babies I could cuddle before giving them back.

On the drive to Murphy and Vee's cabin, I glanced at the passenger side of the truck. I'd brought a bottle of white wine for those who weren't pregnant or trying to get pregnant or nursing—pretty much just me—and now I was wondering if I should've brought more gifts for the twins. I'd already sent over newborn gifts, but what about Vee? I should've thought to pick up a spa package gift certificate for her.

Or...

As I paused at a light, I unwound the pale pink scarf from around my neck, a find new to the shop. Was it tacky to give Vee something I'd worn, even if it was just for a few hours? It was gorgeously soft cashmere and the color would be perfect with her blond hair and blue eyes.

I turned up the street to go toward Ivy and August's duplex, suddenly clutching the scarf like a kid with a pacifier. I should've asked Ivy to pick me up. What was I thinking coming over here while my brain was still full of thoughts about her brother knocking me up?

Even though I was clearly *unknocked*, it hadn't stopped the full action reenactments happening in my brain.

I pulled up to the curb and debated honking. No, I'd send a text. August was supposed to be watching the baby while Ivy had her girls' night out, and Rory was in Turnbull working with his rockstar friend, Kellan McGuire. That meant I could just wait out here and—

Oh for the love of goddess, why was August coming outside with his arms full of baby?

I couldn't do this again tonight. I was already going to be seeing three at Vee's, including her eldest son, never mind all the other children who would be discussed, including the ones still being cooked. Now I was going to be confronted with Rhiannon too?

And August, looking all seductively windblown and wintry in his Carhartt jacket and jeans and that stupidly sexy ball cap pulled down over his head. His nose was red to match his reddened knuckles as he shifted the baby in her bright purple jumpsuit to his hip and motioned for me to roll down the window.

I did as requested and immediately stuck both feet in it.

"Where's Ivy?"

"Taking a bath. You're early."

"I'm not." I glanced at the time on the radio. "Okay, but just by twenty minutes." Who could blame me for not wanting to sit around and brood?

"Come on in and have a cup of coffee."

"I'll wait out here."

Rhiannon squealed and tilted toward me, apparently having decided she'd been well-behaved enough for approximately one minute. I reached my arm out and she grasped my fingers, immediately drawing them to her mouth.

"She loves Aunt Kin." His voice warmed over the words to match the heat in his green gaze. It was nearly dark, and still, his eyes were like lasers, practically searing through my sweater and coat to where my nipples were beading against my dress.

I'd foregone a bra for a lacy camisole since it was winter and that meant lots of layers. But right now, that seemed like an unwise move.

Anything that got my breasts closer to August's sex stares was a big fat heck no.

"As I love her. Look at those red cheeks." I just had to pinch one and she giggled, flailing her hands about in her bright yellow mittens. "Have you been playing in the snow with Uncle Auggie?"

"Not you too," he muttered. "Lucky Charms can't get enough of calling me that."

"Well, he probably does it as payback."

"And yes, we've been building a snowman out back. She hasn't helped much. Kind of being a bum and lazing about, aren't you, Rhi Rhi?"

She patted his chin with one of her snowy mittens and my heart just melted at the smile he aimed at her. He would make an excellent father someday.

To babies born from a woman who wasn't me.

I frowned. Okay, awkward, unnecessary thought. Of course he would. We weren't dating. And even if we were, sleeping together once wasn't enough to consider a future. My needing to pee on a stick might've altered our relationship, but it hadn't. So no harm, no foul.

Definitely no thinking about August's latent parenting abilities.

"Rory bought her this big old-fashioned sled thing, so I've been pulling her around with me while I take care of stuff outside. You know that old wind-damaged sugar maple by the back fence? Think I'm going to have to cut it down and harvest the wood." He rubbed his chin, sprinkling snow into the V-neck of the deep green sweater that offset his eyes. "Could build you another accessory armoire. Narrow and tall to fit your space."

Now he was talking my language.

"How much?" Trying to pay the man was an exercise in futility, so we usually bartered stuff. "I can whip up those pillows for that loveseat of yours you've been squirreling away when you thought I didn't notice."

He arched a brow. "I don't squirrel away. It's an anniversary gift for Seth Hamilton's wife. Apparently, they christened one similar early on in their courtship. At any rate, I don't want it anywhere near the display windows for obvious reasons, and sometimes the shop gets better light than my studio. Much to my consternation."

I wasn't sure what I found hotter right then—a man who toted around in-progress loveseats as if they were Pez dispensers or one who used the word consternation in casual, breath-puffing conversation.

It was cold as balls out. I wanted to roll up my window, but that would've been rude even for me. So I blasted the heat and tried to keep my teeth from chattering.

"Well, what do you say? Trade some pillows for a maple armoire to fit in my space?" Unwisely, I stuck my hand out the window to shake.

Frostbite was a dangerous thing. That was the only reason I could find for such an impulsive, risky move with a man who most certainly wasn't merely a business associate.

He didn't shake. Instead, he drew my bare hand up to his mouth and pressed a kiss to my knuckles. "You're cold. Such delicate skin, out here without protection."

Why did that sound so lascivious in his low, seductive voice?

"My gloves are in my jacket."

I should tug back my hand. Yet I didn't move.

"Put them on." He turned his head, making me stretch my arm out farther from the window as Rhiannon pushed at his face. I had to laugh despite how his command had affected me. Bossy August could piss me off—or turn me on.

"Let me go and I will." I darted a glance toward the duplex just in case, and annoyance crossed August's face.

"Fine, I'll warm you up myself." He kissed my fingertips and moved his broad thumb over the back of my hand in distracting circles.

Parts of me were warming up nicely, but not my hands.

"August, Ivy could—"

"We're adults." But he released me just the same.

The loss of his touch hit me harder than I expected as I tucked my hands under my lap. The scarf I'd decided to give Vee had fallen to the floor of the truck.

Along with my sense evidently, or I never would've agreed to pick up Ivy in the first place.

At least she was now rushing across the snow-encrusted front lawn, her bright red hair trailing behind her from beneath her knit cap.

"There she is."

For a second, I thought she meant me. I grinned as she quickly turned toward her baby, who was making grabby hands for her mother. Of course she wanted her little sweetheart. I'd never thought of Ivy as a mom, but she seemed like such a natural, cradling Rhiannon against her chest and kissing her ruddy cheek.

"Hiya, Kin. Sorry I took a few extra. I had to shave, but that's what I get for wearing a dress." She pointed at the knee-length sweater dress she had on with cute ankle boots.

August held up his hands and backed up. "That's my cue to leave. Have fun, ladies." His voice dipped on the last word.

"Jeez, I didn't say I'd given myself a Brazilian." Ivy rolled her eyes and skidded up the driveway to hand off her baby before he escaped entirely. "There's enough bottles made. More than enough. I pureed her bananas. She gets cranky without them. Don't put her down without her stuffed tiger. The one with the blue bow tie. Her daddy brought it back for her from California."

There was more, but I tuned it out, as adorable as it was to hear my freewheeling friend being such a mom. She'd clearly been cut out for the role.

I picked up the scarf from the floor to give myself something to do that didn't involve thinking about motherhood or watching August hold his niece. Either one was problematic.

When Ivy finally slipped into the truck, I held out the scarf. "Think Vee would like this? It's a new find. I've been so distracted lately that I totally forgot to bring her a present beyond the baby gifts I already sent."

I didn't mention *what* had distracted me, and thankfully, my best friend didn't ask.

Ivy touched the material and let out a wistful sigh. "She'll love it. I sent over a wine-o-gram a few days ago." She picked up my bottle and checked the label. "Classy. She'll love this too."

Turned out I loved it even more, since shortly after we arrived at Vee's, I started hitting the stuff hard.

I wasn't a budding alcoholic. In the past year, I'd only gotten lit on New Year's Eve after the wedding and tonight, but those two times had made up for all my alcohol-free evenings.

I blamed Vee's babies. No children should've been that cute. Never mind the twins, Theodore and Elijah, who had super fine blond hair and angelic expressions that only vanished when Vee made the mistake of removing one too early from the milk bar. She wasn't shy about nursing, and why should she be with this crowd? Macy was a mama-to-be, although she wasn't showing yet. Rylee and her sister

Kelsey were both moms, along with Ivy of course. Ally Hamilton and her BFF and sister-in-law Sage were too.

Gina and I were the only singletons present, and she championed the nope, never, not into babies group.

Where did that leave me? On social media, you could put down single and looking. When it came to parenting, saying you were considering options sounded weird. It probably wasn't as strange in a town like Crescent Cove where hormones hung in the air like fog, but still.

So I drank.

I was two glasses in when the appetizer tray was served. Three glasses in when Macy suggested we play pin the penis on the action movie star until Rylee reminded her anything could be used as retribution at her upcoming baby shower.

"Why do you need to pin it on some random movie dude when you already have a fine man who hands out condoms?" I tacked on a breezy laugh when silence descended on the living room.

Murphy, the lone male in attendance, became very interested in the taco dip.

"He did what now?"

I waved a hand and studied my wine glass. I was pretty sure it had a leak. Hadn't I just refilled it? No matter. I tossed the rest back and smiled. "Oh, nothing. So are you sure you have a real baby in there? You are still as flat as a pancake."

Macy's brows knitted together as she glanced at Ivy. "Are you driving her home? Not thinking she should be behind a wheel."

"I'm perfectly fine. No slurred words. Do you think I'm a lightweight? I mean, I get why John didn't need the condom. It makes sense he'd give it to August."

Even as the words exited my mouth, I knew I was digging deeper. But I couldn't find it in me to care. Why should I be ashamed we'd had sex? Everyone else did right and left. I mean, I didn't want Ivy to know—

Ivy was shoving in tortilla chips at the speed of light and looking anywhere but at me.

"What condom are you talking about?" Macy glanced at Rylee.

"Not a clue, man."

"The night of the wedding. It wasn't a gag one, was it? Because totally not funny. People use those and stuff happens. Or…doesn't happen."

Macy grabbed the bottle of wine. I suspected she wanted to keep it out of my reach, which probably wasn't a bad idea. "I do not have one clue what you're going on about. John handing out condoms makes zero sense to me, but he's male and they do odd stuff. Sorry, Moose."

He just held up a hand and kept on eating, much like Ivy.

Was robotic snacking an avoidance technique? I probably should've investigated that instead of trying to drown in vino.

"It's not like I actually saw the exchange. August told me about it after."

Rylee sucked taco dip off her thumb. "Why did August talk with you about getting his latex from John anyway?"

Oh, shit. Now what did I say to *that?*

TEN

KINLEIGH

I TRIED TO GET MY DISORDERED THOUGHTS IN LINE.

August and his condom.

Me putting it on him.

His hiss of breath as I made sure it was seated just right.

Don't want any swimmers sneaking out.

Except now I wished they had. Just one. So I wouldn't have nearly wept while I took the tests that were supposed to give me my freedom back.

Yay, still not a parent. Yay, I can keep living my wild and free life.

Yay, no babies for you, Kinleigh. Good luck next time.

If there was a next time.

As the silence stretched out, Sage nudged Ally. "Did he need help getting it on?"

Oh, if she only knew.

Ally shook her head. "Don't mind her. Her ovaries are being flooded with all these baby distress signals."

Apparently, Sage wasn't the only one.

Sage snorted. "We're working on it. Besides, Kinleigh is the one who's on the hot seat right now. Maybe she's an expert in condom application. What say you, Kinleigh?"

I opened my mouth and fumbled about for an answer. Before I could, help came from an unexpected place.

"He has a latex allergy." Ivy's voice was matter-of-fact.

Macy cocked a brow. "Well, that's gotta suck."

"Not so much in Crescent Cove." Kelsey grinned. "He's probably the most popular dude on his block."

Everyone laughed, including me. But my mind was whirling.

"I'm sure he was commiserating about how much it sucks." Ivy gave me a pointed look. "I'm sure they had a good laugh."

Not so much.

August definitely hadn't mentioned an allergy. Dear goddess, had August ended up with a painful rash or something after our night?

I shifted toward Ivy to ask about such a development. She didn't give me the chance. Instead, she yanked out her phone and held it up. "Gotta check on Rhi."

"Um, okay."

While she texted up a storm, the awkward as heck conversation moved on. Murphy went off to check on their older son Brayden when he woke up crying, but it turned out he only wanted his mother. Somehow I ended up with an armful of Theodore and he proceeded to stare at me owlishly like Rhiannon tended to do.

He was so warm and soft and snuggly in his fleece onesie with moose climbing all over it. I started to laugh as I got the reference to his father, startling him out of his almost snooze, and he let out a wail.

Yet again the party ground to a halt.

Go, Kinleigh.

Vee came back to take Theodore, but eventually, Elijah landed in my arms. He was blissfully asleep, so I could rock him and whisper whatever popped into my wine-addled head without him being offended. By then, I'd had a fourth glass and was feeling no pain.

Other than over the fact that my best friend was spending more time with her phone than talking to me, but who could blame her? She had a precious little girl at home, and I was a fully grown adult, capable of making an ass of myself without anyone's help.

At least Vee loved the scarf and wanted me to find her half a dozen more in different colors. I agreed, because anything seemed reasonable right then.

Including texting August while Ivy got our coats from the front hall closet.

You have a rash? I hope it didn't hurt.

After I sent it, I frowned. That wasn't how I should've worded that. A little tact, jeez.

Does it still hurt now? Sorry, didn't know it made your *eggplant emoji* sore.

I was rather proud I'd used the eggplant emoji rather than some sophomoric term for a penis. Ivy and I referred to them in all manner of ways that didn't work for a text with August.

"All set?" Ivy asked brightly as she held out my coat. Too brightly actually.

Did she know something?

I let her help me on with my coat, although I was the taller one. But my addled brain was on overdrive.

August wouldn't have told her. Unless maybe he'd had an allergic emergency and he had no choice? No man would want to be caught with his pants down, literally.

I yanked my coat into place and whirled to face her. "Did August talk to you?"

Ivy whipped her hair out from the collar of her coat. "He does often, since he's my brother. As does Caleb, for the same reason. Caleb not as much because he's on the 3 P patrol."

I tried to chill out as I grabbed my purse. "Oh, some school thing?" August and Ivy's brother taught at the local elementary school.

"Um, no. Try parties, Pabst, and pussy."

"Hey now." Sage sidled up to Ivy, her blond brows raised to her hairline. "Is that any talk for a lady? And if not, let's be friends." She giggled and slipped her arm through Ivy's. "We've already bonded through our shared enjoyment of torturing Rory. Did you know they made their very first love nest in my bed and breakfast?" They shared a secret grin.

I did know the story of how Ivy and Rory had hooked up a few times at Sage's inn, but right now, I was feeling left out on about sixteen different levels. I would've sworn there was some private baby mama society I hadn't been invited to and would probably never be granted access.

You aren't drinking again. Ever.

As if she could read my thoughts, Sage reached out to rub my coat sleeve. "You're okay to get home? Ivy's driving you?"

"Yeah."

I didn't even argue. But I did after Ivy's next statement.

"She's also going to stay the night."

"What? No. I can't. My apartment has—"

Nothing. Not even a plant, although I had a couple in the shop. Why didn't I have any plants at home? I needed some.

"Your apartment will be just fine overnight."

"Patches!" I exclaimed as if my shop cat required tending.

She liked her solitary lifestyle during the hours the store was closed. The few times I'd tried to corral her into coming home with me had ended with me sporting an interesting collection of war wounds. I was as isolated as the cat, if not by choice in my case. At least not entirely.

Ivy rolled over that as if I hadn't spoken. "Just for one night, Kin. You can stay in the guest bedroom."

"The one next to your bedroom? Where you sleep?"

As inane as the question was, Ivy seemed strangely nonplussed. "Usually, yes, bedrooms are for sleeping. Unless you're worried about privacy."

"What? Me? Why would I need privacy? I'm alone. Hello."

Sage cleared her throat. "I'm just going to go," she gestured vaguely, "somewhere. See you both soon." She gave Ivy a quick squeeze.

"Do you want to say goodbye to Vee?" Ivy craned her neck. "Not sure where she disappeared to."

"I shouldn't be away from home. I can't sleep near where you and Rory are, in case you need sex."

Yet again, Ivy disregarded my protests.

I couldn't even blame her. I sounded like a drunken drowning woman.

Who was freaking the heck out at being in my nightie with just a few walls between me and August. And with boundaries lowered by alcohol. Again.

Although in all fairness, the wine hadn't done much except make me looser. It didn't make me want August any more than I already did. I'd wanted him long before we slept together.

No wine goggles here. More like I saw everything so much clearer when I didn't let my concerns run the show. As I did almost always.

Except for that one incredible night…

"You go ahead," I mumbled as Ivy waited for my response. "Say goodbye to Vee for me too, please."

"You sure?" She was already moving away.

"Yeah, thanks." I tucked my hands in my pockets and moved to the door to wait for her.

The buzz from my phone made me jump and I had to laugh at myself. That much wine and I was still as jumpy as a cat.

Then again, who could blame me at the prospect of being so close to August and not being able to do anything about it?

I mean, I *could,* but if he had this latex thing and I wasn't on the pill…

No. I could not. That was a recipe for danger.

A danger I might have wanted to lean into, just a little bit. Especially when I tugged out my phone and read his text.

You been into your cups? Need me to come rescue you from too much girl talk?

And a wink.

A wink from August sent my mind straight into the gutter.

Ivy reappeared and I quickly pocketed my phone. "Is 'into your cups' a Rory saying?"

"A variation of that, yes. Why?"

Rory's Irish-isms rubbing off on August despite himself made me smile. I tucked my hair behind my ears and shook my head. "Just curious. Is Vee okay with us leaving?"

"Since everyone else is also going and Vee and Murphy are slow dancing in the kitchen to Frank Sinatra, I think they're very okay with it." Ivy grinned.

I grinned back even as sadness crept into my chest and my belly and everywhere in between. I was lonely. More than that, I was…yearning.

For August. Merely for sex, of course.

Lots and lots of sex.

Trying to play it cool, I waited until we were back in my truck to ask the question lingering in my mind. Ivy was complaining—loudly —about not being able to drive a stick while I snickered and made jokes about finding out if her husband agreed.

She flipped me the middle finger and managed to make it out of Vee's driveway without leaving my engine on the blacktop. Narrowly.

"Did August tell you about his latex issues?" I asked finally.

"Better question is, did he tell you?"

She accelerated and I looked behind us to see if I was missing a muffler on the street. "I'm thinking I'm still better off driving. Or Uber?"

"Or we could call Rory. Or better yet, August. What about August, huh? Then you can get the straight skinny on all his thoughts on latex and proper usage and such. Unless you already contacted him. C'mon, you know you did."

My face started burning to match the fingers I was currently twisting in my lap. Who needed gloves? Embarrassment clearly created warmth.

"I have no need for such information."

"No? Seems like you might, since he decided to chat condoms with you at the wedding. That's what you did, right? Talk?"

Among other things.

"How did you forget how to drive a stick?"

"Oh, you never forget. Comes right back as soon as you climb on the...horse." She shot me a blazing grin with her jaunty pompom knit hat askew.

"I just bet. Your dad taught you on that old truck of his. Didn't August inherit it for a while?"

"He sure did."

"Whatever happened to it? I'm surprised August didn't pass it to Caleb and then to you."

"Oh, he passed it to Caleb, all right, and then it had to be fumigated after he went to the lookout point in it one dozen times too many." She wrinkled her nose and lurched around a corner, making me brace myself in case we suddenly became airborne.

I nearly asked about August's history with the old truck before I bit my lip to stifle myself. Then he picked that moment to follow-up on the text I had not yet answered.

I ignored it, staring straight ahead as my phone buzzed in my pocket.

"Aren't you going to answer my brother?"

"What? Huh? Why?"

"You texted him to ask about the latex allergy, right? I mean, why else would he be texting you, except to answer your question?" A pregnant pause filled the truck. "Can't think of any other reason, can you?"

I frowned. Was Ivy baiting me? Did she know something? Probably just my guilty conscience kicking into gear.

"No, of course not. But how do you know that's August?"

"He's texted you before when I was with you and had my phone off, remember? That's the tone you said you gave him."

No. I didn't remember much right now. Except that I should've stuck to water.

At least the text buzzing stopped.

"We're actually doing a...project." There, that sounded nice and tidy.

One where my legs hook over my ears.

"Oh, yeah, like what? And why didn't you tell me about it, you hussy?" She smacked my thigh, and I guess my guilt decided to hop in the driver's seat and steer us off a cliff.

"Well, I have to do something with my time now that you have a husband and a *baby*." Somehow those words sounded like a vile accusation. Which was so not my intention.

Or was it?

More like I was lonely and out of sorts and on the edge of drunk. Unfortunately, I'd skipped the happy, excitable part and shot right into confusion and woe.

Seemed like an accurate depiction of my life at the moment.

Without warning, Ivy swerved to the side of the road. At first, I thought she'd tried to avoid a cat, but nope, she did it intentionally. She shifted toward me on the seat, her face serious. "Are we okay?"

"Um, yes?"

"You don't sound sure."

"Of course we're okay. Why wouldn't we be? You know I'm happy for you. I love you. I just…"

"What?"

"I just miss you," I whispered, feeling about three inches tall.

Her eyes welled up. "I miss you too. I didn't plan on the baby or the husband."

"I know." And now I was full-blown sniffling, like a complete fool.

"It was all unplanned. But you're still my favorite. You're still my sister."

I undid my seatbelt and lurched across the seat to hug it out. "I am. We are. You're my favorite too."

"And sisters tell each other everything."

I stopped sniffling and patting her back and probably did crazy eyes that she thankfully could not see because her head was on my shoulder.

"Right. So does having a baby make you more horny?"

Ivy's head reared up so fast, it was a miracle she didn't bang it

116

against the roof. She frowned and yanked her coat into place before sliding back into her seat. "If you are referring to last week, Rory had been gone for a while. We needed to reconnect."

"Yeah, I know, I know. I get that."

"Then why are you asking?"

Like I knew. It was as if for one crazy moment I'd thought—maybe even hoped—I was pregnant and so maybe my jumbled mindset toward August had something to do with that, even though I wasn't. Perhaps my libido had been momentarily fooled into thinking he was my baby daddy, so I couldn't help wanting to jump his very fine bones.

It was a theory.

"Just wondering for someday."

It took Ivy grabbing my arm for me to replay what I'd said. *Uh oh.* "Do you want to have a baby?"

"Um, sure, maybe someday." Someday was the best answer.

"Really? Like you're planning to have one? I didn't know you were even considering it."

"No," I said slowly. So slowly I made it into a many-syllabled word. "Just that you know, it's what everyone usually does. Baby and then," I swallowed hard, "well, at least a baby."

That didn't require being madly in love. You could just be in like enough to do the deed—all right, serious freaking like—and then you could just...let it happen.

Especially if the guy couldn't use latex. And you weren't—*I* wasn't —on birth control, since my sex life was as sporadic as sunshine in February in Crescent Cove.

Sometimes happy accidents didn't need to be planned out years in advance. Women had unplanned babies every day.

Besides, the idea was forming in my head, so that kind of counted as a plan, right?

I pressed the backs of my now ice-cold hands to my flaming cheeks. Oh my God, what was I *thinking*?

You're thinking you could still have that baby with August. The one you weren't ready for and now want with all your heart.

ELEVEN

THE BOOKCASE WAS PISSING ME OFF.

To be fair, it was a perfectly reasonable piece. I'd fashioned it out of oak I'd polished to a fine sheen and added three shelves that could expand to hold a book that would face out. A perfect item for a bookstore or to my thoughts, a child's bedroom. It was a good height to go under a window, with carved moons and stars and ladybugs on the fascia dropdown from the top shelf. Like a child's mobile might look. My currently sleeping niece had something similar on the bed I had for in her my apartment.

I didn't have a child of my own, although I was set up as if I did. Technically, I hadn't needed to do so with Ivy's half of the duplex mere feet away, but they wouldn't live here forever. Their new house was being built and come spring, the work there would pick up the pace. By the summer, I'd probably be thinking about renting out the other half of the building.

Unless I expanded it into a proper workshop. Mine at the store was big enough for all but the largest projects, but lately, I was chafing at the bit. The idea of spreading out into a more spacious area was appealing.

I sat back on my haunches and traced my fingertip over the moon and stars cutouts. In the meantime, I should give this to my sister and move onto the next. Even if I selfishly had this idea brewing to keep it for myself as the prototype for the line of children's furniture I had in mind.

Sure, some I would gladly gift to my niece. Some I could certainly sell, especially in a town as prolific at making babies as Crescent Cove.

But that wasn't the only reason I wanted to keep it. Ever since Kinleigh had almost been pregnant, I couldn't get the idea out of my head. That it could be reality. I could start a family of my own. Start building something for myself, not just pieces to give to other people for *their* families.

Granted, I had tons of my own work in my place. Half the time if I wanted something, it was just easier and more enjoyable to create it to my own specifications. I also gave pieces to friends and family all the time. But to do things for my own family, one I'd built from the ground up just like the hunks of wood I made into something entirely different…

Well, that would be incredible.

I picked up my silent phone off the side table and tossed it down again. Kinleigh's bizarre text had led to a whole lot of nothing. I'd replied thinking she was either bored out of her mind or drunk—or both—because why else would she ask something so ridiculous?

Then again, maybe my sister had put that thought in her head from what I'd said to cover my ass back in high school. My mom had found a bunch of condoms in my jeans pocket when I was probably far too young to have them, and I'd lied and told her I was carrying them for a buddy. I wouldn't be using them, since I'd discovered I had a latex allergy after using gloves in science class.

It was the lamest excuse ever, and I didn't even know if she'd bought it. She and my dad had spent inordinate amounts of time making sure I was the next thing to a monk, so I didn't accidentally impregnate some unfortunate woman who wasn't on birth control. To the point that I was almost certain they were pulling my leg, but I'd been too embarrassed about the whole thing to ever ask.

Little did they know I'd never gone without a condom.

Ever.

My mom had also made sure to oh so considerately tell both my siblings and my dad, however, and the lie still seemed to resurface at the worst times. Like Thanksgiving when my ninety-eight-year-old great aunt Irma was in attendance.

Rather than staring at my phone all night, I took a couple snapshots of the bookcase. Didn't mean I intended to sell it. Didn't mean anything except if someone saw them on my site and inquired, I might end up making another in their wood of choice.

Or else I could just keep the pictures to myself for a while.

I circled the piece, inspecting it for flaws. For needed improvements. Places where the wood could be smoother, or if a particular scratch seemed more like a design flaw than a unique enhancement. I was never fully happy with my work, but eventually, even I had to pronounce a project done and put it up for sale.

This one? I was moving to my bedroom, where it would sit at the foot of my bed until I decided what to do with it.

I moved to my Mac to take care of some customer emails. Then I checked on a blissfully sleeping Rhiannon before deciding I'd kick back with a beer and some TV. Which really translated to grabbing my phone five times to make sure it was still working while channel surfing.

Finally, I gave up and tossed my cell aside. Ivy would be home eventually, and I could pump her for details. In a casual, cool, practically blasé way.

At the sound of grinding gears, I shot straight up in my chair.

I'd been halfway to sleep. I was restless on a good night, and lately, my hours of rest had been precious and few. But I was awake now.

I moved to the window and pushed aside the drapes to peer out like a proper creeper. Instead of Kinleigh's truck idling at the curb before heading off into the night, it was parked in the driveway. And Ivy and Kinleigh were shambling up the walk as if they were drunk.

My sister was nursing. Had she imbibed too? And one of them had driven home.

I charged to the door and yanked it open with enough force that Ivy leaped back. She would've stumbled off the top step if Kinleigh hadn't caught her—and giggled as if it was the most amusing thing ever.

One of them was drunk for certain.

"Ivy Beck, if you're drunk right now, we're having words."

She propped her hands on her hips. "It's Ivy Beck Ferguson, cretin. And if I am, so what?" She got in my face—well, as much as she could considering her petite stature—and growled. "What are you going to do about it? Huh? Huh?"

There wasn't so much as a hint of alcohol on her breath. Just the scent of many, many spices. I waved a hand between us and she flipped me off before marching to her side of the duplex, tugging Kinleigh along as if she was as capable of independent thought as Rhiannon.

Possibly less.

"C'mon, Kin, we aren't talking to him right now."

"We aren't?" Kinleigh glanced back. "How come? He's kinda cute when he's clueless."

I started to grin until the rest of that sank in. "So sue me if I worry about you, Ivy."

"I worry about you too, you know, and I don't see you filling me in on squat. Kinleigh, let's go." She opened the door to her side of the duplex and yanked Kinleigh inside before slamming the door shut.

I crossed my arms and waited.

A moment later, she popped her head out. "I want my daughter back."

"Are you sure you're lucid enough to care for her?"

"I haven't had a drop to drink. Do you honestly think I'd drive Kinleigh's death trap home if I had?"

From inside, I heard Kinleigh call out a protest.

"It's my duty to watch out for you."

"Yeah, uh huh, fine, but who's watching out for you?"

That made me frown. "I don't need anyone watching out for me."

"Why, because you have a rashy, warty penis?" she asked in an undertone, breezing past me into my side of the duplex before I could even begin to unpack what she'd just said.

And the implications of her even implying such.

"What did Kinleigh say to you?" I demanded, following Ivy inside to where she was comforting her now wailing daughter.

It took everything I possessed not to detour to the bathroom to verify everything looked as it should. I knew that it did, but at times like this, a man had to wonder.

"Why, nothing. Should she have?" Ivy pushed Rhiannon's ginger curls away from her streaming eyes. "There, there, sweetie. Don't worry. We'll stay far away from the shouty mean man."

"I am not mean. I am not shouty."

Ivy glared at me. "You're shouting right now."

I was not. Was I?

"You inferred...inappropriate insinuations about things that are not for you to know."

"Your rashy, warty dick? Damn straight I don't want to know about that." She grabbed the diaper bag beside Rhiannon's bed and slung it over her shoulder. "Thank you for watching your niece. Goodnight."

"My dick is just fucking fine!" I insisted before Ivy quietly shut the door.

I dropped into my armchair. How much beer did I have? I was going to drink all of it. Right now.

Turned out I'd drank my last can. I rarely drank alcohol and therefore never kept much in the house.

Served me right.

I went to the window to see if Kinleigh's truck was still in the driveway. Yes, indeed. Truth be told, I probably would've heard it if she'd left, although she never drove a stick with as little finesse as my baby sister. Not sure anyone did.

Grabbing my phone, I quickly texted Kinleigh.

What did you tell my sister about my dick?

Almost immediately, a flurry of bubbles appeared, indicating she was typing. And typing. And possibly erasing and typing some more. It lasted so long I nearly demanded she spit it out before her reply finally came through.

Huh?

That was an awful lot of typing for a three-word letter.

Sorry. Thumbs r broken. Texting iz hard.

Why?

Y you think? I had a couple. Mebbe 3. Or 4?

A couple what?

Just wine. But Ivy holding me in prison 2nite.

I still hadn't gotten an answer to my dick question, but Kinleigh on the other side of the duplex held some very intriguing possibilities.

If only she hadn't been drinking. We'd run that scene once before, and the next time we slept together, I intended for her faculties to be operating on all cylinders.

She texted me again before I'd decided how to respond.

I didn't say anything about your penis to her. I swear. How awk would that b? Anyway, issa secret.

It was a secret we'd slept together, even if I would never truly understand why. We were all adults. There was no reason for this cloak and dagger stuff.

Not even to call it warty and rashy?

WHAT? God, no. Your specimen was practically perfect.

I grinned. I didn't love the 'practically' part, but I supposed there was a margin for error.

My specimen? Weird, Kin, but thanks. Do I dare ask why she started the latex shit?

Not sure. You know how women r when they get 2gether.

Did I ever. Men too.
A moment later, she texted again.

Is it true? Did u have some kind of reaction from using a *eggplant emoji*?

I definitely hadn't used an eggplant for any reason at all, but I assumed she was referring to what went *on* my eggplant. God save me.
I started to reply, but Kinleigh was on a roll.

Because you don't need 1 if it's a prob.

I couldn't type fast enough.

What?

More text bubbles that produced no actual words.

Dammit, say something.

This time, there were no text bubbles at all, just a blurted response as if she'd already typed it and had been gathering her courage to press send.

We could just make a baby.

TWELVE

I HAD TO BE HALLUCINATING. DID HALLUCINATIONS INCLUDE SOUND? I didn't know, but I certainly had cause to wonder.

It took me a minute to remember how to type.

Exactly how much did you have to drink? For real. Sounds like more than a couple.

Or *mebbe* 3. Or 4?

Not that much. I'm still lucid. Ish.

That *ish* was what was concerning me. But it also wasn't shutting me down. Far from it.

Kinleigh kept going.

I never got to float away. More like a lift then a crash & so many thoughts.

Here came the text bubbles again.

I tapped my fingers on the arm of my chair to try to keep myself from pacing while I waited for her response.

She couldn't just ask me to make a baby with her and then leave me hanging.

Then again, why was I even still here? We could have this conversation in the guest room of Ivy's half of the duplex, where she was likely spending the night. Ivy would probably be in bed by now, since the slam of a car door outside a little while ago meant Rory was home.

I didn't want to think about their possible nocturnal occupations, but if they were busy, at least Kinleigh and I could talk in private.

Maybe make babies in private too.

Damn, what was I thinking? And I'd only had one beer.

I took another pregnancy test.

My fingers stilled on the arm of the chair.

Neg of course. Still neg. Why am I so sad?

I exhaled. I couldn't answer that question, since I was just as sad. And it didn't make any sense.

We'd never had an official date. We'd flirted—sort of—for years and we'd slept together once, but that was hardly a solid basis for creating a lifetime relationship.

Our nonexistent dating history wasn't for lack of trying on my part. Yet I was good enough to father this baby she suddenly wanted? That *I* suddenly wanted?

I pushed a hand through my hair. God, we were both fucked up.

You were surrounded by babies and mothers tonight. Probably part of it.

Yet I hadn't been, so what was my problem?

The baby-obsessed town we lived in was probably influencing me too, but I'd never had an issue with controlling my urges for procreation before our near miss. It had made me think. Wonder about a different kind of life beyond just working and spending time with my friends and watching Rhi. I loved all of those things, but hell, I could have a family too. Gideon was proof enough that you could make a relationship work, even with an occasionally...challenging woman.

If he could, dammit, I could too.

I always wanted 1. Just didn't think it would happen 4 me.

Her words tugged hard at my chest. Even knowing she was feeling the effects of the alcohol, I suspected some of it was sterling truth. That bothered me in some kind of caveman-like way I had no desire to analyze.

Instead, I got up and shoved my phone in my back pocket. I grabbed my wallet, which held two of the condoms I'd bought optimistically and then relegated to my sock drawer.

She'd been drinking, so it wasn't going down like that. Not again. Especially with all of *this* now on the table.

Nope, that would most certainly be a sober conversation. One we would be having in full detail whether or not she'd 'come to her senses' by tomorrow.

She texted again while I snagged my keys off the table by the door, but I didn't slow down. I was a man on a mission.

Halfway out the door, I turned around and grabbed a pair of scissors to ruthlessly trim one of the two violets I'd managed to grow after far too long spent trying. Guilt immediately assailed me at plucking one of the pair, but the end was worth the means.

And the day I showed up at a woman's—*the* woman's—door at past eleven without some kind of offering, pitiful as it was, was the day I wasn't Annie Beck's eldest son.

Fake latex allergy and all.

I went to the other side of the duplex and pulled out my phone. I couldn't just barge in, though I had a key. Maybe Lucky Charms wasn't banging my sister yet and then what?

Yeah, just the thought I did *not* need in my head. Not the lack of banging, but the opposite.

I read Kinleigh's latest text and swallowed a groan.

Not surprised u didn't reply. Heavy shit. Nm. Have a nice nite.

Great time to not answer, genius.
Quickly, I texted her back.

Are you alone?

No. I'm at Ivy's. Remember? Have u been *beer emoji*?

Just one. Are they still awake?

Y?

I had to grin. Even drunk, Kinleigh was far too suspicious. I lo—liked how she challenged me at every turn, even if sometimes it pissed me off.

I'm here to make a baby with you.

The door to Ivy's side of the duplex flew open so fast that I reared back. I had mere seconds to enjoy the sight of Kinleigh with wet hair, wearing only a tight nightshirt that said *Kiss Me I've Got Irish Inside Me* and fuzzy striped knee socks. She leaned out and yanked me inside with a fistful of my shirt, holding her finger up to her mouth.

"*Shh,*" she whispered in case I didn't understand the gesture. She nudged the door closed and dragged me toward the guest bedroom, her hand wrapped securely around mine.

I liked the feeling far too much.

As soon as we were inside, she slammed both hands against my chest and pushed me into the closed door. She inched up on her toes and I leaned down, unprepared for her hard, hungry kiss. The motion literally knocked off my ball cap and sent my senses reeling.

Somehow I found myself cupping her ass, clad in just lacy panties. My cock went from interested to *hell yeah* in a second flat.

"You're so sweet," she gasped between kisses, reaching down to palm my shaft.

I groaned into her mouth. So much for keeping quiet. I was amazed the sound didn't echo through the canyon. Did Crescent Cove have a canyon?

So many questions. So little bloodflow left outside my erection.

She plucked the mangled violet out of my hand and made a noise crossed between a sigh and a squeal. I'd never heard anything similar from Kinleigh, that was for sure.

"You brought me a flower?"

"Yes?"

Her lips curved. "You sound uncertain."

I rubbed the heel of my hand over my chest. "I'm trying to come to terms with not being inside you yet."

She stepped forward and grabbed my belt buckle, pulling my cock flush with the cleft between her thighs. I couldn't help groaning again, even more loudly than the last time.

"That so?" Her question was a purr. "You risking another rash, big boy?"

When I growled, she released possibly the sexiest laugh I'd ever heard from her. So light and feminine and free.

Also, so very tipsy. Unfortunately for me.

"I never got a rash. I don't have a latex allergy. I just told my mom I did because I was messing around with girls at fourteen and didn't want her to know."

"Fourteen?" Her eyes widened. "Early bloomer."

"How about you?"

She was studying my mouth, her focus so intent that my dick twitched. "How about me what?"

I tucked one of her loose red curls behind her ear. "How early did you...bloom?"

She trailed the small, tender violet over the base of her throat, drawing my gaze to where her pulse beat so crazily under her fair skin. "Not very early at all. Twenty-one. Then I think I re-hymenated for a while after he broke up with me."

I knew I was supposed to laugh, but I didn't. I couldn't.

"Any man who broke up with you is a moron." I couldn't stand the guy without even knowing him, because *I* hadn't managed to date her yet. Possibly because of him. "Tell me his name, and I'll go put sugar in his gas tank."

She smiled again fleetingly. "Not worth it. Besides, he has a valet."

Extreme dislike shot right into hatred. And talking suddenly became very overrated.

I scooped her up over my shoulder, expecting her to let out an unholy scream loud enough to wake the whole house. Instead, she tapped my shoulder and reached back to hold up the violet, already halfway to crushed. "It needs water."

Carefully, I set her down on her back on the bed, making her bounce just to see her laugh. She didn't disappoint me, her blue eyes dancing. Still, she never relinquished her hold on my offering until I held out my hand. Worry crossed her features, and my gut tightened as if I was preparing for a blow.

I probably was. She kept sucker-punching me, and she didn't even know it.

Thank fuck.

"I'll get some water for it."

She nodded and placed the struggling flower so gently in the palm of my hand. I was sure it wouldn't last for much more than a couple of hours, but the gesture was enough.

I filled a plastic cup from the sink in the attached bathroom and set the flower in it to bob along the surface. I returned and placed the cup beside the bed where Kinleigh was sleeping in a starfish position, her nightshirt riding up, her tiny panties twisted over her sexy hips and thighs. On the lacy material, a small spot of wetness taunted me, and I had to fist my hands to not yank down her underwear and wake her up with my mouth.

Blowing out a breath, I pushed a hand through my hair. I should just go. Let her sleep it off and see how she felt tomorrow.

She cracks open a door and you're just going to let her slam it shut again?

The door she'd cracked was having a child. It wasn't as if she'd asked me out for ice cream. This would be a lifetime commitment.

And to get there would involve lots and lots of fun practice...

My cock jerked against my zipper. I couldn't help it. Much as I tried to be a gentleman, I still thought with my other head at least part of the time. Seeing Kinleigh sprawled out the next thing to naked with that stupid phrase about having Irish inside her stretched across her tits was *not* helping me think straight.

I frowned. Was that my sister's nightshirt? Had freaking Lucky Charms bought her that?

Pervert.

Yeah, and he got the girl. While you're standing around thinking about right and wrong and being prudent, LC just impregnated Ivy and worried about details later.

Not that I would ever take life advice—mental or otherwise—from my brother-in-law. The guy still called me Auggie and smirked every time as if it was the funniest joke ever.

But my sister loved him. He treated her well. He adored her and their baby. Really, I had nothing to complain about there.

That didn't mean I wouldn't fuck with him every chance I got. It was practically a rite of passage.

I stared down at Kinleigh's long, wavy hair spread across the white and pink bedspread. Uncontained fire, that was her.

I wanted to be in her world. Wanted her to be even more a part of mine.

Already, I knew we were good together. I just had to convince her.

Besides, if she truly deep down wanted a baby, then what? She'd go hook up with some other dude and let it happen then? If it was meant to, of course. There were no guarantees.

I *could* guarantee there was no way in hell I was going to let some other dude slip into the role of her child's father. No way.

And if she woke up tomorrow and decided she really didn't want a kid yet, well, that was fine too. I'd try to forget she'd mentioned it.

Even more, I'd try to forget how much the idea had scared me— and excited me too.

But that wasn't for tonight. I turned toward the door. She needed her rest.

"August, don't go."

I glanced back to find her sliding her arm across the bed, fingers outstretched.

"Come to bed with me."

Fuck, how was I supposed to say no to that?

"You're drunk." My voice sounded like broken glass, and depending how she responded, she would leave me bleeding.

Not the first time either.

"Some. But I know what I want. Just too scared to say sometimes." A faint smile tipped up her lips and she wiggled her fingers. "An orgasm or two would knock me right out." Her eyes closed for a moment before opening again. "It's hard to stop thinking so much."

I sat on the edge of the bed and fingercombed her damp, gorgeous hair all the way to the ends. On the next trip, I let my fingers sink in deeper to massage her scalp, just so she'd keep on making those little purring sounds in her throat.

She smelled like a strawberry sundae. Sinful as fuck.

"I can help you with the orgasm." Could I ever.

She tipped her head back and met my gaze with her slumberous blue eyes. "Please."

That single word was my undoing. Anything she asked me for, I would give. Happily.

I was in deep freaking trouble.

I shifted until I was lying beside her and traced my fingertips down her jaw. I kissed her gently, extending the moment while she made a frustrated noise and grabbed for me. I eased just out of her reach and cupped one of her breasts, rubbing my thumb over her rock-hard nipple. She gasped and grabbed my hand, holding it against her while she leaned up to seek my mouth. This kiss was harder, deeper, longer. Mimicking everything I wanted to do to her, even if I knew that wasn't an option.

Not tonight.

I bent my head and captured her other nipple through the nightshirt, adding a hint of teeth when she whimpered. My hand was already on the move down her soft abdomen, and for a second, the thought of her round with my child lodged in my brain.

I wanted to claim her. Make her mine in a primal way that defied all sense.

Forever.

I kept my touch easy, at least until I reached the scalloped edge of her panties. Then I couldn't wait any longer. I slipped my fingers inside and dragged them down her swollen cleft, groaning against her breast at the slickness awaiting me. She feathered her hand over my hair, brushing it back while she turned her head to nibble on my ear.

"Want you inside." Her breathy voice was going to fucking kill me.

"I am inside. Feel that?" I circled her stiff clit and tried not to be rough. Not to rub her hard and fast just so I could hear her moaning in my ear.

"I do. Do you feel how wet I am for you?" She leaned back and licked her lips. "I want you. Just you. No condom."

I shut my eyes and prayed for strength. When my dick continued to throb against the constricting fabric of my jeans, I went for broke and slid down the bed to kneel between her thighs. Looking up at her flushed cheeks and trembling lips made my fingers clumsy as I struggled to get her panties off.

Finally, I managed it and parted her thighs, swearing under my breath at the wetness coating them.

"Hang on to me," I gritted out before diving in.

She gripped my head with both hands, arching into the strokes of my tongue—and then my fingers. Winding her legs around my back, she tugged me deeper into her fragrant, drugging heat. I was surrounded by her, lost in her sighs and her quaking muscles and the way she dragged on my hair, adding hot spikes of pain that made me redouble my focus. Her pussy was so slick and hot, and with every move I made, she responded. Tightening her thighs, scraping my neck with her nails, begging me in her silk-sheets-and-champagne voice.

"Don't stop, August." My name, over and over. So low and insistent. "Please don't stop."

As if I would. Or even could. What was happening between us was like a tornado, churning up everything in its path.

When she finally broke under my lips, flooding my mouth and chin with her pleasure and torturing me with those mad flutters around my fingers, I nearly followed her. My control was so thin that the wild beat of her clit against my tongue was almost too much. The urge to bury myself deep inside her and soak her in my release too overwhelming.

Nothing between us but skin and sweat and her sweet, sexy moans.

After easing her down, I turned my head to catch my breath. I was almost wheezing, for fuck's sake.

I dared to take a look at her face. She'd come so hard I hoped she'd found some relief from her busy brain.

And oh, she had, but not how I'd assumed. Her eyes were closed, her lovely features slack.

Kinleigh was sound asleep.

THIRTEEN

KINLEIGH

Mmm.

I smiled and stretched my arms over my head, caught in that comfortable space between asleep and awake. I'd just had the best dream, and my body was still all warm and loose.

The sun slanting in through the window helped with that, heating my face and making my smile widen as I snuggled into the pillows. Nothing better than a good sex dream. Waking up to a sunny day afterward? Bonus. Even if the sun seemed especially intense right now.

I frowned. My room never got that much sun. Which meant I was not at home.

Oh, goddess.

I clutched the sheet to my chin and frantically tried to remember last night. It was all a bit fuzzy. Going to Vee's. Drinking wine. Laughing. Awkwardness. Texting August and then him showing up at Ivy's door.

Shit, I was at Ivy's. And August was—

I opened one eye and cautiously shifted my head before immediately snapping my eye shut again.

August was in bed with me.

Shirtless. Possibly pantless too.

I pressed my thighs together and took a quick assessment. Something had gone on down there last night. But full sex? The penetrative kind? After I'd texted him and said I wanted to make a—

"Oh, goddess," I moaned aloud, belatedly wishing I could suck the words back into my head along with my crazy, alcohol-induced baby request.

And Ivy. Ivy had put thoughts in my head.

And Vee.

And all of those happy, glowing mothers who had found their forever while enjoying a forbidden night of pleasure. Or twenty-two forbidden nights.

I wasn't fussy.

Maybe he was still asleep. Guys rolled over and dozed like the dead after sex, didn't they?

If we'd even had sex. All I knew was we'd had *something* that made me feel all tingly and sensitive.

Flashes of memory took root in my brain, and I flushed from head to toe. Kissing August, pushing him against the door. Him making me laugh by carrying me and dumping me on the bed.

I turned my head toward the other side and smothered a sigh. He'd given me the sweetest present, a lovely, tiny violet still struggling to survive in its small cup of water.

He'd also given me one heck of an orgasm with his lips and tongue and fingers, but who was keeping track?

Me. I so was. The only part that I wasn't sure about was if he'd planted a flag inside me. Possibly literally *and* figuratively, since I'd asked him to do so.

August brushed a kiss over my shoulder and I shivered. When he did it again, same reaction.

I was so screwed.

"You're up," I said lamely.

"I am." He rolled onto his back and I nearly gasped at the pole holding up his sheet tent. He was ready for service in all ways.

Do not get wet. Do not get wet.

"It's daytime." My voice was as prim as I could manage while I was flat on my back with my nipples as hard as marbles and my fingers twitching with the need to grab his morning wood.

Caution: wet...not paint.

"So it is." His voice was filled with amusement as he tracked my gaze straight to his cock, clearly visible under the sheet.

I couldn't tell if he was naked under there. Not that it seemed to matter as far as modesty went. It wasn't as if I hadn't seen *it* before either, but there was full sunshine in here.

Ivy's. Sweet heavens, we were in bed together at her place. Where she could knock on the door at any time. Where she could have heard so many things.

"How much noise did I make?" I shot a furtive look at the closed bedroom door. Had we locked it? Could it be locked? How were we supposed to get him out of here undetected?

"You were as delicate as a hurricane."

"Funny, Becks." I sat up in bed and fumbled on the nightstand for my phone, nearly upending the cup of water containing my beloved violet. Crap. "What time is it?"

"Why are you whispering?"

"I'm not whispering." I so was.

When he didn't answer, I shoved my hair back from my face and glanced over my shoulder at him. He was sprawled on the pillows with his arms crossed beneath his head as if he didn't have a care in the world. His muscled chest with just the right amount of dark hair was on full display, along with that interesting arrow tattoo right near his left nipple. Not to mention the winding sleeve of black and gradients of gray ink that swirled around to make his muscles seem even more dense and appealing.

"See something you like?"

I flushed. There was no denying it. With my coloring, anything I felt translated right to my skin. The guy was hot, and it was rather infuriating he knew it. Not even in an egotistical way. He just had a quiet confidence I couldn't even hate him for. It was one more positive quality in an ever growing, ever irritating list.

"Your sister might've heard us, you know."

"*Us?* You were the one begging me to make you co—"

I slapped my hand over his mouth. "Don't say it." He lifted a brow and waited for me to remove my hand. "Did we have sex?" I demanded.

"On top of you passing out the second after you came, you also don't remember?"

I tugged my nightshirt into place, hoping to embarrass him into not checking out my breasts. I was not successful. He gazed at them unrepentantly, and they did me the dishonor of not only not minding but swelling even more against the material.

From how slowly he licked his lips, he noticed that too.

"Of course I remember." My slightly frosty tone was my last defense against not climbing on top of him and riding for glory. I didn't even have panties on, for goodness sake. "It's just hazy."

Hazy was a good word.

"Hmm." He rolled onto his side and propped his head on his hand. With his other one, he drew circles on my bare thigh. "I'll give you some flash cards then. You texted me with a question about my rashy eggplant. Then you came home with my sister and followed that up with a text about us making a baby." His Adam's apple rose and fell. "So I did what any rational, red-blooded male would do when confronted with such a question."

"Which was?" I shouldn't be asking as if this was story time, but I couldn't deny wanting more insight into his thought process.

At least he'd had one last night. Obviously, unlike me.

"I yanked a violet out of the pot where I'd been trying to keep it and its friend alive and came over here to do my duty."

"Aww, you ripped it away from its friend?"

"*That's* the part you land on?" He touched my chest right above my heart. "Soft. I never guessed."

"There's a lot you don't know about me, August Beck."

"I know. I want to learn every last thing." He leaned forward and sniffed. "Your hair smells like strawberries and cream. So fucking delicious."

"Ivy's shampoo," I said shakily.

He fingered one of my ringlets, hanging so close to my breast. "I was going to be a gentleman and leave. Until you asked me to stay. You told me how wet you were for me. How much you wanted me inside you with no condom."

I closed my eyes, because his soft undertone was going to kill me. Every bit of it was coming back to me now. He'd stayed so stoic and hadn't let my pleas sway him. He'd done the thinking for both of us.

Protecting me even as I begged him to rip all the shields away.

"I remember."

He tipped up my chin with his fingertip, giving me no choice but to meet his gaze. "Then what happened?"

"Then you got down on your knees and made me come."

"I definitely did that." He slid his hand around to the back of my neck, massaging the tension out of my muscles. "I want to again."

"You're a very giving lover." It wasn't what I intended to say, but it was worth the mirth in his eyes. He didn't smile enough when we were together.

That was probably my fault.

"I try to be, but gotta say I do hope to receive this time too." He rubbed his lips against mine, so softly I nearly sighed.

Sense kicked in and I jerked back. "One second," I yelped, fleeing into the bathroom.

My mouth tasted like a sewer, and morning needs were making themselves known. There was no way we could make out and possibly do other things before I'd tidied up a bit.

Once I'd taken care of business—including brushing my teeth twice with the spare toothbrush I kept at Ivy's for our occasional sleepovers—I stepped back into the bedroom. My hair was semi-tamed, and I'd even swiped on lip gloss.

August stared at me as if I was a mirage.

"Damn, you're gorgeous." He gestured for me to come closer and I responded as if I had no say in the matter.

Once my knees hit the mattress, he leaned across it and hooked his hand around my hip. He nudged up my nightshirt with his nose and aimed right between my legs, giving me a long, slow lick that weakened my knees.

He was so good at that. And if I let him continue down that road, we'd never talk. We would never set the ground rules we needed to.

Just so everything was nice and clear.

"Wait. You said—you said—" I grabbed my phone off the nightstand and scrolled through texts once face recognition let me in. "You said you'd give me a baby. Why would you say that?"

"You asked me to."

"What?" I nearly shouted the question and then sent up a fervent prayer that the noise I could hear in another part of the house was the TV.

Rory and Ivy didn't know August was here. *No one* knew. So when we flamed out—as we were going to do any moment now—it wouldn't be a thing in town. People wouldn't ask how I was doing after such an awful event, and Ivy wouldn't be forced to pick sides. She probably wouldn't pick mine, because no one ever did.

Not that I knew anything about that.

But I didn't want to put her in the middle anyway. She loved her brother, last night's hushed argument on the stoop aside. This whole situation was messy and unnecessary, even if my inner thighs were quivering and the minty scent of August's soap was making my head spin.

"You asked me to," he repeated calmly, leaning closer to resume licking me as if he had all the time in the world.

I tried to breathe. To *think*. "I was drunk."

"You were perfectly coherent." He moved back and slowly swiped the back of his hand over his mouth in the most seductive way imaginable before tugging me down to sit beside him on the bed. "And you took two pregnancy tests."

Despite the still obvious tingling between my legs, I rubbed my phone against the hollow ache in my chest. "I wanted to be sure."

"Yeah. And you were disappointed." He averted his gaze. "As am I."

He couldn't be serious. Most guys didn't want kids. At least not in a situation like this. We weren't even technically dating, and he had no concerns about a biological clock. It was my egg timer suddenly dinging in my head, not his.

But he didn't even say he *was* disappointed, as in past tense. He'd made it present.

"You were?"

"Yeah. Crazy, right?" He let out a low laugh and scraped a hand over his adorable bedhead. His hair was normally as neat and tidy as everything else was about him. Not right now. Spikes were sticking out in all directions.

Just like my feelings for him. It was getting harder to put a lid on them when he went and said stuff like that.

"We've been on fast forward since the wedding. I guess this is just one more part of it. So if you weren't just drunk rambling, if you want to go for it... Well, I do too."

Shock echoed in the pit of my stomach. Had he lost his mind?

For that matter, had I?

"I didn't suggest eating a gallon of ice cream for dessert one night." I lowered my voice just in case my best friend was standing near the door. "I suggested making a baby."

"Mmm-hmm." He slipped his finger underneath the collar of my nightshirt. "Ivy loaned this to you, didn't she? Her husband is filthy."

"He loves her madly."

"Lucky for him, because he would've been left for dead in a ditch otherwise."

I had to grin, more than a little wistfully. "I've never had a defender like that. I always wanted a brother or a sister. Someone so I wouldn't—" I broke off. Nope, this wasn't the place for those kinds of declarations. I didn't talk about my background, not even with Ivy.

I'd left all of that behind.

"So you wouldn't what?" he asked gently.

"So I wouldn't always get in trouble of course." I forced myself to smile, determined not to let the familiar memories seep in and ruin this. Whatever the heck *this* was.

I didn't know for sure, but there was no denying the mad locusts circling in my belly. He wasn't saying no. He didn't think I was crazy. Or if he did, he was crazy too.

We could make a baby and be crazy together.

"Defenders come in all shapes and sizes. Family is definitely more than blood."

I lowered my head before he could see the quick prick of tears. Normally, I wasn't a crier, but something about recklessly planning for a baby with my best friend's brother was messing with my tear ducts.

"What would Ivy say?"

Almost instantly, his jaw firmed and his eyes fired. "About what?"

"You know about what. Us. This." I gestured between us. "Us having sex and making babies. She'd be shocked and upset—"

"The only reason she'd be shocked and upset is because we didn't tell her. But that's your call, not mine."

I fell silent as his little truth bomb detonated my resistance. At least for a second.

"But I get that you're worried. You love her. You're afraid to rock the boat. Except if we succeed..." He took a deep breath. "If we succeed, she's going to have to know about it. Because there's no way in hell we're creating a child without me being there one-hundred percent."

My chin lifted. "We didn't discuss that part."

"We are now."

I set my phone back on the nightstand, my gaze catching again on the tiny violet. He truly was the sweetest guy. I'd missed so many of the small kindnesses he offered while I was busy snarking and sniping at him.

"I didn't think all this out, in case you figured I'd come up with some big plan. Just after the scare, it stuck in my mind. I knew I should be relieved. But I wasn't."

"Same."

His agreement bolstered me to continue. "I've always wanted a baby. I'd thought maybe it would happen with—"

"Valet dude," he said tightly.

"It didn't. I was too young in any case, and I had other dreams too. Ones I could attain for myself even if the kid thing wasn't in the cards."

"Who said it wasn't? Did he?"

When I didn't answer, he raised my chin until our eyes were level. "You can tell me."

Suddenly, I couldn't swallow. "He said some women weren't marriage material. So, of course, that meant I wasn't mother material either, at least in my own head. I'd always hoped they would go together." I let out a self-conscious laugh. "Yet here I am, setting up baby booty calls. Leave it to me."

"Kin, you know that's bullshit, right? What does that even fucking mean?"

"It means I was too focused on my plans for my business and not on making him happy." I held up a hand when August would've leaped off the bed and punched a wall—or gone to look for a man he couldn't even identify.

August was right that defenders weren't always related. When I wasn't looking, he'd become mine.

"His view," I said carefully. "I knew it wasn't necessarily accurate, but let's just say I had some concerns of my own and what he said didn't help."

"Which means you internalized his crap and boxed away what you wanted. Until you admitted it to me." He grabbed my hand and held it to his chest. "*Me*, Kin. Not just some random dude. You trusted me with that part of yourself, and I'm so grateful. We can do this," he added quietly. "Our way. In our own time. We don't need to ask anyone's permission."

My throat was so tight I couldn't do anything but nod.

"Every step of the way, we'll do it together. Okay? From the tests to the doctor's appointments to the buying baby clothes and picking out schools and—"

It was impossible not to laugh. "We haven't even practiced yet, and you've already got the kid in elementary school. It might not happen. There are so many variables."

But good goddess, I adored him for thinking so positively when it was far too easy for me to get lost in the *what ifs.*

"Of course. However, you remember where we live, right? Crescent Cove is only the procreation capital of the world. And I drink a lot of water from the lake." He shifted me underneath him and cupped my breast, rolling his thumb slowly over the hardening tip. "The question is, do you?"

"I drink a mix of lake and bottled."

"Might want to stop that. Anything to up our odds." August grinned at me and shoved down his boxers.

I goggled. There was morning wood and then there was…*that.*

"Is the prospect of no condom that exciting to you?"

"Still some leftover from tasting that sweet pussy."

Right. I'd just let the bright flags of color surely dotting my cheeks do the talking for me.

"This is my first time ever going bare." He parted my sticky thighs with a groan. "I love the easy access. I was so smart to toss those panties last night. Good fuck, you're wet."

It was hard to argue about the location of my perfectly good panties when his long, insanely skilled fingers were stroking my clit before sliding lower to slip inside me. One, then two. I clutched the sheets, trying to remember if I'd read somewhere that an orgasm first helped swimmers to swim.

Whatever, I was on my way to having one. Quickly. That didn't mean I could stop myself from teasing him.

"Not toss like throw out. Right? Because I loved that—*mmm,* right there."

"They're under the bed somewhere probably."

"We need to find them." The word lengthened to several additional syllables as he slid his hands under my ass and just scooped me up toward his mouth.

He held me there, his gaze locked on mine while his tongue swirled and dipped and made the most beautiful mess of me. I forgot about my panties and what Ivy and Rory might hear, clinging to the sheets with one hand and August's crazy morning hair with the other. He wasn't being quiet, and I couldn't be either.

Right now, I couldn't find it in me to care.

"You taste incredible." Even muffled against me, the words lit a fire in my blood. He finally lowered me to the mattress, but I still felt like I was suspended.

I arched and clutched at his hair, incapable of being gentle. Already lost, I slid my hand down my belly toward where he was so hard at work, belatedly realizing that he didn't need my help. But he captured my hand, daring me with his gaze to do exactly what I'd almost done in my mindlessness.

With those intent green eyes focused on me, I could do anything.

I let my fingers wander lower to where I was drenched. He made a low sound in his throat, pushing his fingers into me harder and deeper. Making me release his hair so I could grip the sheets and rock into his strokes. I couldn't be shy now about touching my clit. Not when I was so close and he was licking at my fingers as they moved over the swollen bit of flesh. Adding more friction and more wetness.

"I'm gonna come."

"Yes, baby. Yes." He swapped his fingers for his tongue and I cupped his scruffy cheek with fingers still damp from me.

Eyes locked, I covered my mouth with my hand and tried to keep it together while the world spun and shattered.

He never stopped.

Wrung out, I writhed against the bed. I was already starting to climb again. He was working me as patiently as he would one of his creations, content to spend as long as it took to get the result he sought. His fingers and mouth were relentless.

Not coming again was impossible. I grabbed the pillow and bit down to stifle my cries.

He coaxed me through my orgasm, still sucking my clit with every slick stroke of his fingers. I was pulsing all over for him and straining for more.

Just the way he wanted me.

When he finally drew back to breathe, he licked his lips. Slow and oh so dirty.

"I could spend my life between your thighs."

His lips and chin were wet with me. I wanted to kiss him. Wanted to share that with him too.

As if he knew, he leaned up and fisted a hand in my hair to bring our mouths together, the kiss all clashing lips and teeth. He tasted like me. Every suck on his tongue just made me crave his cock.

Bare. Nothing between us.

We were really going to do this.

He shifted his kisses to my neck before pushing back my hair. "Look at that." His voice was thick with wonder as he traced the pad of his finger behind my ear. "Ladybug."

"Yeah." I shifted my head to give him more access to explore. "My only tattoo. For luck."

"It's lovely and delicate, just like you. But strong underneath."

"Don't flatter me." I reached down to grasp his insanely tight ass. "Just fuck me."

His cock jerked between us. "As you wish."

I dug my nails into the firm flesh, dragging him on top of me, moaning at the feel of his hard length nestling into the cradle of my thighs as if he belonged there.

Because he did.

"Wanted to make this last," he mumbled against my lips. "I can't."

"In me. Don't hold back."

He planted his fist beside me on the pillow and flexed his hips, sinking into me to the hilt with a long rumble of pleasure. He bit my lower lip, pulling it between his teeth as he drew back and did it again. His big hand enfolded my breast and I tipped back my head to haul in air when he pinched my nipple. The flash of pain shot right to my clit and I tightened around him, so full of him that I couldn't even move. All I could do was press my legs into his sides and hang on as he retreated and drove in again.

I reached up to frame his face in my hands, holding on to him while he thrusted in and out. The bed was rocking so hard I was sure someone would hear. Had to. But I couldn't ask him to stop. Not now.

He grew almost imperceptibly inside me as he scraped his teeth down my throat. "Last chance," he gritted out. "I'm going to come."

"Yes. Inside."

"You sure?" He reared back enough to stare down at me, the cords in his neck defined in sharp relief. Little droplets of sweat clung to his hairline, where the faintest hints of silver were just starting to show.

Every part of him appealed to me. Inside and out.

"Yes. I'm sure. And me too." Yet another thing I couldn't stop. He was taking me with him, possessing my body as if only he knew the combination to my lock. All of them were snapping open for him even as I fought to hold on.

He pushed back into me one last time. "Kinleigh," he panted against my neck before he finally gave in.

I could feel him filling me up. Probably it was half my imagination. Half my own desperate longing. But the sensation sent me careening and I spasmed hard around his cock. He grunted in my ear, praising me for having no reserves left against him.

"That's it. Let it all go."

I had no choice.

He dropped on top of me for an instant before he rolled off onto his back to wheeze for breath. "Give me five and we'll do it again."

I managed to lift my heavy eyelids. His arm was draped over his face and his chest was heaving. "We will?"

In lieu of an answer, he slid his hand between my legs, cupping me where I was so swollen and soaked. When I got what he was doing—metaphorical gesture or not—I had to bite my lip around a grin.

"What's so funny?"

"You, trying to fight gravity."

He shifted closer and pulled down the collar of my nightshirt until my breast flowed over it, obscenely on display. He drew the tip between his teeth, sucking while I squirmed. "I'll make sure you stay nice and filled, don't you worry."

I pressed my damp thighs together, trapping his already exploring hand. "I don't doubt it."

Rather than climbing on top of me, he tucked my breast away and laid his head on my chest, giving us both a moment to settle. And in my case, to contemplate how my life might be changing.

Our lives.

A sharp knock sounded at the door. "Kinleigh? It's past ten. Are you okay?" Ivy's voice seemed strangled. Or maybe worried. "You never," cough, "sleep this late."

More coughing. Almost choking. Had she picked up a bug? That wasn't good with the baby.

No, she picked up you were banging her brother in her guest room, you horndog.

I glanced at August, certain he would be as freaked out as I was at the possibility she'd heard something incriminating. We hadn't been very circumspect.

His eyes were closed. A moment later, he let out a soft snore.

Fabulous.

Then the time sunk in. Past ten? The store was opening at noon. I had so much to do to prepare before I did my walk of shame out of here. If it could be called that when we were trying to procreate.

We hadn't even dated—and probably wouldn't—yet we were attempting to have a child. Made sense.

"Kinleigh?"

August made another sound in his sleep and I smothered a giggle. I didn't have much choice but to pretend to be snoring the day away until Sleeping Beauty roused, assuming that occurred in the next twenty minutes. I had to get ready for work so I couldn't spare much longer than that.

He would have to hide in the bathroom while I lured Rory and Ivy out of the house. Or something. We'd figure it out.

Since August obviously wasn't aware, I gave in to the urge to stroke his hair. As far as potential baby daddies went, so far I'd picked a good one.

Even if I might need earplugs.

FOURTEEN

KINLEIGH

"What kind of spread would you like today?"

I flattened my hands on my desktop and tried desperately to center myself. It was Friday, always a crazy day at the shop with women hoping to find that special outfit. Normally, I tried to do my weekly reading with Luna and Ryan on Sundays, but that day hadn't gone as planned considering I'd woken up from my Saturday night wine bender in bed with August. Add in babymaking practice and a tarot card reading just hadn't been in the plans.

The rest of the week had been a flurry of work and a couple of buying trips to trunk sales in a couple of nearby towns. Then I'd had dinner last night with Ivy after Rory left town once again, and she was in a woe spiral.

Seeing how upset my bestie became when Rory traveled for work had me evaluating a lot of things. Maybe this baby idea with August was actually a really smart plan. We were friends yet we could have a kid and not get tangled up with messy feelings that just complicated matters.

For two busy business owners, this made sense. It was like having the best of both worlds.

And I'd just keep telling myself that.

"I'll take a Past-Present-Future reading, please."

"Okay, Luna will shuffle while you think about your question."

"Hold up." Luna leaned toward the webcam, her bright blue eyes going wide. "You're making a big life change. You're red. Bold red today."

I looked down at my white man-styled shirt with oversized cuffs paired with a long gauzy pink and purple skirt dotted with tiny wildflowers. "Not wearing a stitch of red." I played dumb, though I full well knew she was referring to my aura. Typically, she tended to say I was a cool blue. "But I did pull out my favorite red lacy thong for this weekend."

"I knew it! You're seeing someone."

Ryan leaned in closer, tipping her sleek long dark hair close to Luna's bouncy blond shorter waves. "Oooh, I totally missed it. You're right. She's sexing on the regular. Tell us."

Luna smacked her friend's arm while I fixated on the pendant lights August had brought me and tried not to flush eight shades of crimson. "No, you don't have to tell us." She grabbed the deck of cards and shuffled gleefully. "The tarot will tell us all we need to know. Past-present-future, you said?"

I laughed and clutched the chunk of labradorite dangling from today's necklace. I'd been called to this stone, probably because my spiritual path seemed very shaky lately. "Why do I do this to myself every week?"

"Because you love us and we always help interpret the cards in a way you appreciate."

I frowned at Luna. "Does that mean you tell me what I like to hear?"

"No, of course not. The cards are the cards. We don't lie. But there's always a way to focus on the positive. That's one of the tenets of Tarot Tramps."

Ryan nodded sagely. "We came up with ground rules before we started the podcast. We always try to leave people with a smile, even if they're going through rough stuff. The cards are always honest. We just frame things in the best possible way so we can help our listeners find constructive solutions."

"Right. I knew that." I tucked my hair behind my ear and took a quick furtive look around my store. For this instant, it was empty. I'd known I was taking a risk calling for a reading now, but Luna and Ryan would recap it for me later if I got busy, and I desperately needed some guidance. No matter how many times I told myself August and I were doing a practical thing, my heart was not nearly as convinced.

Mainly because he just kept being so damn *sweet*. Bringing over meals and flowers and offering to make furniture for my shop without asking for anything in return, other than those pillows for Seth's anniversary present for Ally. August was fixated on those. I kept putting him off, but little did he know I'd taken a swatch of the fabric Seth wanted last time I was in August's shop and was already sourcing something close.

"Okay, Luna's shuffling for you. We'll make the preliminary reading quick because we know you're dealing with customers and then we'll film an expanded one for you to watch later. How's that?"

Since I kept looking at the doorway, expecting customers, that was probably smart. "Perfect."

Luna's armful of bangles jangled as she shuffled and cut the deck before shuffling again. "Tell me when," she said.

"Now. And those two cards on the end too, please."

She set down my three cards from the colorful witchy tarot deck she was using and flipped them over. "Oh, this is very interesting. In the past position, you have Seven of Wands. In the present position, you have Four of Pentacles. In the future position, you have Ace of Wands."

"Uh oh. That looks ominous." I pointed to the past card, depicting a witch surrounded by hands holding brooms pointed in her direction.

"A little bit, but it's largely due to your perception. In the past, you felt as if you had to defend yourself."

I nodded. That was scarily on point. "Yes."

Ryan tapped the Four of Pentacles. "In the present, you're holding everything dear to you close. Your valuables, your gifts, even your spirit. Keeping them away from someone, as if you fear losing them if you share yourself freely." She cocked her head, shrewdly narrowing her eyes. "Joy shared is joy multiplied."

I fumbled for my necklace and said nothing. "I'm trying to be freer."

"Sex is but one expression of such. A good one," Luna conceded, resting her chin on her hand. "But it's only a beginning. There's so much more inside you to give."

I didn't even flush. I knew what they were saying was accurate, and I couldn't deny I probably had a sex glow going on. It wasn't hard to imagine since August and I were...active. As in every night and occasionally during lunch times too.

This was just the first week. Things would settle down sexually soon enough I was sure, but right now, my body was happily humming for the first time since probably ever. I'd never had this much sex before, even when I was seeing someone.

Then again, I'd never tried to make a baby before either.

I hadn't even precisely charted my ovulation yet. I had a doctor's appointment later this afternoon and I was going to ask a bunch of questions and hopefully, find out the best dates for trying. I knew there were do-it-yourself methods to pick your best days. I certainly had a clue when I was reaching that point, but I wanted confirmation. I was already taking lots of notes in the new bullet journal Kelsey had helped me pick out a few days ago after we'd met up at the café. I was not so stealthily picking the brains of all the mamas I knew. All except Ivy, for obvious reasons. And I wasn't going to feel guilty about that.

Lies. So many lies. I already was.

I took a deep breath and considered again Luna's words about sex being just one form of expression before I spoke. They were used to waiting me out while I processed their readings. Yet another thing I appreciated about them.

"I've never been particularly free in that area either," I admitted. "I've been locked down in a lot of ways. But the man I'm...with," I finally settled on, "gives me the space I need and encourages me to explore."

Ryan waggled her eyebrows. "Depending what kind of exploring you're doing, I know of some very educational sites. Oh, and videos. There's this one on RedTube where the guy lifts her up over his head and—"

Luna poked Ryan's arm. "Sometimes she misses the finer points in her lust for, well, lust."

"Hey, do you know how long it's been since I've gone for a good ride? Porn is all I have left."

"Tell that to the pink power drill I saw on your coffee table just last week."

"It's a real power drill." Ryan shook her head while I laughed. "She's just convinced if it's hot pink, it has to be an implement of sexual pleasure. Which, hey, not saying I might not get to that point someday. If some people use cucumbers as sex toys, then clearly anything goes."

Luna picked up the future card and held it toward the webcam. "Moving on from Ryan's libido for a moment, if we can."

"I suppose." Ryan's downtrodden expression made me laugh again.

It was so good to be able to laugh and have fun with girlfriends. I'd been blessed with a great circle in town, even if things had been a little weird for me since Ivy's whirlwind pregnancy and marriage. I was so happy for her, but it had been a big change to go from being carefree single women who could hang out anytime and drink wine and watch Netflix to having a baby and a husband in the mix. At the same time, anyone could see she was so made to be a mother and how much she loved her husband.

Watching Ivy with her new family made me wonder. I couldn't help it.

I rubbed my stomach. Maybe I'd know what the baby part was like sooner than I ever expected. August was certainly working hard at doing his part.

"Okay, for the future, Ace of Wands suggests you're being given some opportunities right now that you need to seize with both hands or risk losing."

"Opportunities?" I asked quietly. "Or people?"

Ryan and Luna exchanged a look. "The cards are up to interpretation. Your opportunity could be a person. Could be a choice you need to evaluate with your whole heart. Be open to what comes your way. Unlock any doors you've barred shut and see what flows inside."

Ryan fought to keep her face straight. "She didn't mean that in a dirty way, she swears."

"No, I don't."

I laughed and curled my fingers against my belly under the lip of the desk. "Whichever way she means, she's very wise. You both are." The chimes over the shop door sounded as a pair of shoppers entered. I swallowed a sigh. Break time was officially over. "Gotta go. I'll look forward to the extended session video. Thanks again as always."

"Don't you have someone else who can take over for a few minutes?"

"No. It's me. Just me." I put on my brightest smile and glanced away from the computer toward my new customers. A familiar blond head turned toward me as she hitched her giant bag up on her shoulder and my smile grew. "Hi Vee. Looking for anything in particular?"

"Kin! We're just window shopping right now. Probably. Not sure. I need something va-va-voom for my first post twins dinner date with Murphy. And Bess needs," Vee glanced at her companion, a chic older woman in a smart pantsuit with her snowy hair up in a chignon, "something funky for her new place. Right?"

"Kinleigh, did you say you're looking for help for your shop?" Ryan asked from my laptop. She nudged Luna just as I glanced back. "Go on, say something."

"What's up, Lu?"

She ducked her head, a few of her loose waves falling into her face. "Just wondering if maybe you're looking for an assistant. I'm always on the search for a fun new gig."

Hmm, was this one of the opportunities I was supposed to stay open to? I had been considering bringing on at least some part-time help for the store. I couldn't do everything myself, especially if this baby plan worked. The child would need a lot of my time.

I let out a slow breath. And I needed to take this step by step. No racing ahead. Reasonable and rational Kinleigh for the win.

"Sure, maybe you could come in for an interview?"

That wasn't so reasonable, but what the hell? Sure, she might not have any retail experience, but I knew and trusted her. I did need the help. Besides, the cards wouldn't lie.

I hoped.

"Absolutely. Let's hammer out details later."

"Sounds good. Thanks again."

"Bye!" Ryan's cheery wave was the last thing I saw before the connection ended.

"Are you hiring someone for the shop?"

I shifted on my stool and smiled at the woman Vee had called Bess. She had kind eyes, lined with lots of grooves from laughter. A life well lived. "Thinking about it. You look familiar, but I'm not sure we've met. I'm Kinleigh Scott." I held out a hand. "Nice to meet you."

"I'm Bess Wainwright. Pleasure is all mine. I'm moving into the third floor loft apartment above Brewed Awakenings that's just finishing up renovations. I have a big old house right in town, but at my age, I don't need all that space."

"The apartment with the Art Deco touches," Vee filled in as she walked over to us. "Not sure if you saw the spread they just did in the paper, but it's going to be stunning. I love how they're making sure every apartment and workspace in that building is unique. Guess Gavin Forrester has an eye to go with his massive vault of money."

"Oh, yes, the place is so perfect for me. I've always loved Art Deco."

All I knew about Gavin Forrester was that he was a big shot property developer and landlord in town, but I had other concerns right now.

Bess kept talking and I kept on smiling, but I lost the entire thread of the conversation.

Dear goddess, had August and I *christened* her new home?

From how she was describing it, why, yes, we had. If our luck had been different, we might've even made a baby there.

"Excuse me," I choked out before fleeing into the storeroom to drink half a pitcher of iced water and fan my cheeks.

How was I supposed to face her? I usually had a pretty good poker face—at least when August's faux latex allergy wasn't on the menu—but I'd been taken by surprise.

I yanked out my phone from the pocket of my skirt and sent off a text to August.

We desecrated Bess Wainwright's newly finished apartment!

Yes, even including the exclamation point. It was an exclamation point kind of day.

Only to get a text from Ivy a moment later.

We did? How did we do that? And who is Bess Wainwright?

Oh, goddess, wrong Beck sibling. Must've been my brain was so programmed to text Ivy that I'd pulled up the wrong text window by mistake. Now I had another mess to fix while I'd only wanted to vent about the last one.

Not that said sex with August was a mess. It ranked right up there as one of the best nights of my life. It had led us to the place we were in right now, which I had no complaints about.

Even if I was occasionally—often—freaked out about how my life was changing.

Bess is the sweetest lady. She's here right now with Vee. Hey, what do you recommend for something sexy for Vee's date with her husband?

Classic misdirection. Would it work? Tune in at two to find out.

Bess who? I have no clue who that is. I'm still stuck on us desecrating her apartment. How did we do that?

So the answer was no. It was not working. Not even close.
Next option? Plan B.
I pulled up the right text window and hurriedly texted August.

Text your sister and distract her. Make something up. Tell her your table is on fire. I don't care, something.

He replied immediately.

If I tell her my table is on fire, I have to set my table on fire. I quite like it.

I grinned and thunked my phone against my forehead. He was so ridiculously logical.

Fine, then you come up with an idea. I messed up and I'll only tell you how if you fix it.

Blackmail, Ms. Scott?

Is it working?

Send me a picture of your tits and I'll fix whatever you like.

My throat flushed hot, along with my chest and all the rest of me. Had I really thought of August as sweet? He definitely could be, but then he'd let loose with a little dirty talk or a couple of well-placed sexy words and I turned into a puddle. As soon as he'd realized how I blushed when he said those words—and how much my body responded—he'd made sure to pepper them in as often as possible.

Well? I'm waiting. I'm sure Ivy is too.

I glanced over my shoulder at the door I'd shut behind me. At least no one would come in. But I had customers, including a new one whom I felt immensely guilty about already since we'd christened her apartment without her permission.

Even so, I didn't send up a token protest. I definitely didn't consider ramifications. I just…opened a door.

And my shirt.

For good measure, I pushed down the cups of my pale purple bra so the slightest hint of my nipples peeked over the satin material.

I took the picture and sent it, after double and triple-checking I'd picked the right text window again. Ivy and I were super close, but I was pretty sure she didn't want to see how I truly flushed all over when I was embarrassed.

And so turned on my panties needed to be wrung out.

Quickly, I nudged my breasts back into my bra and buttoned my shirt. I almost wasn't fast enough, since August called me instead of texting.

"You realize I'm going to save that picture for the rest of my life." His voice had dipped about three octaves lower than it normally was. The low timbre skated over my nerve endings and made my already hard nipples tingle.

"I didn't even look at it." Because if I'd looked, I would've analyzed it. If I'd analyzed it, I wouldn't have sent it.

I didn't want to be that cautious *look-eighteen-times-before-you-leap* Kinleigh any longer.

"I sure did. I'm looking at it right now. In a minute, as soon as my last customer finishes browsing, I'm going to go into the back and pull out my—"

"You are not. You're not going to waste that in your hand." Was that really me sounding so breathless and needy and *seductive?*

Somehow it was.

"Then come down here and climb on top of me and take care of what you started."

I swallowed over the dryness of my throat. "Technically, my clumsy fingers started it. I meant to text you and I texted Ivy."

His rough chuckle was equally arousing. "I hope you didn't tell her how much you love my—"

"*Shh.*" A laugh escaped me as I re-tied the shirttails of my shirt. "No. My text said we desecrated Bess Wainwright's newly finished apartment the night of Macy's wedding. Bess is in the shop right now, and when she told me where she was moving in, I fled into the back like a criminal."

"So that's what started your gorgeous flush this time. Made your nipples that deep dark pink I love."

"Flush yes, but she didn't have anything to do with the state of my nipples. That was all you, Becks. Oh, shit!" I let out a gasp as Patches jumped down from the third shelf of the bookcase where I kept odds and ends. She liked to wedge herself in there and not move so that she looked like a statue to go with the other bits of glassware and crystals and knickknacks I'd collected, some of which would be rotated into the store's stock.

"Are you okay?" When I didn't immediately reply—since I was rushing across the room to scoop up my cat—August's tone took on an edge. "Kinleigh, answer me."

Patches decided to meow loudly enough to respond for me. August laughed. "Guess I don't need to call the cavalry."

"What cavalry? You know you would've run up the steps in a single bound yourself."

"Got me pegged, woman. So any chance of you coming down here? Soon?"

I couldn't deny enjoying that thread of desire in his tone. Knowing he was as turned on by me as I was by him was so intoxicating.

A text came through with Ivy's ringtone. *Uh oh.*

"I have customers. I'd like to." I shifted the cat while trying not to drop the phone. "I'd *really* like to."

"Show me your panties too. I'll know if you mean it."

A laugh bubbled out of me as I set down the cat, who skulked away with an irked glance over her shoulder. She wasn't used to me choosing anyone over her.

"Quickie one," I murmured before tugging up my skirt and snapping a picture of my hip and the curve of my backside. I hit send.

He laughed. "Cheater. But I like that view too. Your ass is stupendous."

"Am I supposed to say thank you?"

"No, that's my job, since you gift me with the present of your body daily."

"Flatterer." I twisted my hair over one shoulder. "I have a doctor's visit today."

"Already?" There was no mistaking the excitement in his voice. No hesitation at all.

When August went in, he went all in and then some.

"I have some questions."

"Is everything okay?"

Then there was that too, that inherent kindness in him that sneaked out at the most unexpected, wonderful times. "Everything is fine, but I set up an appointment for a consultation to let my physician know I'm trying and to find out next steps. Not an exam or anything. Just to nail down my ovulation days and all that, even though I have a pretty good idea already. She mentioned taking a pregnancy test, but I told her it wasn't necessary yet. Too soon." The others had been negative, so the door from New Year's Eve was closed.

"Good plan. Always prepared Kinleigh, dotting all her I's and crossing all her T's." He cleared his throat. "Let me know what she says."

"Actually, I wanted to ask you to come."

Until that very moment, I hadn't planned on that at all. I was used to doing everything alone. But he was so interested and invested that there was no way I could close him out—at least when it came to the baby.

Our baby. Maybe. If the fates aligned.

"Yes. Of course. Really? Oh, wow."

I giggled like an idiot. "It's just a doctor's appointment. My doctor is very professional. She won't ask any probing questions about us or anything."

"Probing like what? Like how'd I get so lucky?"

I didn't know how to react when he said stuff like that. His words gave me a nice warm glow, but I didn't want to set either of us up for a fall later on. Better to stick to the parameters we'd established and enjoy them without building up false hopes—on either side.

"You know, like if we're married or seeing each other or whatever you want to call it."

"Far as I'm concerned, I don't see you enough. So yeah, count me in. What time?"

"Four. She's in Syracuse."

"I'll swing down at three-thirty. Three-fifteen if you think you can fit me…in."

His lascivious tone made me take a deep breath. "Before my appointment?"

"Time enough for a shower."

"In your world, speedy."

"That's not always a compliment but in this case—is that Ivy texting again?"

"Yeah. Distract her. I don't want to tell her we had sex in Bess's apartment."

"Wonder if it's still open?"

I grinned. "Seriously? You're a pervert."

"I'm a sentimental guy. What can I say? Later, Kin. I'll deal with Ivy. But you owe me. And I always collect."

He clicked off and I held the phone to my chest, smiling like a hopelessly in lo—lust, slightly crazy, hopefully soon to be pregnant woman.

But not too soon. I was a fan of the practice part.

And now I would sell my unique, hard to find items to Bess Wainwright, possibly with a small guilt-induced discount. Assuming she hadn't gotten annoyed at my awkward response and left.

I walked to the door to the sales floor and opened it. There she was, still shopping with Vee. Thank goddess.

"Hi there, Bess, my apologies. I remembered an urgent call I had to take care of."

Speaking of which, Ivy was still texting up a storm. I had no clue what August had said to her, but whatever it was, it hadn't worked yet.

Bess turned toward me with a funky pair of Art Deco bookends. "I want these."

"Why, of course." My smile grew. Those were one of the priciest items in my shop. "If you truly love Art Deco, let me just show you—"

I pivoted and caught sight of Vee in front of the item in question, a long mirror on a stand done in Bess's preferred style with beveled edges and glimmering stones set along the frame. She was twirling back and forth in a dress in shades of pink that brought a lovely flush to her skin and highlighted her new mom glow. The flattering V-neck top clung to her curves and flared out into a kitschy skirt I'd repurposed from a retro Halloween costume. On top of it, she wore a cropped denim jacket that made her look young and fresh and happy.

So happy with her husband and her babies and her new business helping other women find their way to their dream of having a child. We all lovingly teased her about the "baby club" she'd started matching potential parents, but she was a godsend to those women. And some men too, I'd heard. She truly had it all.

I touched a trembling hand to my throat. "Oh, Vee, that's perfect for you."

"You think so?" She turned toward Bess and me. "I was planning on seducing Murphy, but tastefully, you know? Not with the crotchless panties just yet." She laughed. "That's for Saturday night."

"Two date nights in one weekend?"

"Yeah, Macy is taking all three kids until Sunday morning because Dani is with her mother. Something about learning how to deal with a 'houseful of rugrats'. I think she's super hormonal right now, but she won't admit it. Just wants some baby cuddles and is getting a dose of Brayden with it."

"Aww, Brayden is the sweetest baby himself. Just a little older." Bess smiled. "He's around the age of my great-granddaughter Lily. Of course my newest great-granddaughter Rose is a cutie too. Nothing like that baby smell, is there? Here, I have new pictures."

Bess pulled out a purple leather wallet from her expensive purple leather handbag and flashed half a dozen pictures at me of two giggling baby girls, one closer to toddler stage. Vee crowded in to see the pictures too before pulling out her phone to scroll through some snapshots of her own.

Normally, I would've felt awkward. Out of place. Unhappy, if I was truly being honest.

Today? I didn't. Because I had August and the plan. I could have everything too—or a reasonable facsimile of it.

"There he is," Vee said with a sigh as she looked at a picture of her husband.

I swallowed hard. That was the one thing I didn't have. A man who looked at me as if the sun rose when I appeared and set when I left the room, as Murphy did with Vee.

My phone sounded with August's ringtone and I pulled it out.

Ivy forgot all about your random text when I promised to build her a custom bookshelf like my newest piece, which you gotta see. It's special. ;) You helped inspire it.

Then a pause.

You're helping to inspire a lot lately.

I clutched my phone tighter. I didn't want to believe in unicorns, but I couldn't help wishing now and then. I hadn't believed the baby thing could happen for me either. But maybe.

Just maybe.

I typed out a quick reply, barely resisting adding a smiley face at the end. And a heart.

I'm excited to see it. See you soon.

Can't wait.

I glanced up and realized both Vee and Bess were grinning at me.

Bess tucked away her photos. "Nothing will put a look like that in a woman's eye except hearing from her lover. I've worn that expression a few times myself."

I didn't flush for once in my life, and only because it was shocking to hear Bess use the word *lover* as if she was discussing bookends. Clearly, I needed to get out more. Or be more brazen about having a lover of my own.

Finally.

Vee's smile was encouraging, not prying. "I hope so. You deserve someone special, Kin."

"We'll see." I slipped my phone back into the pocket of my skirt.

But I couldn't help smiling. Maybe.

Just maybe.

FIFTEEN

I soaped up my face. I swore every part of me was coated in gritty fibers.

Which was why I preferred working with wood instead of MDF. But did my client want to listen to me? Nope.

Did I try to argue with him?

Yep.

Did I win?

Did I ever?

The sound of wind chimes in my bathroom immediately brought my dick into my internal debate. And my dick won. Because thinking about Mr. Connor was definitely pushed aside for that particular ring tone.

I ducked out from behind my shower curtain and snagged my phone.

Your services are requested at Molly Street. Please bring post-coital ice cream.

I laughed and swore when soap streamed into the corner of my eye. I tucked my phone on the top shelf of my shower. It was water resistant, but all I needed was to have to replace it.

I finished rinsing off and took a little extra care with grooming. Kinleigh said she liked my manly scent, but I was pretty sure she meant the soap version. And maybe after I treated my furniture with eucalyptus-scented sealer.

She seemed to really like me then.

It had been a few weeks of booty calls, and I couldn't say I minded them. The doctor's appointment had been enlightening. So many things to know and worry about if—when—she got pregnant.

Even if I was her dirty little secret. It was always me going to her apartment, not vice versa. And okay, so I enjoyed the many—and I do mean many—different versions of after work outfits I found when I went to Kin's apartment.

My favorite was naked, of course.

But I'd really liked peeling her out of her footie pajamas last night. She tended toward cozy clothing on the cooler nights. I was unaware footie pajamas were a thing outside of the kids' department, but she made them work.

Especially when red lace was hiding under the fleece.

I quickly typed back an answer and tucked a towel around my hips. Before I got to my bedroom, she answered with her ice cream flavor preference.

Guess it was a chocolate swirl kind of night.

My previous annoyance slipped away as I whistled my way over to my closet for a pair of my oldest jeans and pulled on a T-shirt to go with my sweatshirt. Spring was thinking about making itself known, but the brutal wind off the lake always reminded me it was still early March.

I tugged on a winter cap instead of my usual ball cap, grabbed my keys, and was out the door in ten minutes. Night didn't drop like a curtain quite as quickly as it used to, but it was well after six when I stopped into the café for ice cream.

I couldn't exactly raid my sister's fridge like I usually would.

Luckily, Macy had started carrying Ivy's ice cream all year

round. And because I hadn't had time for dinner, I ordered a pie from Robbie's while I was in line. Then what was a pizza without beer?

By the time I was on the road toward Kinleigh's apartment, the front seat of my truck was full. I caught the bunch of tulips out of the corner of my eye. Maybe that was going a little over the top.

I sighed. I wasn't exactly good at the booty call kind of dating. Especially when I wanted so much more.

"Long game, man," I muttered to myself once I arrived and gathered all of my contraband. I hip-checked my door shut and tucked the tulips more fully in the bag with the ice cream.

Kinleigh lived in a rehabbed old Victorian that had been sliced up into six apartments. It suited her funky side with the old dollhouse-style. Or gingerbread, give or take the historian.

Her window glowed with twinkle lights and bright pink curtains framed out each of the four windows that made up the tower jutting out from the side of the house. Kinleigh was in the center of it, her hair making a wild silhouette in the glass.

I swallowed hard.

Hair down Kin tonight. She was doing something with one of her dress forms. Slowly circling it in that way she had when she was deep in thought. I understood her design mind, if not always the output she came up with.

She never stopped working. We had that in common at least.

One of her neighbors was coming out as I was climbing the stairs to the porch. She was an older woman I didn't see often in town. Not overly friendly, but she seemed to recognize me and held the door open.

"Thanks."

She gave me a brisk nod and rushed down the stairs to the driveway.

I took the stairs to Kinleigh's floor, two at a time. My hands were full so I didn't get to text her ahead of time, but she should be expecting me.

The closer I got to her apartment door, I heard music. It was one of Kinleigh's favorite singers. I heard her singing along upstairs a lot. Tonight was no different.

I knocked with my boot.

Her music was too loud, evidently.

I tried again and finally, she swung the door open. Her golden-red curls haloed around her, and her endless legs were showing under a pair of short-shorts in a girly pink. She wore a cropped purple sweatshirt with The Misfits slashed across the front.

Was she even old enough to know who they were? I barely did.

Best part? It fell off her shoulder and she wasn't wearing a bra.

I was a damn lucky man.

She was makeup free and smiling up at me. One of my favorite Kinleigh expressions. Then she glanced down and saw the food and the flowers. Her cheeks pinked and she snatched the bouquet of pink and purple tulips out of the bag.

"How did you find tulips?"

"Just lucky, I guess."

"They're beautiful, thank you." She buried her face in the blooms before going onto her tiptoes to give me a soft, almost shy kiss. An all too brief one.

"Nuh uh. I'll take some more of that." I grasped her arm when she would've slipped away too soon and lowered my mouth to hers once again.

After a moment, she slid back and cleared her throat and turned on her heel to go to her small kitchen. "I was beginning to think you weren't coming."

I followed her in. "I hadn't had dinner yet." I set the pie down on her tiny kitchen island and nudged a three-tiered rack full of crystals, rocks, and plants over a little. At the top was a colorful diffuser pumping out the crisp scent of lemon I was so used to. "Figured I'd share."

She busied herself with putting the flowers in a trio of mason jars. She set one by her sink in the window, then dragged her thumb along the edge of a bloom before turning away to take the other two into the living room.

I dragged my hand through my hair. Was she upset? Flowers were the go-to for my mom. And while I wasn't exactly a serial dater, I'd had girlfriends before.

Flowers were just...thoughtful.

And I was overthinking everything because she drove me crazy.

I tucked the ice cream in the freezer and followed her into her living room. She kept fussing around the room. She placed one of the jars in the front window and still another on the little sideboard table that held crystals and another diffuser. Decks of colorful cards, tall glass candles, plants, and dried flowers were scattered around every crack and crevice in her place.

In front of the bank of windows was her sewing area. It took over almost half of her living room. Her dress form was decked out in a sparkly formal dress with lots of flowing see-through material. She was picking up bits of fabric and tucking them into one of the half dozen baskets that always seemed to litter her space.

"Kin."

She wouldn't look at me.

"Kinleigh."

She stopped, tucking her fingers into the sleeves of her sweatshirt. "I'm almost done."

I went over to her and slid my knuckle along the smooth skin of her back. I eased her back against my chest. "What's up?"

"Nothing."

I teased the soft skin of her her midriff, my thumb coasting up over her ribs to the underside of her breast. She shivered in my arms. I dipped my head to taste her shoulder. "It's something. You won't even look at me."

Spicy lemons and freckles filled my senses. I followed the star pattern they made on her shoulder with the tip of my tongue. I kissed over to her neck, my tongue dragging along the fragile chain of sunny yellow gems dotting along every few inches of her necklace. I lifted her hair up and traced a figure eight along the nape of her neck.

She swayed against me with a sigh.

I'd never had to work so hard to woo a girl in my life. Sex was easy between us, but the minute I offered her more, she turned into a damn turtle. Even if the more I offered was just a fistful of flowers.

I wouldn't let her slip away from me. If I could be patient and find the perfect design in a slab of wood, I could certainly wait out Kinleigh.

I hoped.

But for now, I knew how to make her open up for me. Even if it was just her body.

I slipped under her sweatshirt, cupped her breast and gently tugged at one tip. I let her hair fall and used the other hand to slip between her thighs. I groaned into her neck when I found just skin under the loose hem of her shorts.

Her curls teased my cheek as I searched out that little spot that made her purr against me. Her pulse fluttered under my mouth and I bit down softly, adding more pressure as I circled her tight little clit.

In this space, I knew her. I understood what she needed. I didn't have to chase her or search through layers of emotion and truth. Here, she was honest.

And so was I.

She gripped my thigh, trying to reach around to find me. But right now, it wasn't about me. All too soon, I'd lose myself in her and we'd race to the finish. And she'd try to push me away again.

I wasn't ready for that. Even if it meant blue balls for an hour, dammit.

I held her closer, dipping two fingers into her sweet, perfect heat. Her head fell back, and one of her hands came up to cover mine on her breast. "August."

The song changed from the tongue-in-cheek lyrics to a soft, acoustic song. I let the music lead me with slow, searching explorations of her body. I drew her sweatshirt up and off, gazing down at her pale skin in the golden light of her living room.

I eased us away from the windows. No one should see her but me. Even on a nearly deserted street, it didn't matter.

She was just for me.

I drew my fingers from her and traced lazy circles up her belly.

Her necklace was long and hung between the gentle swells of her breasts. I dragged a small yellow gem over the tip and watched her nipple tighten even more. She sucked in a breath as I used the light abrasion of the chain to torment her.

To torment me.

She swayed against my jeans. Her ass fit me so perfectly. Curved enough to cushion the length of my shaft between her cheeks through the nylon shorts. I ground myself against her, swaying lightly to the song as I used the chain on each of her breasts, while I toyed with the other with endlessly patient tugs.

"You're making me crazy."

"Good." I dragged my nose along her jawline. "Exactly how I want you."

"Touch me."

"I am." I nipped her ear.

"More." Her head rolled along my chest, her hair teasing me just as much as I was teasing her.

I let the chain swing back to its spot and turned her in my arms. I cupped her face, and those huge blue eyes were unfocused and soft. Lost in the pleasure I could give her.

Her busy brain buried for now.

I lowered my mouth to hers. Sipping lightly, and nipping her lower lip. She smiled into the kiss and I used it to ease my way in until we were tangled. Tongues twining and flicking, her fingers pushing at my sweatshirt and T-shirt until it joined hers on the floor.

I hissed as her water-soft skin skimmed mine for the first time tonight.

She swayed into me, her nipples digging into my chest as she went onto her toes and wrapped her arms around me. It was just enough for me to hook her leg around my hips and lift her.

"What about the pizza?"

"Later," I mumbled into her mouth.

She laughed and hung onto me. I turned down the short hall to her room, kicking in the door. More candles and scents hit me here.

These lighter and softer, with fabric and pillows everywhere. Her bed was too damn small for the both of us, but I made it work.

I stretched her out on the patchwork quilt and her hair was like fire over the peach sheets and pillowcases. She dug her purple-tipped toes into my jeans. "Off."

"Or?" I knelt between her legs and leaned back.

She sat up and reached for my fly. "I can help if you want."

I grinned down at her. "Is that right?"

Her long, nimble fingers raced over the zipper and quickly reached in to draw me out of my boxer briefs. She swiped her tongue over her lower lip and peeked at me through veiled lashes.

"Kin."

She flicked her tongue under the head of my cock. "I love the way you say my name so many different ways."

She took me deeper and I threw my head back. Her name was more of a strangled moan this time. I was quickly losing control of the situation.

"Yes. Like that. All dark and gravelly." She peeled down my jeans to get to more of me, digging her nails into my ass as she took me deeper.

I fisted my fingers into her curls, holding her there.

Her huge eyes were a little wild. Not the hazy and unfocused from before, but drunk on power. And I couldn't even care at that moment. Because she had me wrapped, if only she'd see it. The truth was I'd do anything for her.

This was so much more than just baby-making practice.

I tugged on her hair and she took more of me, her nostrils flaring as she breathed in and around the invasion of my shaft. She swallowed and pumped me with her strong hand until I was wet from her mouth and the need to empty myself between those pink lips roared through my brain.

But as much as I loved her mouth, there was only one place I longed for.

I eased back and swiped my thumb along her swollen lip. She greedily pulled my thumb into her mouth and I swore. I kicked my jeans away and hooked my arm around her waist to roll her under me. Those long legs quickly curled around me, drawing me where she wanted me.

"Inside me," she said against my lips.

There would be no drawing this out. As much as I wanted to, she made me too insane.

I hiked her knee up higher and sunk into her with one long thrust.

Her nails dug into my shoulders and she caught my mouth on the next stroke. "August," she breathed.

At least here I knew she wanted me. Knew she needed me. Not just for the baby-making. *This* was where we made sense—in each other's arms. The slow glide of our bodies in our own rhythm. Total oneness.

I didn't have to worry about finding the right spots or stressing about whether she was with me. Here, we were always right—she was my true north. And my perfect match.

I buried my face in her hair to find that little spot along her neck that drove her crazy. Just below the tiny little ladybug tattoo behind her ear. She arched up under me and cried out my name. I drove into her, chasing the heady and overwhelming undertow of pleasure that took me down every damn time.

My name was a steady litany between her gasps, and I wore the tattoo of her nail marks down my back as I tipped up her hips and emptied myself inside of her. My brain absolutely flatlined as I gave her everything, as I had nearly every night.

Part of me wished for the baby she wanted. The other half of me knew that I could lose her once it happened.

Her arms slipped from my shoulders as she went boneless underneath me.

I was tempted to do the same. Just roll her to the side and crawl behind her and find the blissful sleep I couldn't seem to find anymore.

But then my stomach growled—loudly.

Kinleigh giggled under me. "Guess I should let you have that pizza now."

I withdrew from her and dropped onto my side. "Now that you got what you wanted?"

Fuck.

I wanted to snatch the words back, but luckily, she didn't take offense. Instead, she curled her arms around her knees and tucked them against her chest.

"What are you doing?"

"Making sure all those guys stay put for a bit. Maybe do their job."

I dropped my arm over my eyes.

"What? I was reading on this site that said you should put your legs up if you can. I was thinking about moving my bed over there so I could put my feet up on the wall."

I shook my head. "Next, you'll have me doing headstands for blood flow."

"Well, that's the wrong way for blood flow."

I rolled off the bed and went to the bathroom to take care of...well, it surely wasn't a condom. It was still weird to actually be that close to anyone. Condoms were a necessary evil for guys. At least the smart ones.

I had a few friends who were diehards about hating condoms. More than half of them had kids earlier than they'd intended.

Me? Here I was, actively tempting fate.

I was still waiting for the warning signs to blare in my head. So far, the only one that was tripping me up was squirrel Kinleigh. Also known as when she clammed up and tried to put distance between us.

Was it wrong to want to hold her down and tame her?

Probably.

Did I really want to tame her?

That was a definite no.

I quickly washed up. I hated to actually scrub her from my skin, but if I was going to worm my way into staying a little longer, I should probably freshen up.

When I returned to the bedroom, she was gone and the scent of spicy sauce overrode the need to analyze everything.

I snagged my boxers and left behind my jeans, and then followed my nose into the kitchen. The pizza box was open and several pieces were missing.

Kinleigh was just shutting the oven. She was a woman after my own heart—cold pizza was gross.

The music was playing again. Kinleigh's slow hip roll as she sang along to JLo was adorable. The fact that she was only wearing my shirt was another point in this evening's favor.

She danced her way over to the fridge and pulled out two beers—the ones she stocked just for me—and wiggled some more.

I had to grin. Damn, my woman was hot.

She jumped as she noticed me. "What are you doing, creeper?"

"Enjoying the view." I crossed to her and slipped my fingers under the hem of my faded Chevy T-shirt to pull her closer. I hissed as the cold beers pressed against my nipples.

Her blue eyes lit. "Cold?"

"Care to try it and find out." I lifted the soft cotton.

She shrieked and tried to move away. "No. No, Aug—"

I pushed the bottle against her breast and watched her nipple tighten and darken with the cold. She tried to squirm away, her laughter filling the space.

The best sound ever.

Still smiling down at her, I took both beers with one hand and put them on the counter behind her, and then lowered my mouth to her icy breast. I drew it deep into my warm mouth and she sighed, slipping her fingers into my hair.

Hard again, I lifted her up onto the counter.

"Again?"

"How long do we have on the timer?"

She swallowed. "Four minutes."

"Think we can?"

Her blue eyes twinkled. "Should you be proud of that?"

I barked out a laugh and freed myself, slipping into her. "The correct question is can I make you come in four minutes?"

"Probably in two." She groaned. "Goddess, you feel amazing."

I shoved her—my—shirt up and latched onto her nipple. She threw her head back. "August."

I knew that sound. I grinned around her tight nipple and tugged her closer to the edge of the counter and drove into her. My spine twinged at the angle and that I actually had to go onto my toes to get the angle I knew she needed. "Hold on," I managed as I gritted my teeth against how good she felt.

She gripped the counter and lifted her legs around me.

"No. Me," I growled. I curled my arm around her lower back and jerked her against me so I could get deeper. Until I bottomed out inside her.

Her arms went around me, her nails scraping my shoulders. Shock flashed in her eyes. I gripped her hair and dragged her mouth to mine, swallowing her surprised shout. I followed her lead and the room darkened, spots dancing along my periphery as we raced to the edge.

She clasped me tighter, inside and out. My heartbeat seemed to echo in my head. Throbbing endlessly. Beating only for her.

I let out a roar as I came so hard that the world went silent. Then suddenly, my hearing came roaring back with the shrill pitch of the timer.

"Done," she said weakly against my shoulder.

"Yeah, you are."

She giggled. "You're a terrible man."

"So terrible I made you come that fast, then twice before?"

"It was not twice."

I caught her mouth. "Sure about that?"

"Pizza's burning."

"I don't care." But then my stomach growled again. I backed away from her, tucking myself back into my boxers. "Stay."

One golden brow arched. "Do I bark next?" She swung her legs as she opened one of the beers for me.

I shoved my hand into the pink fish-shaped oven mitt and pulled out the perfect mushroom and cheese pizza. I burned the tip of my finger when I sneaked a mushroom before dumping the lot of it on the stove. Then I turned and grabbed my beer, taking a long swallow before returning it to her.

"Aww, backwash just for me?"

"So says the woman who took my dick inside her mouth like it was her favorite lollipop."

She grinned. "Different. Besides, I'm just holding this for you while you look all studly and chef-like handling that gooey pizza."

"Since you're calling me a stud..." I opened her knees and wedged my hips between them. "Care for a fourth?"

She didn't say a word, just set aside my beer and licked her lips. Her look of dubiousness was enough for me to forget my pizza again and bury two knuckles into still swollen pussy. I found her clit, squeezing again and again. She gripped the counter, still playing it cool. But her body told the truth. It always did. She coated my hand and her breath hitched. She never broke our eye contact.

Looking into her eyes as she quivered for me made me crazy.

She gripped my forearm, my name a hiss as she dragged me down by the back of my neck. I let out a low laugh as her control broke and she shattered on a long moan.

It took everything inside me not to slide into the fisting grip of her body. To bury myself inside her again and forget the rest of the world existed.

But this was enough. Touching her, bringing her pleasure, being here with her—all of it was more than enough. And I needed her to know that.

I backed away from her and went to the sink to wash my hands before grabbing my beer again. It was almost empty and had gone warm, but I drank it down like the parched man I was. I'd be after the second one in a minute. "Pizza?"

She blew out a slow breath. "Yes, please."

I hid my smile from her as I snagged plates from her cupboard. "Gonna wash your hands?"

"Just as soon as my knees reform their bones."

I laughed and held a mushroom out to her. She bit the tip of my finger when she took it. "So mean. Is that any way to treat the man who left your knees boneless in four minutes? And then again in like two?"

"This is going to be a thing, isn't it?"

179

I took a healthy bite from my slice. "Maybe."

Finally, she hopped down, and maybe my smile was a little smug when she wavered a little. I moved to the island for a napkin and got a smack to my ass for my trouble.

We laughed over half a dozen slices between us. Topics included customers—we both had stories there—and more than a few about Rhiannon. In the end, I hauled her back to bed for another round of baby-making gymnastics.

When she was draped over me and I resumed the ability to take in oxygen, I stroked her hair until she settled against me.

"You can't stay."

"I know."

"If Ivy found out…"

"*Shh.* Just a few minutes and I'll head home."

She snuggled down beside me. "Okay, just a few more minutes."

And because sleep hadn't been one of my top priorities with all the custom orders I'd been working on along with being on call for Kin… Well, it wasn't shocking that I passed out.

Especially with a warm, delicious-smelling woman sprawled on me.

"August!"

"Mmm." I rolled over and shoved my arms under the pillow, flipping it to find the cool side. My knee almost fell off the edge of the bed, for fuck's sake.

"August, it's three." Her whisper was strained.

"Good, that means I can sleep for another three hours."

"No. You were supposed to go home." She hopped off the bed and then my jeans hit my head.

"Jesus, Kin. Who cares?"

"I do. Goddess, my neighbors will see your truck out there and…"

"What? You have a boy—guy over. Big deal." I almost said boyfriend, but that was asking for an argument this late at night.

"And what if Ivy notices you didn't come home?" Her hair was wild around her shoulders, and she kept pushing it out of her face as she looked under the bed.

"My boots are at the foot of the bed."

"Right. Thank you." She scurried around and found them, setting them on the floor beside my side of the mattress.

I sighed and sat up. "Kin, just come back to bed. I'll leave before—"

"You know Ivy is up at weird hours to feed the baby."

I flipped the sheet back. "And she knows I fall asleep at the shop all the time."

"August, we've talked about this."

"No, you talked and I—you know what? Never mind. I'm exhausted." I pulled on my jeans and shoved my feet into my boots. It was my own fault. I knew she wasn't ready.

I just had to throttle back.

She was twisting my shirt into a mangled mess. I stepped in front of her. The little low watt string lights that framed her bookcase were the only light. "It's fine, Kin." I eased my shirt out of her hand and kissed her forehead. "I'll see you tomorrow."

"Okay. August?"

"Yeah?" I stopped in the doorway, but I didn't turn back to her.

"Thanks for the pizza and the flowers."

"You're welcome." I flashed a smile over my shoulder.

At least that was something.

SIXTEEN

KINLEIGH

I RAN TO THE BACK ROOM. I HAD A SPECIAL INTERNET ORDER FOR pickup, and the wind chimes on my front door jangled again.

It was a busy day. And I was grateful for it.

So very much. Even if my shirt was now sticking to my back and my Spotify playlist had run out and the app was picking music for me.

Unfortunately, it still hadn't learned what I loved. It definitely wasn't Justin Bieber. But I was too busy to even check my phone and choose another playlist.

My shop phone rang as I was heading back into the front of the store.

I blew out a breath as I skidded to a stop. A trio of women were holding up different pairs of jeans against them. The ones I'd spent umpteen hours on hand-embroidering—and that I loved with all my heart. Finally, someone had found them.

I'd posted pictures to my Facebook group and website, as well as my Instagram. While I had tons of social proof—and who didn't enjoy likes and hearts on their posts—I still hadn't sold a single pair of them.

In fact, I was ready to bring down the price for the Spring Walk in town.

Almost ready.

I was being stubborn, but for once, I wanted to see if I could get a good profit off something I was upselling. Most of the time, I didn't mind making only a little of the proceeds on my markups. I turned over a lot of items to make up for the narrow margin of profit, but these were special.

My poor pricked fingers said so, anyway. That and my lower back pain from sitting cross-legged and hunched over to embroider for hours on end.

On the brighter side, August was good at massaging away my aches. Depending on angles, he also caused some too.

Whoosh. Not thinking about that right now. Or how amazing his strong hands were.

"These are perfect for your trip. I bet they'd make your ass look amazing." The blond's voice was sweet and surprisingly husky. She was wearing an armful of bracelets and had three of my most expensive crystals in one of the wicker baskets I'd found at a flea market over her arm.

Sales. Yes!

"Let me know if you ladies need anything," I said as I ran past them to the back of the store. Another two customers came in and I felt a headache brewing.

Did I eat?

Was I pregnant?

Get a hold of yourself, Kinleigh.

It was far too soon to know if there was a baby on the horizon. And oh my goddess, there were another two people at the jeans display.

"I saw these on Instagram and had to come in," my new customer said.

I pressed my lips together to hide a goofy smile as I climbed the few steps into the clothing-heavy zone of my shop. It was the only place I could keep clear to do photo shoots for my website. "Hey, Cathy. I found your order."

The customer in question had her arms full of a lamp and was pointing at a chandelier hung in the corner over one of my boudoir setups. Her sweet round face was lit with excitement. "Is that for sale?"

"Everything in here is for sale—well, except for my big pink couch in the dressing area. I know a guy who could make one for you though."

"Oh, that nice young man downstairs maybe?"

"That's the one. August Beck's furniture is beyond compare."

As were some of his other attributes. Which I was not focusing on right now.

"I have been thinking about a new bedroom set for my twenty-fifth anniversary."

"Oh, that's wonderful. When is it?"

"November."

"I'd definitely talk to him. I have one of his beds over here if you want to take a look." I set her box with her online order on the settee I'd moved out of storage yesterday. I'd been stuffing the shop full of items for the last few weeks, hoping to capitalize on the town-wide sidewalk sale.

"Oh, I'd love to."

"Let me take these." I added her finds to the pile.

"Thank you, dear. I just love your shop."

"I'm so glad. I love to go treasure hunting, as you can probably tell."

"Oh, I can. Each time I come in there's something–several somethings—new."

I beamed at her. "One of a kind items are just waiting for the right buyer to find them in my attic."

That sounded a little woo woo, but so what? I truly believed it.

She patted my arm. "I just love that. I could spend all day looking around."

I tucked my arm through hers. "Wait until you see the bed. Maitland Enterprises was tearing down one of the old mansions on the lake. I dragged August over there to gather some reclaimed wood off the beach and what they left behind in the demolition. We ended up with three truckbeds full of prime pieces."

Cathy breathed out a happy sigh as we stopped at the foot of the bed. "Oh, it looks like it belongs on that Joanna Gaines program."

"Doesn't it?"

"Shiplap!" We both said together.

She immediately went to the oversized pillows and linen duvet I'd repurposed.

The four poster bed had been entirely built with the reclaimed wood. The headboard was a simple design of slatted pieces August and I had painstakingly picked out to match. I swallowed at the memory of how long it had taken for us to get the warped wood to straighten out. We'd put it together last fall—before the kiss.

He'd grumbled the entire time about using imperfect wood until the final project came together. The mix of old, weathered ash and August's modern style made for a perfect piece. The posts were simple, but I'd prettied it up with gray muslin and fairy lights to make it even more magical.

Cathy traced her fingers along the little bench I'd convinced August to make out of the last of the scrap wood. "I will definitely talk to your young man."

I opened my mouth to say he wasn't mine, but she was on a roll.

"But I think I need this today." She tapped the bench.

"I can wrap it up no problem. Would you like the vase too?"

She nodded and drew a light touch over the pussywillows and eucalyptus I'd arranged inside the blue glass. "The greenery too."

"You got it."

"You're quite the saleswoman."

That I was. "If you like farmhouse style, I have a lot of wonderful Americana items too."

"My husband is going to hate you."

I grinned. "Might as well make it worth it."

"I like how you think."

I led her over to where I kept most of spring-themed pieces near the front of the store. By the time I got back to the women picking through my pile of jeans, the five of them were chatting like old friends. The closer I got to them, the more I wished I'd called Luna back about that position. Especially with the sale going on.

But no one could know the store like I did. And training someone seemed like more work than I'd get back in time and sales.

"Do you see a size eight?" a stunning redhead asked as she flipped over a huge pile of denim.

"I made piles by size to find my own. I think—yep, here you go." The blond with the jangling bracelets plucked two pairs out from the neat piles she'd made.

"Perfect."

"Do you need to try any—oh." Recognition finally dented my fried brain. We'd never actually met in person, only online. "Luna?"

"Hey, girl." She set down her basket, now overflowing with jeans as well as more crystals. "Your place is amazing." Luna rushed toward me, her exuberant personality the same with or without a video chat window. She threw her arms around me, knocking me back a step. She smelled like wildflowers and happiness. "I can't believe it took us so long to take the trip out."

"Mostly because tying her down in the car for forty minutes takes a lot of bungee cords and threats."

I peered around Luna's voluminous curls. "Ryan, you too?"

She waved. "And we brought our friend April."

Another sunny blond, this one with a yard of wavy curls, smiled at me with a little wave. She also had an armful of clothes. "I can't believe how many cool things you have."

Ryan tucked a glossy lock of long dark hair behind her ear. "April's shopping for her vacation, even though it's not for months."

"I happen to like to think ahead, unlike some people."

Ryan shrugged. "I like to go where the wind blows." She stepped forward and gave me a hug—nothing like Luna's bone-crusher, but it was lovely to know they were both as friendly in person. "Luna wanted to see if she could convince you to give her that interview."

"Way to be chill, Ry."

Ryan laughed and flipped a pair of jeans over her shoulder since she couldn't fit any more in her arms. "The only way to get her moving is to push sometimes."

Somehow I didn't think that only pertained to Luna.

Luna sighed. "Being a cardslinger doesn't steadily pay the bills. Though I am pretty flush at the moment," she lifted the packed basket, "hence the shopping."

"You could make a steady income if you marketed like I told you to," April piped up.

"I'm choosy who I read for. You'd know that if you let me do your damn cards."

April's eyebrows snapped down and she folded her arms over a sizable pile of clothes including my jeans. She'd chosen all of the ones with the crochet patchwork instead of cloth. "Hell no. There are certain things I just don't want to know."

The two other women were obviously listening as they dug through the pile of jeans.

"Sorry, Kin. Not like you want us to shout to the rooftops that we read tarot cards." Luna's wide smile said she was less than repentant about it.

"Actually, would you guys be into doing a tarot night here at the shop? Maybe we can do a little class on crystals and incense. Then maybe you can do some readings?"

Before Luna could open her mouth, the two women on the other side of the table practically shouted, "Yes."

I laughed. "Looks like we might have a little bit of interest."

The redhead held up a finger. "I, for one, have a whole book club who would be into it."

"Oh?" Luna turned toward her with a tilt to her head. "What do you read?"

"Sexy romance novels and drink lots of wine."

Luna reached out and touched her arm. "Tell me more."

The two of them started chatting animatedly about a half dozen books and authors I'd never heard of. Then again, I didn't have a lot of time to read between the store and my own projects—and August.

I shook myself out of my stupor. "Can I unlock a dressing room for you?" I asked the reading club girl's friend.

"That would be great."

"Ry, I'll be right back."

Ryan waved me off. "I have plenty to keep me entertained."

It was even more obvious I needed to get some assistance in the store. Even if they just ran the register while I took care of the floor, it would be a huge help. Foot traffic would only be increasing with the nicer weather and the monthly farmer's market that cycled into the park this summer. I just hated to spend money on the business that didn't include merchandise for the floor.

But then there was Luna right there. As if I'd asked the universe for her.

I made small talk with the short-haired woman and set her up with a glass of lime water. Then it was a mad rush to check out people and I had to SOS August to help me take down the chandelier Cathy wanted. There was no way I could monkey my way up there with the now ten customers in the store.

I was ringing out the book club girls—who were holding business cards from both my counter and Ryan's stealthy pass—when I heard the chimes of my door again.

Instead of a customer, August's wide shoulders blocked the streaming rays of late afternoon sun. I stood up straighter and the exhaustion and overwhelm dissipated when he smiled at me.

Ryan gave me a narrow-eyed glance then followed my eyeline. Her eyes widened and a slow smile spread across her face. "Huh."

I looked back down at what I was doing and refolded the table runner that I'd turned inside out. Goddess, he was a distraction.

He stopped at the desk and flipped his baseball cap around backwards. August in work mode. That shouldn't be as hot as it was.

He nodded to the line of people with a slow smile. "Ladies."

The immediate response of at least half of them made my toes curl in my shoes. Dammit, what were they looking at?

"Which chandelier did you need help with?"

Cathy raised her hand. "I can show you."

"Can I have a store helper like that?" Came a voice from the back of the line.

I cleared my throat and kept ringing people out. Ryan moved out of line with Luna and April. I tried to ignore the fact that they were obviously conferring. They could only guess what was between me and August. Okay, maybe more than guess since my stupid skin was flushed.

I just focused on one customer at a time.

He came around the back of the desk a few minutes later and muscled the heavy fixture into the back room. He'd helped me before when it came to some of the larger things in my shop, so I knew he was capable. Even if the control freak in me wanted to go check on him.

Suddenly, the customer in front of me glanced up over my shoulder.

"Need anything else?" August's voice was low in my ear.

A full body shiver was my first response. Then I lost words. His calloused finger skimmed under my shirt to stroke along my lower back. There was no way anyone could see him, but my nipples were freaking beacons to anyone who was paying attention.

"Kin?"

I swallowed. "I'm okay." I looked up and his cheek was right by mine. The sharp tang of eucalyptus washed over me, and I barely controlled the urge to take a deep breath. It must've been a sealing day down in the workshop.

His lashes lowered as his gaze drifted to my mouth and then to my very annoyingly perky nipples. "I'll see you tonight?" His voice was barely a whisper.

I nodded.

He straightened and his touch was gone. "Mrs. Brown, I'll bring that chandelier down for you." He lifted the bubble-wrapped light fixture and tucked it into one of the oversized boxes I kept next to the desk.

"Thank you, August." Cathy smiled his way before returning her attention to me.

He gave her a quick and friendly smile before he headed to the door.

Cathy handed me her credit card. "I really like your young man."

"He's not—"

"Even an independent woman needs a little help. He's got a very sweet way about him."

Until he flips me on my stomach and fucks me within an inch of my life. But sure, yeah, he's a sweetheart.

I simply smiled. What else could I do?

Especially since the total I punched in for her order would put me well over my sales goals for the week—heck, the month. And I'd figured higher with the Spring Walk.

Ryan, Luna, and April had disappeared. Once I finally rang everyone up, I searched them out. They were in the dressing room area with a pile of shirts, jeans, and a few of the crochet dresses I'd bought from a local crafter.

April had layered the crochet dress on over a flirty black slip that made it seem more like sexy date wear than I'd considered. Maybe I should whip up a few simple tank dresses to sell near the others.

"I knew it." Luna clapped from the floor. She was sitting on one of the bamboo beach mats. A package of trail mix stuck out of the top of her bucket bag and four cans of wine spritzers were sweating on the tray I used for my lime water pitcher.

"Are one of those for me?"

"Yes!" Luna popped up and brought me the green can. "You deserve it."

"I don't know about that."

April was swishing the skirt of the dress in one of the three mirrors I had set up along the side as she munched on a pretzel. "Are you sure it's me though?"

"It's vacation you, which is totally separate." Luna flitted over to her friend. "I mean, look at those miles of legs. And we know you can tan, you bitch."

April grinned at her through the mirror. "I sure can."

Luna gave a lusty sigh. "Takes me three weeks of daily beach time for a hint of beige and then it's gone in three days."

"I just burn, then maybe keep a freckle or two." I took a sip from the bubbly wine and hummed out my pleasure then took another sip. "I need about three more of these." Not that I would be having them, but a little was okay during practice time, according to the doctor.

"Handily, they're from that cute little wine bar a few buildings down."

I turned the can around. Sure enough, it said Ashes and Wine with a mix of scripty and heavy masculine fonts. "Guess I'll have to text my order into my friends who were coming in for a photo shoot tonight."

Luna spun around. "Photo shoot?"

I leaned back on the big pink hassock. "Yeah, for those jeans you guys went wild for. Do you guys want to stay and help? The more models the better."

Ryan dropped into a bean bag chair in front of me. "That sounds like fun. However, what sounds like much more fun is if you tell us about that tall drink of handyman-slash-carpenter-slash-booty call, August."

I flushed and stood up. "Nothing to tell."

"Right. That's why your aura is a neon pinkish-red right now." Luna lifted her can and took a long drink.

Ryan nudged me. "So how much after-hours treatment are you getting?"

"It's not like that."

"Oh? Then how is it like?" Ryan batted her eyelashes at me.

"We're friends."

Luna snorted and popped the top on another spritzer. "Naked friends."

"*Shh.*" I looked around to make sure no one had come into the shop.

Ryan tipped her head and studied me. "Hmm."

"We're keeping things quiet." I sighed. For the first time, I had the option of actually talking about August with someone. "He's my best friend's brother."

"Ohhh." Luna dropped down on the mat again. "Well, that makes a little more sense. But he sure didn't seem like he was hiding anything when he was snuggling up to you at the desk. Is there anything more romantic than a guy who can't stay out of your dance space?"

"At all," April chimed in.

I flushed. "It can't be like that."

"Why not?"

"Because. It just can't." I drained my can of wine and stood up to gather their discarded clothes. I couldn't look too closely at that far too appealing fantasy. The one where I could wake up next to August without guilt or panic. Where I could not worry about who saw us together.

It was just smarter to make sure I didn't ruin the one bit of family I could count on for something that was at best a bad idea and at worst, a breakup begging to happen. And I couldn't put Ivy through that. Nor could I ever make her choose sides. It wasn't fair and I knew which side I'd land on. Just like always.

A lifetime of lessons had taught me that.

"I have flipped the closed sign and locked the door, it is time to party!" Came a voice from the front of the store.

"I brought the wine." Gina's sweeter voice followed her sister Gabby's.

"Thank goddess, more wine," I muttered and rushed to meet them.

A little more wouldn't hurt. I hoped. Besides, I wasn't pregnant yet. Probably not, anyway.

"This conversation isn't over," Ryan called after me.

"There's nothing to converse about."

"What are we not conversing about?" Gina rushed toward me, her long hair still tied into her work ponytail. She smelled like syrup and fresh bread with a little extra diner grease.

"Nothing." I hugged her back. "I'm so glad you could come."

"Let me get out of this freaking uniform and drink half a bottle of wine and I will try on all the jeans." She shoved two bottles of wine and a handled brown paper bag at me.

I peeked in and groaned. "Gravy fries?"

"Of course." Gina headed toward the back of the store where the bathrooms were. "I'll be right out."

Gabby linked her arm with mine. "She had a very long day at the diner. The ducks made another appearance and she had to convince Mitch not to make duck stew."

I winced. "He wouldn't."

"Probably not." Gabby grinned as she tucked a lock of her chin-length dark hair behind her ear. "Pretty sure."

"No, don't tell me these things."

"They blocked a delivery van to the diner before they waddled their way over to the park. Then they wouldn't cross the road and I was late with a delivery."

"Not sure why they are so fascinated by the roads in this town."

"Girlfriend, I do not know. But there are a pack of them."

I juggled the wine bottles and followed her to the dressing room area. "Do you call ducks a pack?"

"Flock?" Gabby set her two bottles of wine down where one of my Alexa Echo units resided. "Alexa, what do you call a grouping of ducks?"

"A group of ducks is called a herd, a flock, a raft, a paddling, or a plump."

"Plump like my butt," Gabby quipped. "Because my bestie keeps making glorious food and I keep sampling it."

Considering I'd used Hannah Jacobs's food delivery service myself, I could see how it could happen.

"Girls, this is my friend Gabriela Ramos."

"Gabby," she corrected with a little wave.

"Fresh blood." Luna dragged Gabby over to the hassock. "Hello. You have a very feisty aura. Tell me all about you."

Gabby gave me a *should-I-be-worried* glance.

I shook my head. "Luna is very excitable. She's going to be working here."

Luna squealed. "I am? Really?"

I laughed. "Well, you said you wanted to."

"I do." Luna detangled herself from the stack of clothes hemming her in. She hugged me, hopping around until I was laughing and hopping too. "You won't regret it."

"More like you're the one who might regret it. This place is insane and only getting busier. And you will have a trial by fire with the Spring Walk tomorrow. Sure you want the job?"

"Definitely. I'm so excited."

"There's no real time for training."

"I don't care." She squeezed my upper arms. "I'm an apt pupil, just ask Ry."

Ryan crossed her long, shapely legs and kicked up her red-heeled foot. "It's true. I've never known anyone who matched intuition with book learning like Luna."

"See?"

"Oh, what do you do?" Gabby asked.

"I'm a cardslinger." Luna bounced back over to Gabby. "And I'm about do yours." She reached into her huge pink bucket bag and pulled out a rainbow and glitter drawstring pouch.

Gabby's eyes went wide. "Cards? Are we playing poker?" She rubbed her hands.

Luna grinned. "That could be fun later, but now?" She dipped her glitter-tipped fingers into the bag and pulled out a colorful deck I recognized very well. "I'm going to do your tarot cards. And maybe a few oracles because you look like you could use it."

"I could?"

"Definitely."

Ryan rolled her eyes. "She doesn't ease anyone into tarot. Just shoves you off the edge."

"Not this girl," April said and shut herself into one of the dressing rooms.

Ryan waggled her brows. "We get everyone eventually."

"True statement." I took the bottle of Moscato the Ramos sisters had brought with them and opened it. It seemed like today was going to be a mason jar kind of wine night.

There was much flailing as everyone ran around getting ready. I sipped slowly from my jar and set up my cameras and lights.

Ryan ended up tag-teaming poor Gabby, and they both had her laughing and drinking her way through telling them her life story.

Gina nudged me. "I like your friends."

"Yeah?" I glanced over at Luna and Ryan, who were poring over the spread of cards.

"Definitely. I'm so glad you got someone to help out. You really needed it."

I sighed. "I know. I just…"

"No one will do it like you do." Gina hooked her arm around my waist. "It's okay to ask for help. You don't have to do everything alone."

I lifted my wine again. "I'm just used to it."

She took the wine away from me and set it down, her big dark eyes direct and still somehow kind. "You are amazing. Look at what you did with this place. I'm so jealous of what you've created."

"Why?" I couldn't be more shocked than if she'd slapped me.

"Because you've gone for exactly what you wanted."

"More like I had to."

"Who cares? Plenty of us work multiple jobs instead of going for something as precarious as opening your own business."

"I guess." I'd started repurposing and upselling to pay the rent on my shoebox apartment in the shittiest neighborhood in Syracuse. That and avoiding the super because I was underage and he let it be known—without saying it specifically—that he'd take the rent on a barter basis.

I'd never had to stoop to that level, but it had been close a few times. Thankfully, my hustle mentality managed to win out in the end. And that was the reason I barely spent a dime on myself.

"Well, let's see if we can sell some jeans." I turned to face the girls. "You all get a free pair as payment for modeling."

"That's what I'm talking about. Now you girls have to help me find the one that makes my ass look spectacular." Gina pulled two pairs off the pile.

"Try these too." I unearthed a pair with a mix of fabric patches and embroidery that was perfect for her curved hips.

"Thanks." She escaped into the middle dressing room.

I nibbled on the corner of my thumb as I waited for her to come out. Then busied myself with the rack of plants I wanted to use as a backdrop for the photos, along with the exposed brick wall.

"Kin, these are awesome." Gina swung the door open and twirled her way to the beveled standing mirror. "I've never had jeans actually fit me so well."

"Vintage Levis weren't made for stick models."

"Thank God for it." Gina turned to look at her own butt. "Incredible. And I love those little embroidered rosebuds."

I hid a smile and picked up my camera to snap a few behind the scene shots. I took pictures from angles that didn't show exactly what wine we were drinking. But I did include the local winery, figuring the Andreas family wouldn't mind a little free advertising.

My phone buzzed in my pocket and I pulled it out.

Are you having a lot of fun without me?

I quickly answered Ivy, knowing my duty as bestie.

Of course not. We are bored without you.

You lie, but I don't care. I'm woe. I would just bundle up Rhiannon and bring her, but she's been fussing all night.

Is she okay?

Yes, just teething. I wish she wasn't because now she bites and it hurts.

I winced and really didn't want to think about where she was biting. Because goddess, that wasn't good. I supposed I should read about that in one of the four baby books I got from Amazon the other day.

We miss you. Next time we'll do a Mommy and Me photo sesh.

Oh, I would love that.

Okay, I gotta go take pix.
:crying emoji:

I sent her back a dozen hearts and stuffed my phone back into my pocket. I drained my wine tumbler and picked up my camera again. "Okay, girls. Ready to show off that denim?"

Luna hopped to her feet, ringed toes flashing as she flipped off her shirt, swapping it for one of my vintage T-shirts.

At my shocked face, she laughed. "What, they're just boobs. You have them."

"That I do." I laughed. "Alexa, play Julia Michaels."

Shuffling songs by Julia Michaels.

Luna pulled Ryan up off the hassock. "Yes, I love this song."

The next twenty minutes was a flurry of denim from three different decades along with a detour into the crochet dresses that April had rocked earlier. The wine was flowing and laughter was hitting an all-time high when the music dimmed and a voice floated into the room.

"Hello?"

I was crouched with my camera up. "Ivy?"

"Oh my God, the drop in feature does work."

Gina paused the can just before her lips. "Can someone listen in anytime?"

I shrugged. "I'm not sure. Never used it."

"If they have access and I doooo." Ivy's laugh filled the space. "I was jealous. You haven't replied to my texts, and I just know you're having so much fun without me."

"Bring the kid," Gabby said from the floor. She was trying on a pair of velvet boots that had about three thousand laces.

"She's finally just fallen asleep. And I'm up to my elbows in ice cream."

"Then have that hot Irish husband of yours watch him," Gabby replied.

"I wish. Rory isn't home until tomorrow. I'm so lonely." Ivy spread out the word with an extra bonus whine.

"Aww. I'm sorry." Gina tucked her feet under her legs. "Don't look at my toes. I didn't have time to get a pedicure."

"You don't have time for anything." Gabby lifted her leg, showing off the boot. "That took forever, but look at them!"

I quickly lifted my camera and snapped the candid shot. My Facebook page was going to be full of super fun shots. And the rest would go up on my *Take a Peek Into the Trunk* website.

"Being a responsible mom is a pain in the butt sometimes."

"So much better than the alternative," I said and checked my viewfinder to see what kind of photos I had.

"Right?" Luna dug into her trail mix. "My mom was too busy being a socialite. Parties here, charities there—she was never home."

Ryan leaned back on her elbows. "Mine was living up to her name."

Luna giggled. "Rainbow Moon."

Ryan rolled her eyes. "She even made us travel around in an Airstream. She sold beaded jewelry and hemp macramé."

I walked around the large pink velvet hassock and took pictures as they all lounged. The fairy lights around the doors of the changing rooms gave an extra soft glow to the intimate photos.

"Well, we know my mom is living for the babysitting, but she likes her evenings free. So of course I wouldn't ask. Even if I was a teensy bit tempted tonight."

I could hear the longing in Ivy's voice, but there was an underlying happiness too. She loved being a mom. Exactly what I'd wished for as a kid.

"Our mom is now dispatch Bonnie at the station. She's incorrigible." Gina put her head in her hands. "Not only do I have to hear about the goings-on in this insane town at the diner, but now I get extra gossip at Sunday dinner."

Gabby groaned. "Then she tries to say she's not judging."

"Better than my mom. I haven't seen her in twelve years."

Dammit. I couldn't believe that had come out of my mouth.

"Who said that?" Ivy's voice piped up.

Shit.

Shit.

How could I be so stupid?

Everyone was sharing and it just..tumbled out.

I cleared my throat. "It's not a big deal."

"Wait, Kin? Was that you?"

I winced. "Yeah. I swear it's not a big deal."

"You don't talk about your mom, but I just thought..." She sniffed through the speaker. "I should have thought about it more. You just love coming to my house, I just—God, Kin. How could you not tell me about that?"

I heard the hurt in her voice. "It's not like that. I wasn't keeping it from you. I just don't talk about it—ever."

Now silence reigned and a heaviness sat over the room.

Lovely.

"And that's exactly why I don't say anything," I said defensively, wishing I'd glued my mouth shut.

"But I'm not just anyone." Ivy sniffed again then the sound of a baby's cries dented the uncomfortable silence. "I gotta go."

I dropped onto my butt and set my camera down next to me. "Dammit."

"It's okay, Kinleigh." Ryan's voice was gentle. "You don't have to talk about it."

"Good, because I don't want to." I stood and escaped to the front of the store. My eyes were dry and my chest ached.

The music resumed, but the happy chatter was gone and it was all my fault.

SEVENTEEN

I TRIED TO WAIT OUT THE GIRL BRIGADE UPSTAIRS, BUT IF I DIDN'T GET some of the supplies for the front window set up for the Spring Walk the next day, then I would be screwed.

It wasn't that late. And I was used to being Kin's dirty little after hours secret, but it had been a long day of getting stuff ready. Her place was always populated by new items, so it was just a bonus bit of foot traffic for Kinleigh's shop.

For me? I was trying like hell to make the front of my store more inviting. When I'd first opened, I didn't care what it looked like. I'd put a new piece in the window and busy myself with online orders and customs from return clients.

Now?

Well, now everything was about the long game when it came to my store. And if I had a kid to be responsible for, I couldn't be so loose and free with my business plan. Hell, the baby line of furniture might actually be a thing if I got off my ass about it.

"One thing at a time," I muttered to myself as I took the stairs.

The music was playing, but the female laughter was missing. The door was locked, but I'd been the one to change her locks all those months ago. I knew where the hide-a-key was.

I reached above the doorway to the antique key photo in a frame and flipped it over. She was adorable with all her quirky shop features. No detail was overlooked.

I unlocked the door and replaced the key.

"Hey, Aug." Gina was coming out of the dressing room area. "What are you doing here?"

Her sister Gabby brought up the rear. "If it isn't my favorite carpenter."

I tapped the brim of my hat. "Ladies. Kinleigh offered to let me use some of her stuff as props for the Spring Walk."

Gina had a pair of jeans draped over her arm. "Oh, that's smart. You have such nice stuff, but you never pretty it up."

"I'm not really a pretty kind of guy."

"Yes, but your customers are." Gabby set a pair of jeans on the desk. "Need some help picking out things?"

"Uh." I scanned the room for Kinleigh.

"Or are you looking for a certain redhead?"

I cleared my throat. "We were discussing a few different things. I think she set some stuff aside for me."

"I'm sure she did." The brunette from earlier came out of the dressing area. That must have been where party central had been located. "Maybe we should leave these kids to it."

"Oh." Gina glanced from me to the dark-haired woman. "Oh." Her eyes went wide. "Well, then."

I didn't disabuse her of the idea. I was damn tired of lying to everyone about my intentions. But I was smart enough not to add any fuel to the fire. Not that the Cove needed help in that arena.

Two blonds came out to join the little crowd around me. Suddenly, I had the need to flee. I wasn't usually uncomfortable around people, but this amount of estrogen rarely ended well for any man.

The smaller one with the short hair gave me an assessing look. "I'm going to go find Kinleigh before we get out of here."

"Is she all right?" The question was instinctive. It wasn't like my girl to leave people on their own in her place.

The sprite-sized blond stuck her hand out. "I'm Kinleigh's new assistant, Luna Hastings."

I shook her hand and my eyebrows shot up when the jolt of something warm hit me. Not attraction—that seemed to be solely for Kinleigh these days. But something else. A little intense. I couldn't put my finger on it. "August Beck." I stuffed my hands into my pockets.

A little smile tilted up her lips. "Hmm." She glanced to the dark-haired woman wearing all black. "Be right back."

I cleared my throat. "I'm just going to go...over there."

Gabby grabbed her jeans off the desk. "Running, Beck?"

"Yes," I said without shame.

I was instantly drawn to one of the skinny tables draped in scarves. Discreet tags hung from the corners, but resting on top was a long, carved bowl full of wooden toys. A truck, a star, and a moon. I tucked the bowl into the crook of my arm.

I wasn't exactly a *this is a sign* kind of guy, but that seemed like it should go in the window display. I picked out a few more items. Sturdy trays and a few large vases meant to group around a living room design would do well with the rocking chair I'd set aside for the window.

I kept checking near the storeroom where the women had congregated. They seemed to be discussing something a little deeper than when the next meeting of the minds would be. Finally, they waved and left.

Kinleigh seemed lost in thought so I didn't approach her, but finally, she seemed to shake it off. She went back into the storeroom, and then returned with a box. "Hey."

I set my current find down, little wind chimes that reminded me of her. Dragonflies in a soft blue stained glass the same color as her eyes.

Jesus, I was turning into a sap.

I'd almost put them back when she took them from me and set them in the box. "That's perfect. Exactly what your window needs."

"Yeah?"

She nodded.

Her blue eyes were sad. Dry and red like they hurt. I stroked the back of my knuckles down her cheek. "What's wrong?"

"Been a long day."

"Are you sure that's all it is?"

She swallowed tightly. "I don't really want to go into it."

I sighed.

She pressed a hand to my chest. "Only because I need to do some damage control first."

"Ivy?" Maybe she'd finally started talking to her about us.

Dream on, Beck.

"I hurt her feelings. I just have to fix it."

Disappointment stabbed me deep in the gut, but I wasn't used to her being so down. And only one thing made Kinleigh happy. Someday I hoped more than my dick would be in that list. "Giving my store a makeover should cheer you up."

A smile curved her lips. "Anything I want?"

I was probably going to regret it, but I nodded. "Carte blanche."

She did a little wiggle and the silver chains she wore tinkled and scraped against the box. "You're going to need a few more trips then. I have a bunch of stuff in the back."

I sighed. "Just tell me what to do."

She patted my arm. "I shall reward you handsomely."

"Damn right you will."

"I have so many ideas." She twirled on her toes and practically ran to the door. She paused at the doorway. "Well, come on."

I grabbed the few things I'd picked out and followed her.

She definitely hadn't been kidding about trips. In no time, I was sweaty and dusty, definitely hungry, and ready for a beer.

Two hours later, she had her T-shirt knotted between her breasts and the stretchy pants she was wearing were distracting me like crazy. Especially the little purple thong string that kept flashing me when she bent over.

"Stop staring at my ass."

I came up behind her and grabbed her hips. "Then stop shaking it in front of my face."

She glanced out the window and I exhaled, backing away from her. Heaven forbid someone see us in the damn window.

"August."

I held up a hand and went to the small fridge behind my customer service desk.

She blotted her sweaty forehead with the back of her hand. "We're almost done, and then we can go take a cool shower together."

I broke the seal on a bottle of root beer. It wasn't the beer I was thirsty for, but it would do. "Tomorrow is going to be a damn long day. We should probably take the night off."

She came around my desk and hopped up on the countertop. "You don't want to come home with me?" She inched over and trapped me between her thighs. "Sure about that?"

I took a long sip and stared at her.

"Don't be like that."

"Be like what? Even a stud for hire needs a night off sometimes."

She took the bottle from me and set it down a few feet from her. "That's not all we are. It's more than that."

"Really? Because you practically dive for cover if someone sees us together."

"I just want to keep us…between us for now."

"People aren't stupid, Kin."

She stared at my chin, then my mouth before leaning in to lick my lower lip. "I never really liked root beer until it tasted like you." She brushed her nose along mine. "I need you. Not just for these little guys." She bypassed my dick to trace a path around my damn balls.

"Nothing about me is little."

She grinned up at me. "That's for sure." She hooked her knees around my hips. "I mean, making a baby. I love how you make me feel. I would really like to enjoy some of that right now."

I slid my hand over her bare midriff. "You can tell me about what happened today."

"I know," she whispered against my mouth. "I don't want to talk."

Did she ever?

Her tongue flicked along my upper lip. I dragged in a deep breath of her. Fresh lemons and the earthier wood scent of my shop melded. All the things I loved right here. I tried to block out the love part, but it was no use.

After weeks spent touching her, laughing with her, and the history we shared, how could I not love her?

My fingers dug into the back of her pants, getting a good handful of her ass. I tipped her forward to rub against my shaft pressing against my zipper. "Then let's not talk."

I slanted my lips over hers, her taste making my head spin. She arched against me, her breasts pressing into my chest.

"Off," she said breathlessly.

I reached behind my neck to jerk my shirt up and off. I lost my hat in the fumble of cotton and greed.

Her nails scraped through my chest hair, the sharp side of her thumbnail coasting around my nipple.

I lifted her to shove down her pants. She tightened her legs around my hips, moaning my name as she bit my shoulder. "Goddess," she panted into my ear.

I knew that was a good sign.

Sometimes I hated the fact that she destroyed me so damn fast, and other times I leaned into it. Tonight was a fucking hard lean.

I peeled down her pants, dropping her back down on the counter. Her huge blue eyes were unfocused and just a little wild.

Here, we never faltered. Even if the back of my mind was crawling with the knowledge it wasn't enough, I rode the adrenaline high. I believed the lie for one more day.

She fumbled with my zipper and then I was free. I didn't even wait to check if she was ready for me. The needy little sighs that followed me into dreams told me she was with me. I plunged inside of her, hard and deep, until there was nothing but Kinleigh around me.

She hooked her arms under mine and her nails dug welts in my flesh as she took each strong thrust. I gripped her hips, dragging her up against me before I turned to find the wall. I couldn't get close enough from that angle. I needed more.

I always fucking needed more.

I cushioned her back and gripped her ass as I pinned her to the wall. Each pummeling thrust was matched by the soft curve of her body, the heightened scent of her arousal, the sharp tang of her taste.

More, more, more. It was a chant in my blood.

I tore my mouth from hers and buried my head between her neck and shoulder, into the curls I loved, the home I was longing for.

"Kinleigh." My voice was a guttural growl as I drained myself into her.

As my mind went utterly blank and my muscles jittered in reaction to such a swift and complete release.

She slid her fingers up my neck to my hair, pulling my mouth to hers. If I could crawl into her bones, I would have.

Jesus, she was going to destroy me. And I was going to let her.

I wasn't sure which of us was the bigger asshole.

Finally, my arms wouldn't hold the weight of her anymore. I didn't want to step back from her. All too soon, she'd make excuses to leave.

I set her down, but instead of rushing for her clothes, she stood on my boots to get closer to me. For God's sake, I hadn't even gotten her shirt off in my haste to get inside of her.

Evidently, I was taking the crown for asshole tonight.

"I'm sorry. I didn't mean to be so rough."

She licked her lips and grinned at me. "Knowing you want me like that—don't ever say you're sorry."

I fisted my hands into the back of her shirt. "I do. I wish you'd see that. I'm always going to—"

She held her finger up to my lips. "Don't say it. Not tonight. Not now while you're still high from this."

"It's not pillow talk, Kin."

She shook her head. "Today was too much. I can't." The sparkle that had been there in her eyes went out and the sad crept back in.

"Tell me."

She cupped my face as tears welled in her eyes. "Please, August."

"Okay, okay." I curled my arms around her and laid her cheek against my chest. Tears killed me and Kinleigh didn't pull that girl card too often. Whatever was on her mind had to be more than just Ivy finding out about us. Everything inside of me wanted to demand to know, but I gentled my voice and forced my shoulders to relax. "It's okay."

If only she understood I'd do anything to make sure that it was.

EIGHTEEN

KINLEIGH

Sleep was for the weak.

At least that was what I told myself as I drank my second coffee of the morning, and it wasn't even seven o'clock yet.

Luna was happily humming as she made the fourth floral arrangement for the stairs. We had an assembly line of pots and baskets overflowing with silk flowers and succulents I'd thieved from all over the store. Since miniature plants were the new favorite thing in everyone's Pinterest, Instagram, and Facebook posts, I figured it was one of the easiest items to use to lead people into my shop.

"I just love these furry brown ones." Luna gently stroked the petal of one of the succulents I'd planted with Ivy.

I swallowed down the ache that had kept me up all night. Well, that and the big, pressure cooker pot of emotions I had no control of for her freaking brother too.

"Aren't they sweet? I can't believe how big it's gotten."

"This place gets so much amazing light." Luna was wearing a pair of Converse sneakers—one pink and the other yellow with a big ol' daisy painted on the top of each. She'd also worn the embroidered daisy jeans she'd gotten as payment for modeling for me yesterday.

She'd paired it with a cute pink polka dot shirt knotted at the waist. Her blond curls were tamed into a pair of braids with daisy elastics.

However, she didn't look the least bit innocent with her winged eyeliner and fuchsia lips. She was obviously a hell of a lot more rested than I was. I wanted to hate her for humming, but she was such a light. I might not be able to pick up auras like Luna did, but she gave off a burst of happiness anyone could see.

She gathered two of the terra cotta pots. "I'm going to bring these down."

"Thanks."

She beamed at me. "I just love this so much."

"I'll remind you of that statement at around ten this morning when we're running around like crazy people."

"I can't wait." She turned on her toes and hurried out the door and down the stairs.

I pressed my forehead to the table. I'd probably gotten a total of three hours of sleep. Between being revved up after August tried to fuck me through his wall and Ivy not answering my texts, I was a hot mess.

But work always saved me. I straightened and gathered the leftover flowers and silks. That was what I could focus on. I dug out my phone and checked on my texts. Still nothing.

I popped open my music app and set my 90's playlist on repeat. No Doubt played from the store speakers.

Footsteps stomped up the stairs and Luna burst through the door, singing along with "Don't Speak" in a perfect mimic of Gwen Stefani's voice. I laughed and we sang along to the best of pop and hip hop for the next hour.

I peeked down at the town from the back of the store where it overlooked the park and the pier. The gazebo was decked out with various vendors selling their wares. I had the windows open to soak in some of that spring air. It had been a cold winter and I was happy to push all that stale air out.

It was a rare sunny day without a cloud in the sky. The wind was a little chilly off the water, but we were running around enough that it felt good on my skin.

I had on white tank top under a pair of overalls. Huge colorful flowers decorated the pockets and bib section then danced down one leg in a rainbow of colors. The cheery outfit helped me push back the uncertainty of everything for now.

By the time people started to drift up from the sidewalk, Luna and I had fallen into a surprisingly easy rhythm of customer service and ringing. What she didn't know, she asked or figured out. She seemed to have an intuitive way about finding what customers needed. She chatted them up and sales were multiplying.

The morning flew by. We'd sold so many of the little floral pots that I stole twenty minutes to make a few more.

"I'm going to bring these down."

Luna waved me off. "Go take a walk. Maybe get some of that fried dough I keep smelling."

"I don't want to leave you alone."

"I'll be fine."

"But—"

"Go. Get some food. Then I'll go take a break too."

I huffed out a breath and took my zip-up hoodie off the hook. "Text me if you need me. I'm just going to check everything is—"

"Seriously, Kin. Take a break."

"Fine. If you're sure."

I brought three arrangements downstairs and tucked the smaller pots along one side of the stairs. I double checked the huge wine barrel full of ice and free bottles of water for the people walking by, then refilled the three huge bowls of water I'd set out for dogs.

Since I shared the space with August, we'd agreed that it was worth losing a little sidewalk space to put an old glider swing between our doorways.

A couple with a wiggling puppy was currently swaying gently on it while they licked ice cream cones. I waved hello and left them to it. Across the street, Ivy's truck had been brought out from winter storage behind the café.

My stomach flipped as a head peeked out from the window of the truck, but I couldn't decide if it was relief or regret when I recognized Jodi slinging ice cream instead of Ivy.

"Looking for me?"

I spun around toward Ivy's voice.

Rory was next to her, rubbing her back lightly as Ivy gripped the stroller handle.

"Hey."

She gave me a half smile. "Looking cute, Pippi."

I rolled my eyes and played with the tail of my braid. "Didn't have time to tame the crazy." I probably looked like I'd had no sleep while Ivy seemed rested. Her cheeks were rosy and matched the pink spring jacket she was wearing.

"About yesterday."

"It's too pretty a day to get into that right now." Ivy's face was a little closed off, pain still shimmering in her eyes, but there was understanding there too.

It wasn't a hard leap to make. I never mentioned family and I always changed the subject, deflecting with questions about *her* family tree instead.

I hadn't lied, but my not sharing was just as hard to swallow. Shame wasn't an easy thing to live with when you lived in a place like Crescent Cove, which was basically a postcard for a family town.

Oh, it wasn't perfect. No place on Earth was really Pleasantville. But the Cove was damn close, especially with the baby boom putting a shiny happy glow on everything.

I looked down at my sensible shoes and tightened my hoodie around me. Maybe we just wouldn't talk at all. What exactly could I say to her?

"Can you walk with us? We were going to meet August at the pier."

I quickly looked up. "Oh, I shouldn't leave the store. Luna is still so—"

"She'll be fine." Ivy eased around the stroller and gave Rhiannon an absent pat, tucking her stroller blanket around her ever flailing legs.

She smiled at her daughter then came around to me and linked our arms together.

My dry eyes suddenly stung.

I didn't deserve the olive branch, but I took it. Heck, I grabbed it. "Sure. I could use a walk."

"You sure could." Ivy snagged three bottles of water from the barrel and passed them out to all of us. "Now let's go see what kind of terrible food there is. I've barely gotten back into my pants, but I'm dying for some fried dough."

Before I could agree, I was getting pulled along into the pedestrian traffic. Most of Main Street was coned off to let the kids run around within the adults' watchful gazes. A soccer ball was being kicked around on the patchy spring grass to the far right of the vendor stalls.

Instead of the usual summer flowers bursting everywhere, there were stalls selling seeds and seedlings ready for planting and pretty baskets full of tools and stoneware pots to create container gardens. Because we lived in the Northeast, planting didn't happen until after Mother's Day, which was some weeks away. April was upon us and my weeks with August were marching on by.

Enough for me to worry about them coming to an end? Maybe. I worried about everything else, so why not?

My stomach grumbled as we ended up downwind from two food trucks parked across from the diner in front of our small town hall. There was enough foot traffic for the café and the diner, which were both overflowing with people as well.

"Is there anything better than the Spring Walk?"

"Farmer's Market?"

Ivy grinned. "Okay, yes, I prefer the veggie stands all summer long, but we've been hunkered down from the cold for so long, it finally feels like we're thawing out."

Was that what I'd been doing? Me, the little seedling poking out. Or would I be the one stomped under a boot, or frozen by the next winter wind?

My breath caught at the wide shoulders in the crowd. I had to stop looking for him everywhere. Not every wide-shouldered guy in this town was August. And boy, did I not need that today. Things had been weird last night with him. Too intense. Not that we knew any other way around one another when it came to naked mambo time.

And it was *always* naked mambo time.

I had to confess that not all of it was purely due to my procreation goals. Some of it was just me wanting to feel close to him for a few minutes. It was all I allowed myself. I couldn't get too attached—no matter how easy he made it.

Ivy dragged me farther into the crowd. I smiled and waved to those I knew, chitchatted with a few others who asked about my overalls. Why, yes, I had a bunch of jeans just like these over at Kinleigh's Attic. I loved them, but I'd definitely worn them as my own particular brand of billboard.

I caught a glimpse of wide shoulders in a dark jacket. The heavy kind August always wore against the elements. I was just being silly—the guy wasn't even wearing a hat.

Then the man turned and the strong jaw and a pair of aviators struck me. Sometimes it stole my breath when I got a good look at him not covered in sawdust and the torn-up, long-sleeved thermal shirts he wore. Today he had on a bright white T-shirt with his logo peeking from the unbuttoned midnight Carhartt jacket.

Our gazes locked, and he smiled at me. No hiding, just a sweet, loaded smile full of promise.

Thank goddess for the bib overalls because it wasn't the cool wind making my nipples tight, that was for sure.

"I forget how hot my brother is."

"What?" I glanced at Ivy.

The corner of her mouth was tipped up. "I mean, look at all the girls looking at him." She nodded to the group of women on the bench. "They're eating him up. I should have brought out some of my spoons."

"Right." I frowned. "He's objectively attractive."

"Objectively, or is that objectifyingly?"

I cleared my throat. "That would be what those barely college-aged women are doing over there. They should have seen him last night."

"And you did?"

"Yes, I helped him with his window. He's cranky and ill-mannered when he doesn't get his way."

"Is that right?"

"You know that very well." I shoved my hands into my hoodie pockets. "He's perpetually cranky."

"Not lately. Know anything about that?"

"Of course not." My heart rate spiked as he cut through the field of people.

He stopped to shake hands with a few and passed out the simple white business card he had stashed on the inside pocket of his jacket more than once before he got to us. He pulled out a tiny bottle of hand sanitizer and quickly doused his hands before he reached into the stroller to tickle Rhiannon's belly.

My heart turned over. That he'd actually think to do that when so few did unwound me.

"Hey, Ive." He brushed a kiss over his sister's cheek, then gave a somewhat friendly nod to her husband. "Lucky Charms."

Rory inclined his head. "Mate."

"Kin." His voice lowered and he caught my hand for a moment before I twisted away.

He fell into step with us but kept veering closer to me. I glanced around and people were looking at us. Knowing smiles hidden behind their hot chocolates.

Did everyone have to assume a man and woman were together if they stood near one another? Or maybe they would because he kept brushing his pinkie along mine. And maybe I wanted to curl mine around his. Okay, maybe our pinkies actually tangled twice.

"Want a pretzel?"

"Me?"

August's lips quirked up on one side. "Lucky Charms has bought Ivy about three different versions of bread."

"My girl loves sweet breads," Rory replied with a smirk.

"And his girl loves eating them." Ivy tugged Rory down and gave him a kiss.

"Aye, that she does."

I slanted them a look. The easy way they were together, the baby they had between them, the way they both checked on Rhiannon even though she'd been sleeping effortlessly through the noise of the crowds. Goddess, I wanted that.

More every day.

My pinky tangled with August's again and I accidentally moved in closer to him. Suddenly, he dropped his arm over my shoulders and dragged me in close. "Or are you hoping I'll go stand in that super long fried dough line?"

"Honey, would you please?" I drilled my knuckle into his ribs like I always used to. Back before we knew what skin on skin felt like.

His gaze dropped to my lips and the teasing *honey* felt far too real. I slipped away from him and shoved my hands into my pockets again. "But a pretzel would be fine, honestly. Don't go to any trouble."

"You want fried dough, you'll get fried dough. Be right back."

He cut through the crowd with his long legs. I really needed to stop staring at him.

"He needs a strong woman."

"Yeah?" I asked absently. Was that what he needed? Should I step aside when he found that particular kind of woman?

My stomach twisted.

Would I even be able to? What if we had a baby together? Would there be split custody, and he or she would have two mommies?

"Yeah, he'd need one so he wouldn't mow them down. He gets something in his head and he just won't change his mind."

I glanced at Ivy. "He's not that rigid."

"No? You used to mention that he'd never bend."

"I just don't think I understood him before."

"Right. Seems reasonable."

Before I could decipher what the heck that meant, there was a startled shout and...was that a quack?

All at once, the semi-orderly lines at the various vendor tables and booths surged forward and people started scattering.

"Where do these things keep coming from?"

I craned my neck to see who'd said that. Then people jumped out of the way and a half dozen ducks appeared. Two of them were fully grown with one quacking maniacally as they cut a swath through the crowd. They obviously were getting confused with all the people and the maze of tables.

A dog yipped and the quacking got louder.

Then there was flapping and squawks. I was pushed aside as Jared, our town sheriff, broke through the crowd. Next thing I knew, a dog got loose.

Chaos erupted.

Gina appeared, cupping something in her apron. She bent and scooped another—was that a chick? "Sheriff Brooks, you save those ducks right now. There are babies over here!"

"Dammit. Okay, folks, let's just back it up please." Jared pointed at a man. "Gary, you get that dog or I'll fine you for Harley not being on a leash."

"I'm trying. If everyone would stop moving." The older man stomped on the grass, trying to catch the end of the red leash.

Ivy and I maneuvered the stroller to the side as the mama duck circled, quacking for one of the babies that had darted under a crate.

"Christian, go left!" Jared barked out the order.

"Got it!" Christian darted around me. "'Scuse me, Kinleigh." He flashed me a charming smile and handed me his hat. "Hold that for me?"

I laughed and took his hat.

"Which way?"

Ivy and I pointed toward the gazebo stairs.

Christian went after the other adult duck as Gina scooped up another chick.

"Are you supposed to touch them?" Rory asked out of the side of his mouth.

"Not sure. Probably better than if one of those poor babies was hurt," Ivy whispered back.

A woman with dreadlocks rushed over to Gina with a burlap bag, and Gina gratefully dumped them in there and darted after Jared.

"What's going on?" August crowded in behind me and held up the mouthwateringly perfect fried dough like a prize in front of me.

I held up Christian's hat and snatched the dough out of his hands and tore off a piece. "Ducks." My ass slid across the front of his jeans and the urge to lean back on him was almost unbearable.

Ivy tore a corner off my dough and I practically growled at her. Until I noticed her gaze sweep up to where her brother was cozied up behind me.

Could I blame it on the crush of people? I glanced around to notice the townsfolk were dispersing. Hmm. Probably not.

"I should probably bring Christian his hat," I blurted out around another bite.

"Why do you have Christian's hat?" August's voice was deceptively mild.

"Ducks."

"Ducks?"

I nodded and took another bite as I scanned the crowd to where people were congregating. "Oh, look, see?"

August followed to where I was pointing.

"I can't see," Ivy said behind me.

I moved over and we both sighed out an audible, "Aww."

Jared was heading down to the pier with the two adult ducks following him. Gina got to the edge of the pier and let go of her little babies as well and the line of them followed Jared.

It seemed way too cold to go in the lake as far as I was concerned, but they all hopped right off the edge and swam toward the bank where there was a bit of brush and a slice of beach.

"Isn't that the sweetest thing you've ever seen?"

August smiled down at me. "Not a bad way to spend the day."

I took another bite from my fried dough. "I should probably get back."

"I'll walk you back."

"You don't have to."

"Handily, my store is right under yours."

"Right. Handy."

I moved to the stroller and smiled down at Rhiannon, whose big blue eyes were finally open. She gave me a drooly smile as I waved. I looked up at Ivy. "Can I leave this with you?" I held out the hat.

Rory took it. "We'll take care of it."

"Thanks." I handed it to him and turned to Ivy. "Today's a little crazy, but we'll talk soon?"

She nodded. "You know you can talk to me about anything, right?"

"I know."

Her gaze tracked up to August. "Both of you can."

August touched my lower back, which got me moving.

"Kin, wait up."

I lengthened my stride. "I need to get back."

"Is everything okay?"

"Of course. Why wouldn't it be?" The doughy sweetness now tasted like sawdust, and Ivy's words filled my brain. She didn't seem mad at me, but she didn't seem happy either.

August snagged my hand and drew me to a stop before I could get to the stairs. "Will I see you tonight?"

I flashed a bright smile at him. "I just watched a bunch of baby ducklings sprint across the park. If that didn't make me want to try to make a baby tonight, what would?"

"Right."

I could see the disappointment in his eyes, but then two customers came up the walk—one obviously who wanted to talk to August.

He heaved out a breath. "I'll find you later." He waved to the couple. "Hello, Mr. and Mrs. Willoughby, it's nice to see you again."

They both smiled and August gestured for them go ahead as he opened the door for them. He paused for a second, giving me a tight smile before he followed them inside.

I tipped my head back, then tossed my cold fried dough into the garbage can before I went up to my own store. So much for a perfect day.

NINETEEN

"Are you serious about this thing?" my younger brother Caleb asked.

I propped my hands on my hips as I gazed at the petite armoire I'd built for Kinleigh without her knowledge. After some discussion, she'd settled on wanting a skinny dresser instead for that spot in her shop where her customers tried on clothes and accessories, so I'd started working on that too. She hadn't mentioned our bartering arrangement again so I figured I'd have to beg for the pillows.

In the meantime, I'd worked on this stuff during the hours I was supposed to be sleeping after Kinleigh sent me home after my sperm insertion duties were done.

But I wasn't bitter. Exactly.

The armoire was a simple piece made from that wind-damaged sugar maple behind the duplex I'd finally taken down with some help from my friends. I'd used some other materials too, since it was colder than balls so my time outside sourcing wood had been limited. But everything from the carved feet to the louvered doors and hand pulls on the drawers had been crafted with her shop's style in mind.

The small moon and stars and ladybug details I'd added in secret places were just for me—and maybe Kinleigh, if I ever shared my idea for a line of baby furniture. For now, I was working on the piece I'd promised my sister and I had the bookshelf in my bedroom, waiting for the day we'd have our own baby.

If it happened. So many fucking ifs. They were making me crazy.

"Spill it," Caleb said when I continued to stare at the armoire and brood.

Something I was becoming an expert at.

"What?"

"You know what. This is for that Kinleigh broad, right?"

"Don't call her a broad, you oaf." I shoved him hard in the shoulder.

"Didn't hurt," he said affably, much as he had when we were kids and I whomped him on the back for taking my bike or swooping in and stealing the fish I'd been trying to reel in.

He'd always been big on being as annoying as possible, and now that he was in his late twenties, he hadn't changed much. Except now he had two main priorities—teaching his students in second grade at the private elementary school and chasing women. In that order.

His popularity in town with the fairer sex was legendary, equivalent to his closest friend Lucky. They were bad influences on each other in the extreme, often trying to outdo the other in whatever way possible.

If Lucky hooked up with some woman within a day of arriving in town, Caleb made it his mission to achieve the same feat on the next hapless newcomer by dinner time. They didn't lie about their intentions and from what I'd seen, Caleb was always a gentleman and careful about respecting boundaries. He just didn't stick to pollenating any one flower for long.

"You ever think about settling down?"

His loud laughter echoed through the store and had a couple browsing the kitchen furniture in back turning toward us with matching frowns. "You serious, bro? Why would I do that?"

"Oh, I don't know. Maybe so Ma wouldn't always have to worry you'll sleep with the wrong woman and some husband will take a shot at you?"

"That was one time. I didn't know she was married. She lied to me. You know I don't do that sort of thing." He held up his hands, palms out. "I have a good time, but I don't poach. Everything is nice and tidy and aboveboard."

"Relationships aren't meant to be tidy."

"Right, that's why I don't have them. Much easier to scratch that itch and roll on, no harm, no foul. Besides, Ivy gave Ma her beloved grandchild, so I'm off the hook there, thank fuck."

"You think Ivy having a baby means you'll never have to settle down? Like that's your goal? To be forever alone?"

He stared at me as if I was an alien life form, plunked down right in the center of Crescent Cove with my spaceship twinkling merrily behind me. "What else would my goal be? Literally every single person of childbearing age in this town is procreating or dreaming of it or wondering who else is currently knocked up. You mad because I'm not joining the water drinkers, son?" He stroked his scruffy golden jaw. Depending on if he was in school or not, that scruff tended to edge closer toward a full beard. "My guess is you're lining up with your cup with that pretty redhead upstairs. Or is she lining up with *her* cup?"

I didn't have a chance to answer. The kitchen browsers had looked through the selection of farmhouse style chairs and stools I had on the premises, along with flipping through my lookbook of custom designs I'd made in the past, and wanted to discuss creating ones to their own precise specifications.

I asked Caleb to give me a few but he was gone when I returned— and so was the armoire.

I hadn't seen him go out the front so he must've gone up the rarely used interior staircase. It was built in a way that carrying furniture up it was a trial, but leave it to my brother to push his luck.

He was a big guy, although not as big as Lucky. I probably could've managed to lug the armoire upstairs to Kinleigh's shop myself, but he'd stopped in and I'd figured hey, maybe he'd help keep things from getting awkward when I presented it to Kinleigh. She got too quiet whenever I brought her anything, from flowers to takeout to furniture.

Not that it stopped me from doing it. I was compelled to offer her stuff whether or not she wanted me to. My swimmers were just the beginning, apparently.

That gift was one she always appreciated though, right on down to times on a chart and breathy phone calls saying, "August, I need you."

I knew what she needed. The same thing I did. But for entirely different purposes, at least some of the time.

My urgency for her burned hot in my blood. Morning, afternoon and night. It didn't matter if I'd just had her. My body was primed to react to her lemon fresh scent.

At the rate I was going, even the detergent aisle at the grocery store was out, because fuck me running if I smelled something citrus. Hard-ons while picking out fabric softeners were never appropriate.

On top of all of that, time was passing and she hadn't gotten her period again yet. Did that mean we'd been successful? Who knew? She'd informed me she wouldn't take a test before the right time, whatever that was, and I was torn between wanting to knock her up and wanting it to take a while so she still needed me.

The shop phone rang and I picked up, barking out a, "Yeah?" without looking at the readout.

"Did you send this strapping young man up here with this fine piece of wood?" She sounded flirty and breathless, and I could hear Caleb's rich laughter behind her.

I fisted a hand on the phone stand. "It's my piece of wood, and it's far finer than his."

"Touché."

"We were supposed to bring it up there together, but God forbid he ever not shoot his wad in a hurry. Kind of his specialty." I deliberately spoke loudly enough for Caleb to hear me if he was standing close.

Which he would do without thinking, because Kinleigh was a beautiful, presumably single woman and Caleb was perennially on the search for a good time. And hey, I hadn't staked a claim on her, so all good, right?

Except it wasn't. Not even a little bit.

"It's a lovely piece, August. Truly. But where am I going to put it? It's too big."

Caleb said something in the background and I could only imagine what shot he'd taken at my manhood in jest. He didn't know that was a particularly sore spot right now when I was doing target practice on Kinleigh's ovaries and constantly wondering if I'd scored.

That was my life now. Times on a sheet. Goals and practice. Being with her was still sexy as hell, since Kinleigh made me hot even when she was unconscious, but I couldn't deny I wouldn't have minded being intimate with her when implantation wasn't an issue.

"I'll be right up."

"Wait, you don't have anyone to man the store—"

I hung up. I usually wasn't testy, especially not with her, but I was in a mood today and my brother wasn't helping.

Once the chair shoppers had stopped browsing for other pieces for their kitchen and went on their way, I flipped the door sign to closed and went outside to march upstairs.

I needed a minute of fresh air to cool off.

My greeting as I entered Kinleigh's shop was her light, airy laughter as she opened and closed the drawers of the armoire. I stopped in the doorway, savoring how she looked for one more moment.

My brother had rested his arm on the top of the thing and was looming over her, probably checking out her perfect little ass in another one of those thin, summery skirts she loved to wear. If that wasn't enough, I could very clearly see the lines of her pale blue thong when she was bent over at that angle.

I took a deep breath and came closer, resting my hand on the small of her back. "What do you think, babe?" I gave my brother a death glare, tempting him to push me over the edge.

Kinleigh's head reared up, bumping the open armoire door at the same time as Caleb raised a brow and held up his hands in his increasingly annoying "no problem" gesture. Maybe everything was casual as could be in his world, but in mine?

Not so much.

"Are you okay?" I palmed the top of her head, feeling for bumps, and she stared at me with wide, uncomprehending blue eyes as if she didn't grasp what was happening. "Sorry, I shouldn't have surprised you."

"It's okay. I'm okay." Her throat rippled. "You can let go of me now."

"No, I really can't." It took everything inside me not to lower my head and take her soft, unpainted mouth. The kind of kiss she couldn't slot away as for fun or reproduction, or maybe some combination of the two. But not anything more.

"You're acting strange." She nudged me back. "You chased off your brother."

I glanced over my shoulder. "So I did. Too bad." Had to hand it to Caleb, maybe he wasn't as absolutely oblivious at catching subtext as I'd assumed.

"He brought that up for you. It's awfully heavy. Why are you mad —oh." She cupped her hand over her mouth, her pupils flaring brighter for an instant. That lively blue practically rendered me mute. I didn't see her that amused nearly enough.

"Oh, what?"

She let her hand drop. "You're jealous."

I crossed my arms. "What do I have to be jealous of?"

"Absolutely nothing." She took a quick look over her shoulder to assess the shop. Finding it empty, she swayed closer, rubbing her nipples against my chest through my T-shirt. "This is the sweetest thing. I love it, even if I'm not sure what I'm going to do with it yet. Or where I'm going to put it. Thank you." She rose on her tiptoes and rubbed her lips against mine. "You don't have to do stuff like this though. I'm a sure thing."

"You're the farthest from a sure thing."

"Not according to my chart."

"Kinleigh, stop."

She stepped back. "Sorry."

I swore under my breath. "Don't do that. Don't shut down on me."

"Seems like you shut down first." She gripped her necklace, a long yellow crystal wand that dangled between her mouth-watering breasts, discreetly hidden away. But I remembered their exact shape. How her nipples bloomed under my touch, whether with my lips and tongue or my fingers. The way they flowed into my hands, soft and perfect. A vulnerability she never hesitated to share with me.

The *only* one she'd share.

"Go out with me."

Her expression turned cagey. She didn't move back any farther physically, but in her head, she was already bolting all the locks against me. "I do all the time."

"You stay in with me. Locked away in your bedroom."

She ran her hand up my chest, her nails lightly skimming the material. My cock jerked against my zipper and her lips lifted. "Not just in my bedroom. Pretty sure we've enjoyed a few other inventive spots."

"I want to walk with you in the sunshine and hold your hand."

Saying it out loud felt absolutely ridiculous. *This* was what I was making my stand on? I had access to this woman's luscious curves almost anytime I wanted them. Basically, I had my brother's ideal situation, minus the procreation part.

Yet it wasn't nearly enough. I didn't want only her moans in private. I wanted her smiles in public and to be able to just touch her hair or cup her cheek. I craved her innermost thoughts and her dreams and her fears.

I wanted fucking everything.

She held my gaze for a long moment before turning toward the front as the chimes on the door signaled a customer. "Good afternoon. Is there something I can help you with today?"

"Just browsing, thank you. I love your shop."

"Oh, thanks. Are you sure you don't need any assistance? We just got in these new Tibetan singing bowls," Kinleigh added as the petite brunette paused by the self-care section. It led into a space filled with home relaxation items and a couple of padded chairs meant for taking a moment with a cup of tea. "Have you seen them before? They're so soothing. If you're planning a special night, they set the perfect mood for getting ready."

When she turned away, I left the same way I'd come in. And kept right on walking down the street without even locking up my store for the day. It was Crescent Cove, after all. A lovely safe town, made for families.

I might even be on my way to having my own family, with a woman who wouldn't let me in no matter how many times I knocked. Whether I used gentleness or a battering ram, the vault of Kinleigh Scott remained on lockdown.

And I'd really believed having a child with her was the answer? She'd probably lock me out of that too. Then what? We'd need to get lawyers involved, because there wasn't a way in hell I would let her keep me from my baby. It was bad enough trying to understand the distance she put between us. If a child was involved, I wouldn't be able to let her close the door in my face. Whatever tenuous strides we'd made between us would be destroyed.

What the hell had I been thinking?

I strolled down the street in the fading sunshine, my head down. I didn't want to chat with anyone. Definitely didn't want to exchange smiles or waves.

I climbed into my truck and reversed out of the spot and hit the gas.

Without knowing where I was headed, I drove out of town. Aiming anywhere and nowhere, following the curve of the road and the sunshine along the horizon. Spring was coming, but it hadn't quite arrived yet. Even so, the days were longer now and I drove until the sun dipped behind the far side of lake and the already chilly air turned cold.

My stomach growled and I decided I'd get a pizza for one. No delivery service tonight. If Kinleigh wanted me for any reason other than my dick, she could be the one to make the move this time. I was tired of winding up and striking out.

And if she never contacts you, then what?

Then I'd deal with it. I didn't know how. The idea of not being with Kinleigh again was like a physical blow to the gut. Not just sexually. I missed her when she wasn't around. Her voice, her rare laughter, the way she touched me when she forgot her goal and just lived in the moment. I'd spent years watching her and Ivy's bond grow and deepen, but now if I wasn't mistaken, even that relationship was faltering. Probably because of me too.

Weird as fuck to be both the cause of Kinleigh's problems—in her mind—and her solution to yet another one. Where for me, she was just the answer. The meaning that made everything else make sense.

I went into Robbie's and ordered a large, sad pie for one with extra cheese and pepperoni and green peppers. Kinleigh hated them but she wasn't around.

Might never be around in any way that didn't include her legs in the air. Hard to complain about that but here I was, complaining in my own head.

While I waited at the counter, a text came in from my brother.

Why didn't you just admit you want her?

Such a loaded question.

Banging the sister's best friend is on half the movies of the week. You know, it's just enough taboo to juice the panties but not taboo enough to get you thrown out of church.

I shouldn't have laughed, but I couldn't help it as I replied.

Don't tell Ivy your theories, all right? I have enough problems.

If Ivy went to Kinleigh with suspicions about us, Kinleigh would probably not only decide she didn't want a baby any longer, she was also done with me and men in general. She was so afraid of losing Ivy, when anyone who knew my sister would understand she would never begrudge someone's happiness. She only wanted all of us to find what she had with Lucky Charms.

So why was Kinleigh so spooked about the Ivy thing? Did it have to do with valet guy somehow? She'd lost someone important to her, and her family didn't seem to be a factor in her life, so maybe she was convinced deep down she'd end up alone.

She refuses to see you'd never leave her. Maybe she just doesn't feel the same.

Caleb responded but I didn't take time to read it since my pizza was finally ready. I snagged the box and headed out to my truck, head still down in case anyone felt chatty. But it was the Cove, so of course I was stopped a couple of times just on my short walk to where I was parked.

I slipped into my truck with a slip of paper with a phone number for a potential new customer. Jude Keller was a recent transplant to the Cove. In fact, he hadn't even landed yet. He was still scoping out the area as far as potential places to live. I gave him a tip on the apartments over the café—and not because I wanted to make sure that Kinleigh and I had time to break it in first—and he mentioned he needed furniture. And voila, I had a line on a new piece to fill my nights.

Pathetic, Beck.

I'd no sooner pulled into the duplex's parking lot when Kinleigh's name flashed across my in-dash screen. I intended to let the call go to voicemail, as rare as it was. Maybe it was petty, but I had no intention of giving her any more inches when she'd seen fit to not make use of a mile.

And for once, I wasn't thinking of my penis.

Then I heard her breathless, frantic voice and I forgot about anything but making sure she was okay.

Aug, if you're there, pick up, please. I know you're mad at me, and you probably have a right to be, but I need you.

Those three words were always my undoing when it came to Kinleigh. She probably fucking knew it too.

I snagged the call. "What is it? Where are you?"

"At Ivy's. It's the baby. I didn't know who else to call—"

I left my pizza in the truck and shut off the engine before jumping down and running inside. I didn't disconnect the call. Nor did I keep talking to Kinleigh. I had no idea if she was still there. All I could focus on was getting inside to my niece.

As soon as I opened the door to Ivy's side of the duplex, Kinleigh rushed forward with a sobbing Rhiannon in her arms. My girl's eyes were stark and frightened. "Ivy had to run to the store because she was out of Rhi's baby food. She warned me she was super fussy today and wouldn't sleep, but I figured I'd sing to her and try to put her down anyway. But she just won't stop wailing. And then I saw this." Carefully, she peeled the pale yellow blanket wrapped around Rhi away from her head. There was blood on the material.

My chest seized. "From what? Her mouth? Where?"

"I think her ear. Oh, God, what's wrong with her? Did I do something? All I've been doing is rocking her."

"Come here, sweetheart. Come to uncle August."

Instead of reaching her arms out to me as she always did, she just flailed in Kinleigh's embrace, swatting her hand against her head again and again. More blood trickled from her ear.

"We need to go to the hospital."

Kinleigh stared down at the baby, her mouth trembling.

"Kinleigh, are you listening to me? We need to take the baby to the ER. Grab Ivy's baby bag, and I'll go get the truck."

She nodded, her eyes overflowing. A tear splashed on the baby, but she never stopped jerking around long enough to notice.

I took a second to cup Kinleigh's cheek. "You did the right thing, baby, calling me. It's going to be okay."

She nodded again, her tears still running freely.

I hated leaving them for even a moment.

I hurried to the lot and stowed the pizza box next to the car seat before backing out of the space. They were waiting on the porch when I pulled the truck around. Luckily, I kept a car seat in it all the time in case I needed to babysit Rhiannon, so it was just a matter of getting her situated.

Rhiannon sobbed the whole way to the ER. Kinleigh texted Ivy that she should meet us at the hospital, and my heart gave a painful lurch at the panic my sister would feel getting that text. But it couldn't be helped. I didn't want to delay any longer. When blood was involved —even a small amount—I wasn't taking any chances.

"Can you text Rory too? Do you have the number? I think he's down in the city for the day, back tonight."

"I have the number." She typed frantically while I tried to focus on the road.

Every minute or so, I glanced back at my niece and crooned softly to her, hoping I could find the right combination of nonsense words and her name and anything I could think of to try to calm her down. She just continued to let out huge wrenching sobs that made my throat constrict and my shoulders ache.

"She's going to be fine, baby." I reached over to take Kinleigh's hand as she stared morosely out the window. "I promise."

Instead of shoving me away, she wrapped her fingers around mine and held on tight.

TWENTY

KINLEIGH

I PACED UP AND DOWN THE SMALL WAITING ROOM WHILE AUGUST WAS IN the examination room with the baby. We'd been together for most of it while the doctor did the necessary checks, August and I taking turns soothing Rhiannon while the other helped keep the fussing baby still. Then Ivy's frantic texts had started coming in, along with Rory's, and August had suggested I wait out here for Ivy to arrive.

Since the little girl's anguish was tugging hard at my chest and belly, I hadn't argued. August's steady calm had soothed me as much as it had the baby.

Oh, it hadn't happened quickly. Rhiannon was still uneasy and crying, but she'd definitely started to calm down. The doctor had mentioned a likely ear infection, with a probable ruptured eardrum. That sounded much worse than it actually was apparently, especially when it came to babies that young. But I didn't blame Ivy for freaking out. Add in the mom guilt that she'd chanced running to the store and now her baby was at the ER and she was a mess.

I couldn't seem to stop pacing.

As soon as Ivy rushed into the waiting room, the emotion in her expressive eyes so like August's, I started to cry. She'd stopped momentarily, her cheeks blotchy and red. But the instant our gazes connected, it was instant waterworks on her side too.

She hurried toward me and we hugged, any earlier awkwardness forgotten. "She's fine," I repeated over and over, stroking her hair. "She's with August in with the doctor. Everything is going to be okay."

As if I'd summoned him, he came into the waiting room, toting a now subdued Rhiannon. "She had a shot," he explained sheepishly before Ivy wrenched away from me and hurtled herself at her child.

Rhiannon's chin wobbled and she immediately started crying again as she saw her mother, extending her arms in a universal gesture my already maternal heart recognized.

And yearned for, as much as it made me ache.

"There's my darling. There's my sweetheart. Mama's here. I'm here, baby. I won't ever leave you again, I promise." Ivy cradled Rhiannon gently, brushing her ginger curls away from her flushed forehead.

August and I exchanged a glance over Ivy and Rhi, the moment plunging me back into the past to the day of the baby's birth. He was so good with her. So good with Ivy as he rubbed his sister's back and told her softly what the doctor had said. But his eyes remained riveted on me.

If I had to say one moment had changed everything between us, Ivy's baby's birth had been the start.

"Rory's on his way," I said into the momentary silence. "He's catching the first flight back he can."

"Yeah, he called. We spent a few minutes crying and going crazy while I drove here." Ivy let out a sniffly laugh. "He tried to be strong of course, but I heard him sniffing. Said he had a cold. He loves her as ferociously as I do." She tugged her daughter's blanket up more tightly around her. "Isn't that right, Rhi-Rhi? Daddy's hurrying here to see you. He'll be here to put you to sleep tonight." She sighed. "First, we have a prescription to get."

Again, my gaze clung to August. It was impossible not to think about what kind of father he'd be to our child. Would it be a girl or a boy? Better question—would I be a hopeless mess every time he or she got a skinned knee or the flu?

I hoped not. Practice made perfect, right? In time, I'd find a modicum of chill.

If not, August would be there to be my balance. As he'd been today. As he was so often lately without even realizing it.

Just don't get too used to depending on him. He said he wanted to be involved in the kid's life, but the baby hasn't arrived yet.

The baby wasn't even confirmed. I was late, but I hadn't taken a test. Not quite yet.

"I can drive you back. Kinleigh can take my truck."

Ivy waved him off. "You guys have done enough. Surely you have a better way to spend the evening, right?" She looked between us, her expression probing.

What was she getting at?

"I called August when I didn't know what to do with the baby. He has more experience with her," I said quickly.

"Right."

"He does. He's her uncle, isn't he?"

"And you're basically her aunt."

I crossed my arms. "He babysits more often."

August remained stoically silent. Funny how I didn't appreciate that quality in him as much right now.

"Just saying I'm sure you guys want some privacy. I mean, to be alone." Ivy's voice was even, but her eyebrows were on the verge of waggling.

"I'll call Mom and see if she can meet you at the house." August withdrew his phone from his jeans. "Just until Rory gets there."

So August wasn't even making a pretense of going back with his sister. He let her make statements that somehow sounded pretty freaking incriminating and just rolled with it.

Sounded like Ivy's brother in a nutshell.

"I'll go get Rhiannon's carrier." Before anyone could argue, I snagged Ivy's keys dangling from her jacket pocket and rushed out of the waiting room and down the hallway to the double doors that led outside.

We'd gone into the hospital without the carrier, newbie parents that we were. We weren't even that yet technically.

Despite my desire to run a hand over my belly and to give in to the urge to buy another one of those pee sticks, I had no concrete reason to suspect anything. Sure, my breasts seemed heavy in my bra. My nipples were almost sore. I was so tired, on the edge of cranky.

My body was sending out signals. Some of them might've been due to the stress of hiding far too much from too many people I lo—

Cared about.

Some might've been wishful thinking. But if not, if August and I having sex at truly Olympic levels had worked this quickly, everything was going to change.

Maybe even me.

I crossed the lot to Ivy's car and unlocked it. I was getting the carrier out of the back when a cool, purportedly friendly voice made my whole body turn cold.

"Kinleigh, is that you?"

I jerked so hard I hit my head on the ceiling before hurriedly backing out of the backseat. Just as that nightmare upper crust voice had confirmed, in front of me stood Percy Maitland. Tall, lean, impossibly rigid in every way with his shock of dark hair that dipped into brown eyes and lips that curled too easily into a sneer. But he wasn't doing that now. He was far too interested in the item I'd been wrestling with.

"Hello, Percy. How are you?"

"Doing quite well, thank you. And yourself?" He smoothed a hand down his already impeccably placed tie as he cast a glance into the still open backseat of Ivy's car.

"Fine." I was pretty sure I stuttered on the reply and I hated myself for it. For feeling about five inches tall with the hole in the sole of my shoe as I'd been the day Percy had glided into the shop I'd been stocking shelves in so many years ago. His suit then had been top of the line, just as it was today. He'd worn Italian loafers then and now and expensive cologne followed him like a signature.

The same. Always the same.

Just as you are. Same not good enough Kinleigh, pretending you've earned your place.

"Do you have a baby?"

I hadn't expected that question at all. Instead of saying no, instead of saying anything at all, I let out a sound that bordered on a hiccup.

"Yes." August somehow appeared at my side and took my elbow.

I stared up at him, as perplexed at his sudden presence and how he'd known to agree to the lie—yet another lie, at least as far as we knew at this very moment—until I noticed the man in black standing beside a limousine parked at the end of the lot. The driver's attention was squarely centered on Percy, who couldn't seem to decide if he wanted to focus on me or August.

Or Ivy, cradling her beautiful, now sleeping daughter with the red hair so like her own—or like mine when Ivy stepped forward and wordlessly passed the baby to me.

My eyes filled and I started to shake my head, but she pressed her lips into a fierce line as she determinedly offered up her daughter.

Ivy knew who Percy was. I'd told her the story of my ex a long time ago. Leaving out some details of course, like how deeply he'd scarred me with the way he'd dismissed and dumped me. But she knew the Maitland family. Everyone in the Cove did. They were wheelers and dealers and power brokers that even the likes of the Hamilton brothers couldn't quite rub shoulders with—and they were one of the richest families around.

"She's yours?" Percy frowned, his dark eyes narrowing. "And yours?" he asked August, who merely stepped closer and wrapped his arm securely around my waist. The warmth from his body made me want to burrow into him. To let him shield me from the world.

I'd never had anyone who wanted to. It had always been me against everyone else. Fighting to prove my worth and that I belonged. I'd started out as the outsider foster kid, but I'd finally made something of myself.

August didn't answer him. I didn't either. I couldn't. Because August was tipping my chin up with his free hand, his thumb exerting gentle pressure against the corner of my mouth. As if he was searching for the lever to get me to open up for him and let him in.

With those intent green eyes on mine, I couldn't do anything else.

His lips were so warm and soft. He didn't push. Didn't demand. Just coaxed me so sweetly to accept what he offered while the baby between us let out a gurgle.

She wasn't the only baby between us. I knew it with a certainty that had me leaning up for more, lost in his kiss and his touch and the wonder he wrapped around us like a cloak that would never ever let anything in but light and heat and promise.

"Mine," he whispered as we reluctantly drew apart, and I knew the word was for me alone. It trembled on my tongue to give it to him in return. I couldn't help myself. It might've even slipped out if Rhiannon hadn't grabbed a fistful of my hair and tugged hard enough to make me yelp.

All at once, I remembered our audience. Ivy. Percy, who'd mercifully turned to go back to the car. I didn't know if he'd been visiting someone in the hospital or just ambulance chasing for his law firm.

And for once, I realized I truly didn't care. He was my past, dead and buried.

What he'd left behind and embedded in my psyche would be harder to root out and dispose of. But I was trying. Goddess, I was trying so hard.

I just needed a little more time.

"Kinleigh." Ivy's soft voice brought me back to the present with a thud.

She didn't sound mad or accusatory. She was every bit as patient as her brother, at least on the surface. But her blue eyes were wounded.

I started to explain. It was all for show. She had to understand we'd kissed to kind of give the middle finger to Percy. Even if he'd long ago moved on with someone named Priscilla—yes, I'd ferreted out that fact years ago—and even if they'd bought a townhouse together—I'd also dug that up—and owned a Shiz Tsu named Sally—yeah, found that out too. It was amazing what someone with long, lonely nights could unearth online.

An easy explanation was right there.

Oh, August, aren't you the sweetest for helping me out. Thanks, buddy, old pal. Here's your baby back, Ivy.

Scene over.

I just couldn't form the words. Couldn't look at August and dismiss the significance of that kiss while what we'd made together was inside me. At that instant, I almost would've dared any test to prove me wrong.

But I also couldn't declare my feelings either. Not when my emotions were hot and edgy and my faith that this would last was so shaky.

I'd never had any good role models growing up. Nor did I know how to be the sort of woman August could devote himself to. The idea of ever disappointing him was crushing.

How could I expect his trust when I didn't even trust myself?

So I didn't say anything. I returned Rhiannon to her mother and leaned toward Ivy for a long hug that I hoped conveyed what I couldn't say. Not only about August this time. About her too.

I love you. Please understand. Please don't hate me.

You're both all the family I have left.

TWENTY-ONE

THE FIRST PART OF THE DRIVE TO KINLEIGH'S WAS MADE IN SILENCE. I hadn't even turned on the radio.

What was there left to say when I'd just met—sort of—the man Kinleigh had allowed to help her become a shell of herself? He'd torn her down with words she'd not only listened to and believed, she'd made them into a life motto and slapped them onto a T-shirt.

Some rich prick who hadn't even introduced himself to me or done anything but look through me as if my only use was as the possible father of Kinleigh's progeny.

Seemed to be a lot of that going around right now.

Every time I slid a glance her way, she was cupping her stomach. It probably wouldn't have been noticeable to anyone who hadn't been trying to plant a baby in her for almost a month and a half now. But I saw far too much when it came to Kinleigh Scott.

And yet not enough to understand all the reasons she was so quick to push me away.

Regardless, we'd been working on this long enough that she could give me a progress report for how I was doing. Because, yes, I was the caveman who expected results when I went without a condom.

Even if I wasn't sure this whole plan wasn't insane. If I wasn't insane to agree to it.

But God, I ached to see her belly full with our baby.

How could I get angry with her for allowing Percy-flipping-Maitland to jerk her around when most of the time, I was no better? She didn't tear me down with words. Far from it. Her most often wielded weapon was indifference.

"When are you going to take a pregnancy test?"

Her head whipped toward mine and the hand protectively wrapped over her stomach flexed. So much for giving her time. "I will when it's the right moment."

"You haven't, have you?"

"Do you really think I'd take one without telling you? We're in this together."

"Oh, really. If we are, then why does Ivy know that punk ass's name and your history with him when I don't?"

"I told you what he said."

"Telling me what he said when you were drunk and your guard was down is not the same as a rational, adult conversation about our exes when you're sober."

"What about Serafina?"

The name was like a blast from the ancient past. "What about her?"

"You think I wasn't around when you kept pingponging back and forth out of her bed? Ivy said she yanked your chain all the time."

"Yeah, well, you'll notice we aren't together anymore. We haven't been for quite a while. You'll also notice I never mention her, never see her, never even think about her until you brought her up. Unlike your ex who I just watched render you speechless. You so badly wanted to impress him you even let me kiss you in front of my sister and God and country, so that says the hold he still has on you."

"He wasn't the reason I couldn't speak. He thought I had a baby. That Rhi was mine. And you and Ivy—"

"We made sure he understood you were loved. It's nice to do that for someone, you know?" I hated, absolutely hated, the edge to my voice, but it couldn't be helped.

I'd tried to put a choke-chain on my impatience and irritation for weeks now. I understood that I'd been blessed to come from a decent family with good, hardworking parents, an amazing sister, and a halfway respectable brother. Not everyone had such a secure foundation. I *got* that. But Kinleigh never spoke of her family, which was the only tip I had that she'd had a difficult home life. She never gave me anything about herself that didn't involve taking off my damn pants.

"I really appreciate you two stepping up for me. I understand that someone like you can't grasp how my confidence could be knocked by Percy."

I tapped my thumbs on the wheel. By nature, I was not a violent man. Today was testing that theory. "Percy is the most inane name I've ever heard. And what do you mean, someone like me?"

"Someone who has a solid base. You've never had to struggle, August." Her prim tone rankled the last nerve I had that wasn't already pissed the fuck off.

"You think I've never had to struggle? Look at the last few months. I can say you are very wrong."

"Speaking of inane, you think Serafina isn't? Isn't that a Disney princess?"

"Difference is I didn't make her my excuse for not living my life."

She fell silent, her cheeks leaching of all color, and I wanted to rip out my tongue and feed it to the hounds the snooty Mrs. Whaley was walking three-deep across the street.

I didn't want to hurt her. Anything but that. The idea of Kinleigh in pain caused an answering reaction inside me. I wanted to give her everything. Make her eyes light up and hear her laughter and offer her anything she'd ever dreamed of. Right every wrong, even the ones she wouldn't tell me about.

But she wouldn't let me, and I didn't know what she could've done that would have stung more.

Once we reached Kinleigh's place, she unclicked her seatbelt and climbed out. I didn't know if she wanted me to leave. That was probably a good guess, since she went inside without even glancing back at the truck.

I couldn't leave her like this. Couldn't leave *us* like this.

We'd been trying for weeks to build something. Beyond the child we wanted to bring into the world, I knew we were creating something of our own too. Sometimes the steps we took were so small no one could see them. *I* couldn't even see them most of the time.

But I knew she was trying. I knew she loved my sister, and whether or not she would ever admit it, she felt something for me too.

I turned off the ignition and dropped my head into my hands. Forcing her feelings out of her was never going to work. A promise demanded wasn't a promise at all.

It took me a couple minutes to get myself back in line enough to follow her inside. When I knocked on her door, I was prepared for her to not answer or to flip me the bird before slamming the door in my face.

What I wasn't prepared for? For her to grab a handful of my shirt and drag me inside.

She booted the door shut and boosted herself up on my hips, fusing her mouth to mine as her arms locked around my neck. Her taste poured into me—the fizz from the soda she'd had at the hospital while waiting for Rhiannon to be examined, the burst of fruit from her lip gloss, the wild hint of more that was simply Kinleigh. I clung to her because I was afraid I'd wake up alone in my bed, and I honestly wasn't sure I'd survive it.

We stumbled into the living room. Fell onto the couch, still kissing, hands roaming, buttons flying, zippers sticking. A couple of tugs and it loosened. Thank fuck. She scooped her hand into my jeans and boxers to find me hard and straining. Ready for her as if I'd been born for exactly that.

I expected even in the midst of madness for her to roll her hips and take me inside—we had a purpose, after all—but that flash of pale skin above her waist was a sin I couldn't resist. I was so fixated on touching every bit of her I could reach that I didn't grasp where she was headed until she'd shimmied down the sofa and her thong-clad ass was in the air, her airy skirt slipping down her body to pool at her waist.

And her mouth was around my cock, sucking hard, one hand gripping my shaft and the other toying with my sac. Teasing me with her nails while she drew on me with enough heat and pressure to make me fist the cushion.

"Baby, I can't last."

Between the worrying and the fighting and the fucking dream of having Kinleigh's hot, wet mouth clasped around me, I was too close to the edge already. My thigh muscles bunched beneath her as I sunk a hand into the thick ropes of her hair to guide her where I needed her to go. Farther, faster. She went, her big blue eyes never leaving mine as she pleasured me. Her tongue dipped into the slit on the head of my dick and my touch grew rougher. I couldn't control it. Couldn't keep from watching her perfect ass bounce in time with the strokes of her hand and her mouth.

The tingle at the base of my spine warned me to stop. Stop flexing my hips. Stop fucking her throat. Stop rocking toward a moment we couldn't come back from.

In so many ways.

If it wasn't about a baby, it was about us. Just us.

"Kin, I'm going to come."

I waited for her to climb astride me and finish things the way we meant to. My balls were so full, my length throbbing. But she kept right on sucking me, adding another layer of torment when she reached down to fumble her breast out of her bra to pluck at the beaded tip. She made a deep sound of almost pain and I would've stopped her if she hadn't started circling her nipple restlessly. I covered her hand with mine and helped her, squeezing her flesh, absorbing her moans humming around my length.

Dropping my head back, I let out a shout as she took me exactly where she wanted—straight into a dark, drugging place where all that existed was Kinleigh drawing out every drop of my release. She swallowed again and again while I shook and gripped her fingers like the last lifeline to my sanity.

But she didn't release me then. She kept right on licking me, sliding her tongue up and down to chase whatever she'd missed.

All I could do was groan and pray that this never ended.

That *we* never ended.

When she finally slid her body up mine, I rued the few pieces of clothes left between us. We'd rushed and skipped steps and now her soft, used lips were teasing mine, transferring my taste mixed with hers as if it was ours to share. I cradled her face between my hands, pouring my gentleness into her the same way I'd fed her my anger and hurt. Cherishing her to erase the harsh words I would wish forever I could take back.

"Kin," I whispered, tracing my fingertip over her swollen mouth. "I lo—"

The sound of crackling filled the room. "Kinleigh? Are you there?"

For one final instant, Kinleigh kept moving against me, her body flowing as sinuously as water against my spent shaft. She drew back, the flush of arousal fading from her cheeks.

"Ivy?" She covered her mouth with her hand and frantically shook her head.

I should've been far more relaxed. My jagged edges should've been dulled. But my cock was already hardening again, and beyond that, the white-hot ball of frustration in my gut hadn't gone anywhere. She'd soothed it, soothed me, but nothing had changed.

My sister's voice on a speaker was enough for her to go ice-cold in my arms.

"Yeah, it's me. Sorry I'm doing that Alexa drop in trick again. Is it a bad time? If it is, you could just tell me, and I'll leave you alone to do... whatever. But if you don't tell me, I'm going to be really pissed because seriously, hasn't this gone on long enough?"

Kinleigh's gaze swung to mine as I nodded although my sister couldn't see me. And thank God for that, since my state of undress was inappropriate, to say the least. But she was about to hear me.

As was my girl.

246

"Yes, it has." I didn't lower my voice when Kinleigh rose to yank on her blouse and tugged her skirt back into place. I couldn't stand the fear that telegraphed on her face, and I didn't have the slightest clue if what I was doing would help or hurt even more.

But I had to do it. No more waiting.

"August?" If I wasn't mistaken, my sister didn't sound surprised I was at Kinleigh's. Far from it.

"Yeah. It's me."

I shut my eyes. I just hoped for the sake of her sanity—and mine—that she hadn't dropped in to Kinleigh's living room any sooner than she'd made herself known.

Dear God.

Ivy didn't ask why I was there. Somehow she already knew. Granted, I'd kissed the hell out of her best friend at the hospital, but still. Putting it together with some of the odd little looks and comments she'd made recently, it all added up.

"You know we're together, don't you?" I asked while Kinleigh buried her face in her hands much as I'd done in my truck.

The difference was I'd been at the end of my rope. She didn't realize it yet, but this might be the thing to finally free us.

"Yeah." Ivy sounded hurt. "I just don't know why you've been lying all this time."

"It hasn't been that long," Kinleigh began.

"Since the wedding," Ivy corrected. "That's pretty long to me. Three months? Really? And you thought you were pregnant and didn't tell your best friend?" She let out a sharp laugh. "At least I thought I was your best friend."

Kinleigh turned her face away but not before I saw the accusations fly across her face. She looked as if she'd been slapped.

By me.

"I didn't tell her." When Kinleigh wouldn't meet my gaze, I shook my head. "Ivy, did I tell you one damn thing?"

"No. You lied to me every bit as much as my best friend. Really makes me feel good. What I don't understand is why. Do you both trust me that little?"

"We trust you. Kinleigh just somehow thought you wouldn't be happy."

Kinleigh rose and walked out of the room, taking a chunk from my chest with her.

"Are you freaking kidding me? When Rory and I heard, I basically wanted to beg you two to try again for a baby. That would be unreal." She sniffled. "At least it would've been, if anyone had bought a clue and realized I want nothing more than for you to be happy. If you're happy together, bonus round for me. Another cousin for Rhiannon would be wonderful, since God knows Caleb won't ever settle down. Like…ever."

I laughed at the truth in that statement as I sat up and stuffed myself back into my boxers and jeans. Talking about having babies with my baby sister while my dick was hanging out was skating too close to about fifty lines.

Then the rest of what she'd said hit home.

"Wait a second, when you and Rory heard what? How did you hear anything? From who?"

Kinleigh chose that moment to reappear, her face scrubbed of all makeup. My cock still jumped in my jeans as if I hadn't come ten minutes ago. She lifted a brow at my obvious erection as she sat at the opposite end of the couch, but she didn't say anything.

Neither did I. I just moved toward her and wrapped my arm around her shoulders and kissed the top of her head. She was board stiff, but I didn't care. We were having this out once and for all. Time to let the chips drop all over the damn place.

And my sister still wasn't spilling.

"Ivy? Hello? How does Lucky Charms know about my sex life?"

"We were at the bed and breakfast, okay?" Ivy blurted. "We figured we'd use the time you guys were babysitting to—"

"Don't say it." I covered my ears. "Do not violate the fragile balance of my well-being that comes from imagining the stork visited my baby sister."

Ivy laughed and I was almost positive Kinleigh joined in. Quietly. Since it was better than her sobbing in the corner, I'd take it.

When I dropped my hands from my head, I took one of hers between mine and rubbed her knuckles. She was so cold. Freezing.

She's afraid, you asshole. What she's been all this time.

I just didn't understand why. Ivy and I weren't monsters. We just wanted to love her. That was all.

But she wasn't relaxing. If anything, she was turning a lovely light shade of green.

"I don't feel bad for you though. How do you think I feel imagining my brother and my best friend having sex?"

Kinleigh and I looked at each other. Her expression said clearly *told you so.*

Until Ivy spoke again.

"If you think I hate it, you're wrong. I kinda skip imagining the actual process part, because icky, but the fact that it's you two, that you guys are together, well, that makes me ridiculously excited. It's basically the most amazing thing ever. Minus my own wedding, giving birth to Rhi, and opening Rolling Cones of course."

It was my turn to give Kinleigh a *told you so* glance of my own.

Not that Ivy's declaration had helped much. Kinleigh didn't seem any more at ease. Worry lines pinched her forehead and her lips were pressed so tightly together they were white.

"Anyway, Rory had gotten into town early that day. Of course we wanted some alone time, so if you and Kinleigh were watching Rhi anyway, why not take advantage?"

I grunted.

"So we get there and Rory decided to check the app so he could see the baby. Because he missed her that much. Isn't that the sweetest thing?"

"Ivy," I warned. "What app?"

She cleared her throat. "So, um, we have the entire place wired with cameras and sound."

"What?" I was pretty sure I roared it. "What kind of perverts are you two anyway?"

"Oh my God, does your mind live in a sewer? It's not for that. It's for the baby. You know, Rory's into the audiovisual side, and this was a prototype for the system for the house when it's done so we can make sure Rhi is safe. He wanted to be able to check on her from his app when he's not home. Just that day, well, we both got more than we expected. I can't believe you didn't tell me you could've knocked up my bestie. And Kin, that whole baby convo in the car the next weekend when you got wine wasted. Do you have any idea how hard it was for me to act like I didn't know anything?"

Kinleigh chose that moment to escape. I couldn't begrudge her leaving the room. I wished I could too. Thank God we hadn't done anything too lewd that day at Ivy's.

Physically, we'd behaved perfectly. I'd just mentioned us fucking half a dozen times and she'd taken a pregnancy test.

I covered my face with my hand. No big.

"What baby convo in the car?" I demanded. It was about the only way I could act when I couldn't get the idea of Rory and Ivy listening to my private conversation with Kinleigh out of my head.

"Look, I know you're mad we overheard. We didn't mean to."

"Did you turn it off?"

Ivy cleared her throat again. "Not exactly?" A thud echoed across the speaker. Then another. "Look, I couldn't find out the goods any other way. God forbid either of you tell me. So I took matters into my own hands."

"And Rory's hands."

"I swear, he didn't say one thing about you not hitting the mark when he did the very first time."

I growled.

Kinleigh reappeared in the doorway, my ancient red sweatshirt dwarfing her as she clutched her belly. "So, uh, yeah, that might actually not be true."

TWENTY-TWO

I STARED AT HER BEFORE JERKING TO MY FEET. "WHAT'S WRONG?"

"I'm sick. Tossed my cookies twice." Kinleigh rubbed her hand over her mouth. "My boobs are sore too. Big time. I barely could stand when you touched—" She shut her eyes. "Whoops. Sorry, Ive. Blame the evening sickness. Maybe."

I crossed the room to her, already forgetting everything but the reality standing before me. That the loveliest, most irritating, most perfect woman in the world was looking up at me with hope and nerves and emotion in her eyes. She lifted her hand to touch the spot behind her ear with her tiny ladybug tattoo and I had to swallow hard before I dropped to my knees. I couldn't speak, so I just laid my cheek against her stomach and closed my eyes.

Someone let out a sob. I wasn't entirely sure it wasn't me.

"Oh, Kin! Are you serious? Oh, God. This is literally the *best* news. Eeeep!" She broke the sound barrier with a cheerleader-worthy squeal. "I'm coming over. Did you take a test? Can we take it together? I'm coming. Don't do anything until I get there." A pause. "Make sure you're both dressed. There are boundaries, you know." *Click.*

I grinned up at Kinleigh, well-aware my eyes were wet. So were hers, that sunwashed blue that never failed to make my heart skip. "She gets excited."

"I hope I'm not a disappointment. I'm pretty sure it's a lock. But on that small chance I'm wrong…"

"How long?"

"What?"

"How long have you suspected?" With Kinleigh, anything could be possible—from an hour to a week to more. Her poker face belonged on the Las Vegas Strip.

She swallowed hard and scooped her hand through my hair, her touch so gentle that it eased the part of me that wanted to insist on hearing her every truth. "I haven't taken any tests. I have one. I just didn't."

"So you can't see the negative again."

"No. More like I know it's going to be positive, and once I see it in black and white, everything changes." She swallowed audibly again. "I feel the differences in my body. I *know*, August."

Staring up at her, feeling her utter certainty permeating into my bones, I knew too.

Holy fuck, I was going to be a father.

For real.

With shaking fingers, I pushed away the familiar cotton of my sweatshirt and undid the buttons on her button-down shirt to spread the sides wide. Her stomach was still so flat, the pale skin dotted with freckles. I pressed a kiss just above her navel and she sucked in a breath, quick and deep.

"It's early for the practice to be kicking in," she whispered, feathering her fingers through my hair again.

I didn't hear her at first. I was too busy trying to see with my X-ray eyes if there really was a baby inside her. In the meantime, I was quite happy molding my hands to her belly to see if there was even the most minute of changes. Already I was beginning to know her body so well.

"You're right," I murmured, awed. "You are changing."

Her eyes overfilled and a tear slipped down, splashing on the back of my wrist. I reached up to smear them away, finally really comprehending what she'd said. "Wait. You don't think this is from—but it was negative. You took two tests."

"And I thought I got my period, but now I don't think so. Oh, goddess, I have to sit."

Before she could move, I stood and scooped her up, making her release a watery laugh as I carted her to the couch and set her as carefully as spun glass on my lap. When she would've buttoned her shirt, I slid my hand into the gap, cupping her stomach as protectively as she'd done in the car.

I should've known. Even when she didn't tell me things, I could pay more attention.

If I wanted to be with Kinleigh—and I did—I was going to have to.

"Anyway, I had a little spotting and I assumed it was my period, but it was super light and didn't last very long. I figured it was just stress making it weird."

I didn't even let her finish before I was rising again with her in my arms. "We should get you to the doctor."

Her laughter stopped me in my tracks. "It's after hours now, and we don't even know I'm pregnant yet."

"Yes, we do," I argued. "You said you were and I see it."

"You see it?" She gazed down at the slice of her stomach revealed by her open blouse. "I don't see anything."

"Yeah, well, I spend more time in that particular area than you do. Some nights a damn lot of time." And I didn't mind when she blushed, because it was the truth.

She could never say I didn't keep her well taken care of, that was for certain.

"The bleeding was weeks ago and it wasn't much. I got it right after I took the tests."

"You mean—whoa." I sank back to the sofa, still holding on to her.

"Yeah, whoa. So maybe, just maybe you did hit the mark the first time. Or *we* hit the mark. The male doesn't cause pregnancy alone. Just a FYI to all you penis-wielding members of society." She shook her head again. "Then again, John Gideon's trick condom probably played a part too."

"It was a real condom."

"So you think. Could've been five years old."

"You really think he got that little action?"

"I haven't considered it. But I got pregnant somehow. Maybe I'm all wrong and it's from practice. Maybe the condom slipped. So many maybes. But I'm choosing to blame John."

"It could've been my incredible thrusting powers."

She rolled her eyes. "Goddess save me."

There was one point I just couldn't let go. "But the tests..."

"Tests can be wrong. Could've been a little too early." She ran her fingertips along my scruffy jaw. "Also, as an aside, I shouldn't be turned on by the way you can hold me as easily as a sack of potatoes while standing up and sitting down, but I kinda am. Good thing I'm not nauseated anymore."

I shut my eyes and dropped my forehead to hers. The timing for this was so crazy. Probably all wrong. I should wait until I was certain she wouldn't mix it up with my excitement over the baby.

Holy shit, was I excited. I could barely sit still. But that wasn't why I was about to say what I was going to say.

This moment was all about Kinleigh.

"I love you. So much it makes me act like a jackass." I felt the shock go through her body, but I didn't stop. Now that I had the freedom to say the words that had been lodged like a splinter in my throat for too many weeks, I wasn't backing down. "You're going to think it's because of the baby. No, the reason I wanted to have a baby with you is because I love you. I've probably always loved you."

Her lips trembled. "Why?"

"Why?" I repeated dumbly.

"Yes, why? I've been so scared of losing everything that all I've done is push you away. I set up this baby goal thing because, I think, I wanted to have you in a safe way." A soft hitching laugh escaped. "Well, and I did—do—want a baby too. But if I had one, deep down I wanted it to be yours."

If she'd pledged undying devotion to me, I couldn't have been more floored.

She brushed tentative fingers through my hair. "You're easy to lo— care about," she added, thereby deflating my momentary joy.

Not entirely, since she'd just admitted to wanting my baby. But she was Kinleigh, so she always had a pin at the ready.

This pin was that she couldn't say the word *love*. I wasn't even convinced she didn't feel it for me. Saying it was harder. I got that. I'd wait.

I'd wait forever if I had to.

"Why do I love you?" I picked up her hand and kissed her fingertips, one by one. "Because you can turn a pair of worn-out jeans into a masterpiece."

"Huh?"

I had to laugh. "You have a vision. An eye for seeing how to remake the broken into something new. Something special. You have a way of unearthing all the hidden nooks and crannies that were overlooked. Someone else might see a pile of junk. To you, it's a treasure."

She curled into me, laying her head on my shoulder. I only gripped her hand harder.

"Even though you're so good at finding beauty, you've never seen what Ivy and I do when we look at you. What so many people in this town do. You don't see your wit or your kind heart or your wicked sense of humor, when you relax enough to laugh. You don't see that I'd be willing to wait forever for you to realize you love me, because I know there will never be anything better than being one of Kinleigh's treasures."

She made a sound caught between a laugh and sob, and my chest ached as if she'd pummeled it with both fists.

"Oh, August. Don't worry, I brushed my teeth," she added before she pressed her lips to mine.

Arousal and need and longing swam into me in equal measure. On top of them all was love.

I cupped her head, taking her mouth in a kiss that was deep and sweet, long and slow. The kind of kisses we hadn't had nearly enough of.

That was going to change.

Dimly, I heard Kinleigh's door opening and a flurry of footsteps a second before my sister's delighted laughter. "Yay, I got here just in time to see the credits-worthy kiss."

I eased back and rubbed my fingertips underneath Kinleigh's eyes. She was still crying silently. I hoped they were mostly happy tears now, but I just didn't know. "No, we're not to the credits yet. We still have a test to take."

Kinleigh laced her fingers with mine as she held out her other hand for Ivy, who rushed over to take it. "And I have a story to tell you." She bit her lip, glancing between us in turn. "Both of you."

TWENTY-THREE

KINLEIGH

I WASN'T SURE IF IT WAS NERVES JUMPING IN MY BELLY OR IF IT WAS THE remnants of a soda and stale coffee cake. Though I'd have to assume all of that was out of my system at this point.

Baby.

I was really pregnant.

Goddess, all this time?

I let go of Ivy and her brother and with shaking fingers, I quickly did up the buttons on my shirt and zipped up August's hoodie. I didn't want to own up to how many nights I'd fallen asleep with the soft cotton wrapped around me like a security blanket.

I turned toward Ivy. "Is Rhiannon okay?" I'd meant to ask before, but it had been pure chaos.

"Rory won't put her down, so they're both sleeping in the rocker." She curled her fingers around my hand again. "Now stop stalling."

I gripped hers back. "Yeah, okay." I swallowed tightly and glanced at August, who slung his arm around my shoulders and tucked me closer. Immediately, his warmth seeped into my bones. It wouldn't make the telling any easier, but there was nothing but trust in this room and I wouldn't waste it.

"It's not like it's a long drawn-out story."

"It doesn't matter, we just want to hear it." Ivy laced our fingers tightly.

"I was a foster kid for a while. My mom—if you want to call her that—wasn't exactly the most loving woman. Most of the time, she left me alone or just ignored me. Those were the good times."

"Oh, Kin."

"There are far worse stories out there. She never hurt me. Not physically. She was just not there. I'm not sure why she even had me, to be honest. Then finally, she got tired of me." I looked down at the folds of my skirt. The echoing click of her heels was the last thing I remembered. Not her voice, not her perfume, not even her face.

"Anyway, she left me with a priest in Syracuse. He was kind to me. Gave me my first peanut butter and jelly sandwich. I'll never forget how lovely he was. After, I bounced around between a few foster homes."

"How old were you?"

August's deep voice brought me back. "Thirteen, I think. My birthday wasn't really a thing. Just another day. In those years, everything sort of blurred together."

"Piece of crap."

I tightened my fingers around Ivy's. "She was just...a void. I didn't look back on it. I just tried to do things on my own. I found a way around the system. I started sewing the hand-me-down clothes I got from the other foster kids. At first, I did alterations so they fit, then I made a few bucks because I used the material to make other things. Hair ties, book covers—whatever I could to make a few dollars so I could buy more and make more."

"And Kinleigh's Trunk was born," Ivy said between sniffles.

I patted her hand. "Yeah, thank the goddess for free apps. The more business I did, the more things I could buy at the Salvation Army or swap meets. I made friends where I could, couch-surfed and then met some art students in college. They didn't care how old I was. All they cared about was how quick I was with a needle. I helped with costume alterations and mending in exchange for crashing in a spare room. I didn't care where." I ignored Ivy's gasp and how August stiffened behind me. "Eventually, I saved enough for a shitty apartment, and I got my GED so I could get a job."

August rubbed his thumb along the back of my neck in soothing circles.

"Oh, Kin." Ivy's voice cracked. "I can't believe I didn't ask you more questions."

I shrugged. "I didn't want you to. It's easier to be the hardworking girl with her own business than to see those pitying looks when people find out I'm a foster kid."

"But I'm not just anyone. And I don't care. I mean, I care." Ivy swiped away tears. "But it doesn't matter where you came from. You're just my sister, my bestie, my person. Well, Rory is my person too now, but you'll always be the first."

I leaned forward and hugged her. "That day you came to my trunk party was the first time I'd ever felt like I met someone who mattered. Then you gave me a family. Annie loves me more than any dream mom I could ever make up."

"She does love you. We all do."

"It was just easier starting over. When I saw that window in my building, I knew it had to be mine." I turned to August and cupped his face. "And you were the annoying older brother who was so bossy. When we both wanted a storefront—well, it was just perfect. I could have everything I ever wanted."

He caught my wrist and brought the palm of my hand up to his lips. "You were everything I ever wanted. I was just too blind to see it at first."

"I'm really good at making people not notice me."

"Oh, I noticed." He hauled me in close. "I always noticed."

I laughed into his neck. "Liar."

"I'm not supposed to look at my sister's friends. It's just asking for drama, but I always noticed, Kin."

I sniffed and tipped my head back. "I hate crying."

Ivy giggled and threw herself into our little circle. "I hate it too, but now I get a sister for real. Not that it wasn't—"

I hugged her back. "I get it."

"But you see why I was so scared, right?" I tucked my chin on Ivy's shoulder. "I just have a really bad track record with guys."

"I'm not some guy," August said gruffly.

"No, you're way worse. You're Ivy's and I couldn't hope for you to be mine too."

He hauled me back onto his lap. "I am yours though. I am."

"I know." I hung onto him because as much as it scared me, I wanted it to be true. So very much. Hope was terrifying, but there was a little bit of it growing inside of me—I just knew it. And my little baby would be so blessed to be a part of this family.

"Ugh, you guys are the cutest. Disgusting, but the cutest."

August laughed. "Thanks, Ive."

"Now I need to go home to my baby, but not before you take that test."

Nerves crept up my shoulders. "I—"

August pressed a kiss to my temple. "It's time, Kinleigh."

"I don't have to pee."

"You always have to pee," Ivy said and crossed her arms.

Okay, that was a fact. I guessed that would be even more fun when the baby started bouncing on my bladder.

I slid off August's lap, tucking my fingers into the cuffs of his sweatshirt.

"Is that mine?"

From the sly way he asked, I was pretty sure he knew the answer. But August being August, he always had to tease me.

I kind of loved it.

"It used to be," I said and headed toward the bathroom.

I pulled down the test I'd tucked behind my tampons and Q-tips. I was pretty sure I'd only need one of those things for the next few months. "Now don't show me up in there." I patted my belly. "I know you're in there and you need to make those pink lines show this time."

"Are you talking to yourself in there?"

I jumped at August's question. "Why are you being a creeper?"

"Do you want me to be in there with you?"

"I think there should still be a few mysteries in our relationship, Becks."

"Okay. Yeah, sorry. I'll be right out here."

I couldn't keep the smile off my face as I read the box for the hundredth time—just in case. I did my business and wiped down my sink before setting the little white wand down on a pile of toilet paper.

I washed my hands and opened the door. August's large shoulders blocked the doorway.

"Is it positive?"

"It takes a few minutes."

"Right." He curled his arm around my waist. "So I can kiss you then?"

"Your sister—*ummf.*" He lifted me onto my toes and that was that. I had to admit, it was a better way to spend three minutes and some change than pacing.

When he finally put me back on my feet, I was a little wobbly for more than one reason this time.

He pushed me aside and went for the wand, but I already knew it was positive. That certainty was a warm glow inside me. I smiled at Ivy down the hallway as he let out a whoop.

I wondered what Luna would say my aura was like right now. I'd go with a joyful, contented pink. Or maybe a rainbow. Was that possible?

August lifted me up to swing me around and we crashed into Ivy, who was crying and hopping up and down. The best kind of insanity.

It felt so much better than the worry and the fear that had dominated the night. First with my niece and then facing all the things I never wanted to let into my present.

The past would always be mine, but it was much easier to deal with now that it was out in the open.

With the happy news shared and too many tears shed to count, we finally managed to get Ivy to go home to her husband and baby.

Afterward, August took me into the shower and we washed away the hospital funk, the last of the pain stagnating between us, and all the bad memories.

Then we tumbled into bed together. There was no need to hide anymore.

I couldn't have been more grateful.

He curled in behind me, sliding a heavy arm over my middle. He slipped his palm over my still mostly flat belly. "You need a bigger bed."

I laughed into the dark. "I think I know a guy."

"Yeah, you do."

"Kin?"

"Hmm?"

"I think we should tell our parents about this little ladybug tomorrow."

My eyes stung again. Ladybug. Goddess, I didn't deserve this man. Then the rest of what he'd said sunk in. "*Our* parents?"

He pressed a kiss to my neck. "Now more than ever."

"Do you think they'll be happy?" I whispered.

"I think we're going to make their year."

"Are *you* happy?"

He pulled me in tighter. "You and this ladybug are everything I ever wanted."

The silence stretched and his breathing evened out behind me.

"I love you, August."

There, that wasn't so hard. Maybe next time I'd even be able to say it when he was conscious.

TWENTY-FOUR

I<small>T TOOK A LITTLE LONGER TO GET MY MOTHER ON BOARD WITH A FAMILY</small>
dinner. I could have blurted out our surprise—and almost had about
four times, but I wanted to actually make things special.

And if the scent of brownies down the hall was any indication, so
did Kinleigh. I was pretty sure that was one of the few things she
knew how to cook.

"Becks!"

I smiled as I pulled the small bookcase out of my closet where I'd
tucked it away a few days ago. It was nice to hear that name again.
The easy Kinleigh used to call me that all the time. The one who
didn't get all squirrelly and weird about secrets and feelings.

Emotions between us were still a little hit or miss. A lifetime of
holding herself back wouldn't be cured just because I'd said, "I love
you". Especially since we were still so new.

But I was a patient man. I could spend three days sanding a
bookcase.

I smoothed my hand down the case in point.

Not to mention the carving. I tucked my thumb into the new bit
I'd just done. A lot of people used 3D printers to make logos these
days, but there was nothing quite as satisfying as carving into wood.

Well, maybe Kinleigh riding me with all that fiery hair bouncing around her shoulders. That was a damn fine way to start my day.

Her voice got closer. "You better be getting ready in there. We have to leave in an hour."

"That's a whole hour," I called over my shoulder.

"I don't want to be late." She flipped a sky-blue towel over her shoulder. "Oh, what's that? And haven't we talked about woodworking in the bedroom?"

I turned to her, sliding my hands around her waist. "It's a special little addition."

She peered around me, but I blocked her. She tilted her head up at me. "What are you hiding?"

"I've had this idea knocking around for a little bit." I stroked my thumb over her middle. "About the same time we had the first little scare."

"Which ended up being a valid one."

The fact that we were pretty much through the first trimester already was a little terrifying, but I was doing my best to not freak out every minute of every day. "Well, I've been working on a little something. Originally, I was going to put it into the shop and see how it went, but I couldn't quite bring myself to show it to anyone." I pulled her farther into the room and let her see the bookcase.

"Oh, August." She went right to the newest carving. Her fingers shook as she traced the ladybug.

"I was thinking of doing a line of kids' furniture. Ladybug Treasures."

She squatted down in front of the bookcase and smoothed her hand over the wood before bringing her fist to her mouth.

"This one is kinda perfect for under the window. It can hold baby stuff on the shelves, some books, that kind of thing. I even thought about doing a converter changing table for the top—*oof*."

She launched herself at me. I laughed and held her tight as she sniffled into my shoulder.

"It's so beautiful." She pulled back and went back to the ladybug part of the logo. "For our bug?"

"Even before I knew she was a thing."

"We don't know it's a girl yet."

No, we didn't know officially, but I was sure. As surely as Kinleigh had known she was pregnant, I knew we were going to be having a little girl. Even if for our first sonogram, she'd been too shy to show us her gender right away. We could do bloodwork things to test it, but Kin wanted to be surprised.

At least until she couldn't take it anymore.

"So I'm guessing you like it."

"I love it. And now we don't even have to barter anymore. I did finish those pillows for you, by the way."

"I'm still open to favors—especially naked ones."

She rolled her eyes. "Making baby furniture in this town is a solid business plan."

I snorted. My creative lady was far more business-minded than people would assume. "Ya think?"

She gave me a narrow-eyed look, but she couldn't stop smiling. "Honestly, it's a wonderful idea."

"I'd love for you to help me with it. We work well together, Kin. And we could find ways to repurpose stuff you find to suit people who maybe don't want traditional baby furniture."

"Now you're going to make me cry." She dabbed at her eyes. "I told you we would make the best furniture together."

"So you did."

She went on her toes and kissed me. "I love it. Goddess, I have so many ideas running through my head. Do you know how many ugly bookcases I could make shine with baby stuff? With sweet, baby blankets tacked up along the back to hide ugly particle board. Not everyone can afford your beautiful pieces."

I tugged her back toward the bed and sat down. "No, but that's what makes us a perfect team. We cover everyone." I lifted her oversized garden party of a shirt. Just how many flowers could you jam into a pattern? I kissed her belly. "And we have you to thank for all this inspiration, my little ladybug."

She scooped my hair back in that way she had. Gentle and loving, with a little extra tug for good measure to make me look up at her. "I love you, August."

My eyes stung as I gripped her hips.

"I have for a long time. You make it so easy." She gave me a wry smile. "Most of the time. When you're not being grumpy or stubborn."

"Even when I'm being grumpy, I'm always going to love you, Kin."

Her lower lip trembled before she pressed them together.

"I really don't care if it takes ten years for you to really believe it. I'm going to show you every day." I pressed another kiss to her belly. "And this little ladybug will always be loved." I let her shirt fall back into place and pulled her astride my lap. "Just as much as her mama."

She cupped my face, kissing me softly. "How in the universe did I get so lucky?"

I stood with her in my arms. "I'll remind you of that on the grumpy days."

She laughed and wound her legs around my hips, her blue eyes lit with something other than tears now. "How long do we have?"

"You guys ready to go?" Ivy's voice floated down the hallway.

I groaned. "I can't wait for them to move into their house."

"You certainly changed your tune about that."

"Sharing a wall with my sister was only good to keep track of Rhiannon while Lucky Charms was out of town."

"He still works out of town, Becks."

"Now that I know about this drop in thing with the various apps, I definitely don't need her all up in my business. Especially when that means you and I get to have way more naked time." I squeezed her ass and let her slide down my body.

She gave me a squeeze back before she smacked my butt. "To be continued."

"Count on it." I nipped her lower lip. "We're back here," I called out.

"Are you clothed?" Ivy's voice was suspicious.

"No," I answered.

The footsteps stopped halfway down the hall.

Kinleigh shoved me away. "We're decent."

"I've got ice cream in the car for your brownies. Don't want it to melt. It's already hot in April, which means we're in for one hell of a summer." She peeked in the doorway. "What are we doing? I mean, you're clothed, so what else are we doing in here?"

"Come look at what August made. He's really outdone himself with this."

I flushed as Kinleigh waxed poetic about my craftsmanship. I wasn't exactly the guy who looked for praise, but it was nice to hear how much she loved it.

Two of the most important women in my life chattered about the future and expansive ideas about how much work they would be adding to my pile. They had their heads together over Ivy's phone like the sisters they were.

Ivy tugged her out of the room with talk of baby ice cream flavors and ways to overlap our respective companies. It looked like I'd created a monster with my initial idea. But it spoke of the future and that was just fine by me.

"August?"

"Yeah, coming." I opened the top drawer of my dresser and pulled out the last thing I'd worked on this week. I tucked the small gift into my inside pocket and followed them down the hall.

We rode together in Lucky Charms' loaded SUV. Rhiannon was back to her old self with the antibiotics taking care of her ear infection. The girls were still bouncing ideas back and forth. I managed to add a few to the mix, but they were definitely blowing past me with a business plan.

I'd probably have a contract proposal for the bank by noon tomorrow with the way they were talking.

We pulled up to my parents' ranch-style house. My dad was taking advantage of the sunny day. I could smell the barbecue as soon as I opened the door.

Kinleigh slid out of the backseat, uncertainty stamped all over her face. I held my hand out and she took it immediately. Lucky Charms handed me our bag with the brownies and…was that a salad?

Ivy came around with ten pounds of baby gear and a grinning

Rhiannon kicking up a storm in her baby carrier. Rory smoothly took the carrier and they fell into step together. They really were a solid unit.

I glanced down at Kinleigh and brought her hand up to my lips. "We're in this together now."

She nodded. "I know."

We bypassed the front door for the side yard, music pumping out of brand new backyard speakers thanks to their new son-in-law. *Suck up.* But I didn't mind the Fleetwood Mac vibe.

Caleb was running around with Bert, my dad's idiot dog. The dog spotted Kinleigh and sprinted to her, tripping on his big, goofy legs before he got to her. She dropped down in front of him and loved all over him. Bert tilted his head and tried to climb into her lap. That wasn't exactly a new thing, but the way he kept butting his head against her middle sure was.

I gave him a quick rub and wondered if he knew something was a little different too.

"There you guys are." My mother came out with a big bowl in her arms. "Caleb, get over here and help me set the table."

"Yeah, yeah." Caleb brushed the grass off his jeans before trying to take the bowl from her.

"Wash those grubby hands."

Caleb rolled his eyes, then planted a kiss on my mother's cheek. He gave me a look, then noticed that my arm was wrapped around Kinleigh's hip. "Finally."

Kinleigh blew out a slow breath.

"Give me that sweet grandbaby." My mother rushed around the picnic table. "It's been—oh."

"Hey, Ma." I slid my hand down to catch Kinleigh's.

Her eyes filled. "Oh, finally."

"What, did everyone know?" I muttered.

She hugged Kinleigh. "Of course we knew. You two were so blind. Or trying not to let anyone see, anyway."

Kinleigh's arms went around Annie. Her obvious relief eased her shoulders. "You're not mad?"

"Oh, heavens, why would I be mad? You're the perfect girl for my boy." She gripped Kinleigh's arms and set her back. "I'm just so glad you two finally got your act together."

"Right?" Ivy tipped her head against Kinleigh's shoulder.

"George, come out here," she yelled through the screen door.

"I'm prepping the steaks."

She shook her head. "That man. The steaks can wait."

My dad came through the sliding door. "They need time to marinate. Oh, well, there's my girls." He was more silver than blond-haired these days, but it seemed like semi-retirement was suiting him well enough. He already had a tan from golfing and there was no doubt he was happy to see every single person in the backyard. "What's the ruckus?"

"Kinleigh and August are finally out of the closet."

"Ma." I laughed.

Kinleigh dabbed at her eyes. "A little more than that, actually."

My dad gave Kinleigh a hug. "Oh? A proposal? Are we planning another wedding? Maybe this time we don't have to go all the way to Ireland." He winked at Rory. "Not that it wasn't lovely."

Rory set the carrier down and unbuckled Rhiannon. "No offense taken. I'll pass on customs nightmares."

Getting so many people to a destination wedding had not been the easiest feat.

Kinleigh immediately covered her middle. "Well, maybe a little more cart before the horse there too."

"No." My mother covered her mouth. "Oh, Kinleigh."

I pulled the little frame out of my jacket pocket and handed it to my mother. "Another Beck is going to be added to the family this fall."

She looked down, her eyes filling. "Oh, this is just the best news." She held the sonogram close to her chest, then looked down at it again. "Is that a…"

Kinleigh peeked over the edge. "You're just going to make everyone cry."

"Let me see." Ivy plucked the frame out of our mom's hands.

269

Our mom pulled Kinleigh close and there were tears and questions and laughter and more questions.

Ivy bumped me, the frame still in her hands. "Ladybug, huh?"

I hooked my arm over her shoulder. "I guess it's going to be a thing."

Caleb was sitting at the picnic table, digging into the bread and dip. "Don't expect me to be adding to the scoreboard. You get all your grandbaby wishes fulfilled by these two." Caleb pointed at me with a piece of bread. "I knew that cup was full."

Ivy frowned. "What the heck does that mean?"

"Ignore him."

"Crescent Cove water," Caleb muttered. "That's why I'm sticking to beer."

I didn't think I would be so happy to have two huge life changes on top of one another, but seeing Kinleigh laughing with a lap full of Rhiannon and my parents fawning over both of them was pretty amazing.

My chest tightened. That was my future right there. Our ladybug would probably have the same red hair.

I'd give Kin a little time to get used to all of...*this* before I asked her to marry me.

A few days.

Maybe.

EPILOGUE

KINLEIGH

Summer

UPSTATE NEW YORK WAS HAVING AN UNPRECEDENTED HEAT WAVE. AND of course it had to be the year I was pregnant. I dabbed the back of my hand against my forehead, then pushed my mask down.

Because of course I had to wear a mask while painting. Even if it was just touch-up paint. August was going to kill me for doing it without him, but I wanted to get the sky done on the feature wall in the nursery. I wasn't exactly an artist when it came to painting, but I could rock the heck out of a stencil set.

He'd done the rest of the room in a soft buttery yellow to highlight the gorgeous oak furniture he'd been creating for our little girl.

I winced and rubbed the side of my growing belly. "Soccer-playing girl."

Ivy was busy getting her own house put together. They'd finally moved into their dream home. Luckily for me, it was only a few streets over. I'd never dared to dream that our kids could grow up together, but now it was all I could think about.

They'd be honest to goddess cousins.

I had a family and everything was almost perfect.

I tucked the paintbrush into the handy little can that kept it from drying out because there were still some places I needed to fix, but it would be good for now. I quickly washed my hands and put myself into some semblance of order.

Being just about six months pregnant meant there was a lot more of me to get organized these days. Not that August seemed to mind. We'd found some inventive ways to deal with the added belly clearance.

I checked my phone. August was on his way home and would be here any minute.

I pushed the bookcase over in front of the window and set the changing table converter on top. The pads of my fingers found the little carved trio in the corner. Our hallmark for the baby line of furniture.

August already had a waiting list for his designs, just like I knew he would.

But our baby would always have the first one.

I stacked the little pile of baby clothes on the changing table and added the carved ladybug August had gifted me for my birthday. It had more than one meaning for me now.

Finally, I set the little onesie in the middle of the table on the blue polka dot pad.

I'd spent all morning embroidering the little ladybug on the white cotton. Not to mention the words below it. Part of me wondered if I should wait until the baby came, but the other part knew it was right.

Will you marry my mama?

"Kin?"

"Back here," I called.

I curled my shaking fingers into my palms.

"I smell paint. Did you paint without me? I told you I didn't want you on that ladder without me around."

I turned around, leaning against the padded edge of the table. "No ladders here, Mr. Bossy Pants."

Goddess, he was pretty. Even if he was getting bossier every day.

He reached above the doorjamb, stretching out his back. He wore a hunter green T-shirt that was minus some sleeves. Sawdust dotted his tanned shoulders and he had his toolbelt slung low on his hips. A tiny pencil was tucked behind his ear and there was more sawdust on his backward ball cap. "You've been busy."

"You too, evidently."

"Yeah, I just delivered the princess bed over at Sage's. Star loved it."

"Of course she did."

He grinned. "You have to say that. You're biased."

"No, I'm just right. Come here."

He looked down at himself. "I'm dirty."

"I don't care."

"Not what you said yesterday."

Goddess, he was a pain in my butt. "That was yesterday."

He lowered his arms and walked in. "Looks really good." He stopped in front of me and dropped a light kiss on my lips. "Exceptional."

"Sweet talker."

He waggled his eyebrows and went for a deeper kiss.

I twisted my fingers into his shirt and nearly caved when he unbuckled my overalls. I pushed him back. "Hang on a second."

He licked his lips and tugged me closer. "We have the whole house to ourselves, we don't have to hang on a second anymore."

I laughed. "I have a question to ask you."

"Anything." He brushed my nose with his.

I moved to the side and turned him toward the changing table.

He grinned down at me. "I love it. Are we setting it up for the Instagram page or something?"

I laughed. "Look closer."

He looked down and his hand went to the onesie. "Kinleigh." His voice was hoarse.

"It could be cute for the Instagram page too, with the—"

August swung me up into his arms. "Yes. Yes, I will marry Ladybug's mama." He let me down and pressed his forehead to mine. "You beat me to it."

I framed his face and thumbed away the tear that escaped down his cheek. "I love you so much, August Beck."

He shoved his hand into his pants pocket and pulled out a box. "I've had this for about two months."

My eyes filled. "Two months?"

"Took a bit to get it made. My girl's not exactly traditional." He went down on one knee. "Not exactly how I meant to do this, but then again, we make our own timetable, don't we?"

I pressed my fingers to his chest. "We sure do."

He flipped the box open. "Marry me, Kinleigh Scott."

Laughing, I simply let my tears flow. There was a simple diamond set with two tiny gold ladybugs on either side. "Yes."

He stood and our hands were both shaking as he slid the ring on. "I love you, Kin." He gathered me in and I held him tight.

I never believed it would be possible to be this happy. But I was about to do my best to make sure this was just the beginning.

Our beginning.

You know that little confession that Ivy knew Kinleigh and August were a thing? Well…there was a wee little scene we took out of the book, but it was just too good to leave on the cutting room floor. Sooo…we made it into a bonus.

Turn the page to read HUMMINGBIRD HIJINKS!

Thanks for reading MY EX's BABY!
We appreciate our readers so much!
If you loved the book please let your friends know.
If you're so inclined, we'd love a review on your favorite book site.

As Sheriff, I'm used to being in charge. But handling changing diapers and two a.m. feedings? Not so much. Luckily, my best friend Gina stepped up when someone left a baby on my doorstep. Now I can't seem to remember we're supposed to be just friends...

After HUMMINGBIRD HIJINKS check out a special sneak peek of DADDY UNDERCOVER - Crescent Cove Book 9.

HUMMINGBIRD HIJINKS

A RORY & IVY BONUS SCENE

My wife was driving me absolutely mad.

Ivy's head bumped against mine as we stared down at the fuzzy camera angle on my phone. Since I traveled so much and we had a newborn, I'd made sure our temporary home was outfitted with cameras and sound so I could check in on my ladies whenever I had a chance.

Plus, the extra cameras gave Ivy a measure of security. They were basically amped-up baby cams with apps that could be viewed remotely on our phones. Everything was top of the line. I was in the music production business, so we definitely hadn't skimped in this arena.

When we moved into our new home—if it was ever finished, for feck's sake—we'd have it similarly outfitted.

The technology was welcome, and along with its intended purpose, we made good, inventive use of it. But a man could only make do with his hand and his wife's lovely visage on camera for so long.

I just hadn't expected that swinging into town early would lead to *this.*

We had a rare hour alone, and I'd even braved a chat with Sage at the Hummingbird's Nest bed and breakfast to secure a room for our brief meeting of the minds.

And other things.

Ivy running out to get a food whatmajig had been pure blind luck. I'd asked her to meet me for a quickie, and instead, I'd had to witness today's daily soap courtesy of August and Kinleigh's secret love affair.

"Oh, no. No. She's not pregnant." Ivy sniffled. "How can this be?"

"Hate to burst your bubble, my ginger fairy, but outside of the Cove, women aren't pregnant every day."

"Actually, statistically, you're wrong. Many women find out they are pregnant every day all over the world. If they didn't, the population would die out."

"Thank you for that tidbit."

"But oh God, her face." Ivy jabbed the screen with her candy pink nail. Nails I wished were currently scraping down my back, not making points I was too jet-lagged to appreciate. "She's devastated. We missed some of the finer points of their conversation in the hall because the speakers suck, but—"

I narrowly resisted informing her how incorrect she was. The extremely high bill for their installation proved that. "The speakers do not suck. Kinleigh and August weren't in the proper position for maximum auditory relay."

"They probably didn't know they were on *Candid Camera.*" She waved a hand. "Doesn't matter. I know them so well, I can tell. Look at them. They're trying to be so brave. I can't believe this." She shoved her fist against her mouth not unlike the worried Kermit the Frog gif I'd been sent via text message from my idiot best friend Ian Kagan upon landing.

"Why is this picture so sketchy? Does your phone need an upgrade?"

I gritted my teeth. "This is a brand-new phone."

"Hmm, the microphones at home are cutting out. Was there some part of the package you missed?"

"I missed no part of any package." Especially the one in my pants on the verge of sobbing, if manfully sized penises did such things. "Perhaps they should stop mumbling and moving around so much."

She'd already rolled on. "Even poor Rhi feels their pain. Look at my baby."

"I'm looking," I muttered. "You mean our baby."

She made a noise in her throat.

I hated listening to our baby wail while we sat on the four-poster bed we had not used for fornication or anything but a swift kiss hello before we'd tuned into the movie of the week. That was my fault. I'd wanted to ensure my child was in safe hands with Auggie. Turned out she was, minus the epic tears, and he was trying to make some offspring of his own.

More information than I needed to know.

"She's so upset. God, does Kinleigh want a baby?"

"I can't answer that question. She seemed to indicate no."

"You're just pretending to care."

"No, not even that."

At my wife's murderous expression, I exhaled. "Look, I do care. Of course I do. Kinleigh is very sweet, and she's Rhiannon's godmother. But your brother lives to harass me, so I'll probably have to work up some caring there."

Her face softened. "He's just making sure you take good care of me."

"I do, don't I?"

She slid a little closer to me on the bed and slid her hand around my neck to toy with the ends of my hair. "You need a trim."

"Ivy, don't I?" I repeated.

"I'm an adult woman with a job. I can provide for myself."

"Of course you can. You know what I'm asking."

"Right now? No. You're doing a crappy job taking care of my needs. Because I'm horny as hell and you insisted on turning on this app when I could be galloping on you like a bull at the fair."

I groaned and closed my eyes. "It was supposed to be a one-minute check on Rhi, not all...*that.*"

"Oh, no, he's leaving. He's walking out. Did they fight and I missed it?" Ivy leaned in again and grabbed my phone, holding it up close to her face. "Kinleigh's rocking Rhi. I think she's on the verge of tears."

I wanted to cry too, but for the utterly shit reason of wishing to have some alone time with my wife.

I understood this desire made me a terrible person. So what if I'd just returned after weeks away and wanted nothing more than to sink inside Ivy and get lost for a little while? There were bigger considerations right now. I truly didn't want Kinleigh to be hurting. Even if the reason she was must be because Auggie's mystical sperm hadn't produced an heir on the first try.

"He can call me Lucky Charms all he wants. One of us is magical, and it isn't him."

My wife scowled at me, her bright red hair framing her utterly cherubic face while flames shot from her eyes. "You did not just brag about your prowess in impregnating me."

I shrugged. "If the condom doesn't fit..."

She whacked me and it hurt. I wasn't even surprised. When a man loved and lived with a woman, he soon understood where her stress points were located. My beloved's involved her family, as well as my sperm and its notable ability to hit the target with little effort.

There was a reason Ivy was on birth control yet I was still going to use condoms. And it wasn't because I appreciated double-bagging.

The Irish had many claims to fame. Apparently in my family, that included remarkably motile spermatozoa.

"Yours won't fit because you won't need one today. Where is your sense of empathy? Is it stored in your dumbstick?"

"My 'dumbstick' as you so lovingly called it misses you just like the rest of me. Do you know what hell it is being away from you and my angel for weeks on end?"

Her eyes welled up. "I've missed you too. We both have."

"Eh, she barely knows who I am at this point." I waved it off. "But she will. That day will come when she can say 'Da' or 'Pop' or—"

"Buzzy," Ivy said with a sniffle as she rubbed her nose.

"Pardon?"

She gave me a misty smile. "That's what I called my daddy when I was a baby. I think there was a bee flying around one day and my mom kept yelling about buzzing and I took that for my dad's name. At least that's the story she told."

"I'd accept Buzzy. Anything from that little girl in my direction and I'm sold."

Ivy leaned her head on my shoulder. "I didn't know Kin wanted a baby. Or that August did."

"I'm not sure they do. They said they didn't want one."

"Their mouths said that, but their eyes said something else."

Of course they did. Leave it to Ivy to intuit meanings I couldn't grasp.

"Oh my God, Rory, they actually had sex. Like...together. They were *naked*. My brother and my very best friend in the whole world." She sat up straight. "Can you believe it?"

"That's usually how it goes." I had to grin at her. "Wonder if they were snowed in too? Since that's what worked for us."

She started to smile before lowering her head. "But it didn't work. She's not having a baby. I wanted Rhi to have a cousin."

I tilted Ivy's head upward. "She already has a cousin, remember? From my sister. And someday my brother will have some, and August probably will too. Caleb, however, is doubtful. He's a rogue one."

Then again, once upon a time, I'd felt the same way about myself. If any town could fix him right up, it was Crescent Cove.

For the sake of his singledom, I hoped he was layering himself in protection like my love layered noodles, cheese, and sauce when she made lasagna.

"Right, but I want him to have one with *Kinleigh*. Now that they put the idea in my head, it has to happen. I can't imagine Kin thought I might not be happy. It's my biggest dream come true."

"Excuse me, I thought marrying me was your biggest dream come true, never mind having our baby. And of course starting your own thriving business," I added hastily.

"Yeah, yeah, sure, but Kinleigh has been my best friend for years, and she's lonely. I don't want anyone to be alone, especially someone I love." She wrapped her arms around her belly. "My brother too. He spends so much time locked in his shop, working with so much care on his projects. He deserves to find what we have."

My wife knew just what to say to tug me kicking and screaming onto her side. Not that I could deny the wisdom in her words.

"I was once lonely too," I murmured, stroking a hand down her long red hair. I'd loosened it from its updo the moment we'd kissed hello. She was a vision, and I wanted nothing more than to bury myself inside her while her ribbons of silky hair surrounded us in our own private world. "Then I drove into Crescent Cove in a snowstorm and found my own happy ending, complete with a ginger fairy. Who gave me the prettiest ginger baby in all the world."

Her smile was worth all the time apart. All the long nights and empty days, no matter how filled they were with work.

She slid her hand up my chest. "I love you, Rory."

"Almost as much as I love you, a stor." I tossed aside my phone and dipped my head to her luscious mouth, more than ready to enjoy this pleasantly firm king-sized bed.

"You want to them to be together too. Don't you?"

I rubbed my thumb over her lower lip. "Of course. Anything you wish. What do you have on under these jeans?"

"Sadly, just granny panties. I didn't expect to see you until tonight after I changed."

"Don't fret. It's what's under the panties I love."

"*Mmm.* So you agree?"

I slid my hand up the slight slope of her belly to cup her breasts through her top. I loved the changes in her body since she'd had our baby. Those extra curves just made me want her more. "Aye. Auggie hasn't exactly made my life easier with his bollocks, but if he finds love, maybe he'll stop poking in our pram."

"He doesn't need to *find* love, silly. He has it. They have it."

"They do?"

"Duh. They had sex. You know what that means, right?"

"Yes, they wanted to shag."

She sighed and dropped back her head, revealing her long neck. I moved my mouth to it, sucking slowly, and finally, she released a soft moan that meant she was present in this room and not plotting Auggie and Kinleigh's fertility schedule. I pinched her taut nipple, relishing how she pushed her breast into my palm.

About time.

"They're perfect for each other. We need to support them in… every possible way. Oh, that feels good."

"Mmm-hmm. Are you wet for me, love?"

"So wet. If this happens, she'll be my sister for real."

I dropped my forehead against hers in defeat. "Should we just go back?"

"No. They can wait." She linked her arms around my neck and pressed her full breasts to my chest. "Let's screw like sleep-deprived parents first."

DADDY UNDERCOVER

GINA

Working at the diner gave me a pipeline into the Cove. I was privy to all the town goings-on, and the hours had given me the freedom to play with a few side hustles over the years. Between working here and bartending at my sister's bar, I didn't want for cash. I preferred a simple life.

"*Mija!*"

I shut my eyes. Of course my family made that nearly impossible, but there was always hope in my heart.

I set my tray down on the counter before turning around with a bright smile. "*Mami.*"

Bonnie Ramos came at me like a freight train, enveloping me in her Lily of the Valley scent and freakishly strong arms. My mom was on a health kick which included food, yoga, and essential oils. I was pretty sure she was driving my father to his backyard garden oasis more each day. I only hoped he survived the winter since upstate New York meant snow as high as the rooftops some seasons.

She pushed me away and squeezed my upper arms. "You're melting away to nothing, *nena.*"

"I am not, Ma."

She *tsked* then turned her attention toward my very pregnant sister. "Ahh, *corazoncita,* come sit down." My mother shooed me away and hauled my sister, Erica, up the aisle and toward a booth.

"Ma, I'm fine." Erica huffed out an exasperated breath as she waddled in our direction.

She'd given up the pretense of closing her jacket. Instead, she used colorful scarves to keep warm. I knew because I'd crocheted three of them for her in the last two weeks. Along with a bunch of baby things she'd find out about soon enough.

"Will you fit?" I winced. "Sorry."

"Hateful," Erica muttered and slid into the booth, but no, her belly definitely didn't fit. Rather than crying about it, she just inched back and put her feet up on the bench-style seat. "My feet are swollen anyway. Might as well put them up."

"I can't believe Jake let you out of his sight." I hurried around the counter for a black coffee for my mother and a large glass of iced water for my sister. Thankfully, it was just before the lunch rush was due to start.

I skirted around the other waitress working today. "Polly, I'm going to take ten."

"Okey doke." She thumbed off a Lifesaver and the familiar clack of the candy rattling in her mouth followed me as I headed back to my family.

I set down their drinks and slid in next to my mom. "What brings you guys in?"

"I've been craving gravy fries."

"We were shopping at Kinleigh's and August's for a bassinet, and she dragged me over here." My mom pulled out a single Splenda from the small dish near the window and dumped it into her mug. "That's too much salt for you."

Erica rolled her eyes at our mom. "I don't care."

"*Nena,* your ankles are already softballs."

"I don't care," she repeated. "I want fries with extra gravy and extra salt. And ice cream." Erica made a big mound with her hands. "Maybe some fudge and extra cherries."

I laughed. "Ivy's truck is only open on weekends, but I can

probably get some from the café. The kind we have here isn't exciting."

She grabbed my arm. "Could you?"

My mom pointed before she lifted her coffee to her lips. "Do not encourage her."

Erica collapsed back against the wall. "I am—"

My mom's mug snapped on the Formica table. "You are not the only woman who has been pregnant. Just look around this crazy town, *mija*. Jacob indulges you too much!"

Erica shoved on her sunglasses, but not without a quick eye roll that I was pretty sure our mother didn't see.

Good thing. We both had a healthy fear of our mother—and for good reason. Being an amalgamation of Italian and Spanish meant she was definitely the hothead of the household. Our father could hold his own, but she viewed his behavior as similar to my brother-in-law's.

We also had our dad wrapped. Put a little Elvis on and sit with him in the garden and we could pretty much get what we wanted. Not that I knew that from prior experience or anything.

Erica rested her hand on her belly. "Jake realizes that a happy wife means a happy life. That and he doesn't like the couch."

"I'll remind you of that when it takes three extra months to lose the baby weight."

Erica's finger tapped on the red sweater stretched to capacity, but she didn't bother replying. We could never win an argument, so it wasn't worth trying. Especially this one. My sister was glowing with health, but she was indeed a bit more swollen than usual.

I knew she'd curse my name later when she was in the bathroom about eleven times, but it would cover us both. "Drink that whole glass of water, and I'll make you a batch of my poutine."

Erica's eyes widened as she sat up straighter. "What?"

I shrugged. "I convinced Mitch to let me do the ordering for this week. I changed up the menu a little."

She lifted the water glass and drained it, and then pushed it my way. "Well, hurry up."

I swallowed a laugh when my mother gave me a narrow-eyed look.

"What is this poutine?" My mother's accent slid out like she was saying something disgusting.

"Heaven," Erica said with a smile.

Welcome to the Ramos family of crazy. There's so much more to come in the book. Sheriff Brooks has no idea what he's in for!

Now Available
For more information go to www.tarynquinn.com

CRESCENT COVE CHARACTER CHART
BEWARE...SPOILERS APLENTY IN THIS CHARACTER CHART. READ AT YOUR OWN RISK!

Ally Lawrence:
Married to Seth Hamilton, mother of Alexander, stepmother of Laurie, best friends with Sage Evans

Andrea Maria Fortuna Dixon Newman:
Mother of Veronica 'Vee' Dixon

Annie Beck:
Married to George Beck, mother of August, Caleb, and Ivy, grandmother of Rhiannon and Vivian

April Finley: Executive assistant to Preston Shaw
Friends with Ryan Moon and Luna Hastings

Arthur Maitland: Real estate developer

Asher Wainwright: CEO Wainwright Publishing
Married to Hannah Jacobs, father of Lily and Rose

August Beck: Owns Beck Furniture, later known as Kinleigh & August's Attic and Ladybug Treasures
Married to Kinleigh Scott, father of Vivian, brother of Caleb and Ivy

Beckett Manning: Owns Happy Acres Orchard
Brother to Zoe, Hayes, and Justin

Ben Sullivan: EMT/Drummer

Bess Wainwright:
Grandmother of Asher Wainwright, great-grandmother of Lily and Rose

Bonnie Ramos: Sheriff's department dispatcher
Married to Enrique Ramos, mother of Damien, Erica, Francesca, Gabriela, and Regina, grandmother of Samantha and Leo

Bryce Johnson: Professor
Best friends with Callum MacGregor

Caleb Beck: Teaches second grade at the Catholic school
Brother of August and Ivy

(Charles) Dare Kramer: Mechanic, owns J & T Body Shop, later known as Kramer & Burns Custom
Married to Kelsey Ford, father of Weston and Sean, brother of Gage

Callum MacGregor: Adjunct mythology professor/painter
Married to Ellie Lawton, father of Faith Mistletoe, brother of Lennox, Hudson, and Finn, best friends with Bryce Johnson

Christian Masterson: Sheriff's deputy
Brother of Murphy, Travis, Penn, and Madison

Cindy Ford:

Married to Doug Ford, mother of Kelsey and Rylee, grandmother of Weston, Sean, and Hayley

Colette Edison: Owns Every Line A Story, art supply and yarn shop

Dahlia McKenna: Designer/decorator who works with Macy

Damien Ramos: Carpenter
Brother of Erica, Francesca, Gabriela, and Regina

Doug Ford:
Married to Cindy Ford, father of Kelsey and Rylee, grandfather of Weston, Sean, and Hayley

Ellie Lawton: Hair stylist/works at Brewed Awakening
Married to Callum MacGregor, mother of Faith Mistletoe

Enrique Ramos:
Married to Bonnie Ramos, father of Damien, Erica, Francesca, Gabriela, and Regina, grandfather of Samantha and Leo

Erica Ramos: Owns Sharkey's
Married to Jacob Mills, mother of Leo, sister of Damien, Francesca, Gabriela, and Regina,

Finn MacGregor: Architect
Brother of Lennox, Hudson, and Finn

Francesca Ramos: Involved in the fashion industry in NYC
Sister of Damien, Erica, Gabriela, and Regina

Gavin Forrester: Real estate owner

Gabriela Ramos: Co-owner Hannah's Helping Hands
Sister of Damien, Erica, Francesca, and Regina, best friends with Hannah

Jacobs

George Beck:
Married to Annie Beck, father of August, Caleb, and Ivy, grandfather of Rhiannon and Vivian

Greta Conrad: Manager of the Rusty Spoon

Hank Masterson:
Married to JoAnn Masterson, father of Murphy, Christian, Travis, Penn, and Madison, grandfather of Carrington, Brayden, and twins Theodore and Elijah

Hannah Jacobs: Owns Hannah's Helping Hands
Married to Asher Wainwright, mother of Lily and Rose, best friends with Gabriela Ramos

Hayes Manning: Owns Happy Acres orchard
Brother of Zoe, Beckett, and Justin

Hudson MacGregor: Graphic designer
Brother of Callum, Lennox, and Finn

Ian Kagan: Solo artist
Engaged to Zoe Manning, father of Elvis, brother of Simon, best friends with Rory Ferguson, friends with Flynn Sheppard and Kellan McGuire

Ivy Beck: Waitress at the Rusty Spoon and owns Rolling Cones ice cream truck
Married to Rory Ferguson, mother of Rhiannon, sister of August and Caleb, best friends with Kinleigh Scott, friends with Maggie Kelly and Zoe Manning

Jacob Mills: Firefighter/Fire Code Chief
Married to Erica Ramos, father of Leo, brother of Kayla

James Hamilton: Owns Hamilton Realty
Father of twins Seth and Oliver, grandfather of Laurie, Alexander, and Star

Jared Brooks: Sheriff
Engaged to Gina Ramos, father of Samantha, brother of Mason

Jessica Gideon: Actress
Ex-wife to John Gideon, mother to Dani

JoAnn Masterson:
Married to Hank Masterson, mother of Murphy, Christian, Travis, Penn, and Madison, grandmother of Carrington, Brayden, and twins Theodore and Elijah

John Gideon: Owns Gideon Gets it Done handyman service
Married to Macy Devereaux, father of Dani and Michael, ex-wife Jessica Gideon

Justin Manning: Owns Happy Acres Orchard
Brother of Zoe, Beckett, and Hayes

Kellan McGuire: Lead singer Wilder Mind, solo artist
Married to Maggie Kelly, father of Wolf, brother of Bethany, friends with Rory Ferguson, Ian Kagan, and Myles Vaughn

Kelsey Ford: Elementary school teacher
Married to Dare Kramer, mother of Sean, stepson Weston, sister of Rylee

Kinleigh Scott: Owns Kinleigh's Attic, later known as Kinleigh & August's Attic
Married to August Beck, mother to Vivian, cousin of Vincent Scott, best friends with Ivy Beck

Kylie Fisher: Bartender
Involved with Justin Norton, lives in Forrester Apartments

Lennox MacGregor: Lawyer
Brother of Callum, Finn, and Hudson

(Lucas) Gage Kramer: Former race car driver, owns Kramer & Burns Custom
Married to Rylee Ford, father of Hayley, brother of Dare

Lucky Roberts: Works for Gideon Gets it Done Handyman Service

Luna Hastings: Works at Kinleigh's Attic,
later known as Kinleigh & August's Attic, tarot card reader
Friends with Kinleigh Scott, Gina Ramos, April Finley, and Ryan Moon

Macy Devereaux: Owns Brewed Awakening and The Haunt
Married to John Gideon, stepmother of Dani, mother of Michael, sister of Nolan, best friends with Rylee Ford

Madison 'Maddie' Masterson:
Sister of Murphy, Christian, Travis, and Penn

Marjorie Hamilton:
Ex-wife of Seth Hamilton, birth mother of Laurie

Mason Brooks: Owns Mason Jar restaurant
Brother to Jared Brooks

Maggie Kelly:
Married to Kellan McGuire, mother of Wolf, best friends with Kendra Russo, friends with Ivy Beck and Zoe Manning

Melissa Kramer: Owns Robbie's Pizza
Married to Robert Kramer, mother of Dare and Gage, grandmother of Weston, Sean, and Hayley

Mike London: High school teacher

Mitch Cooper: Owns the Rusty Spoon

Murphy 'Moose' Masterson: Game designer/construction contractor and owns Baby Daddy Wanted
Married to Vee Dixon, father of Brayden and twins Theodore and Elijah, brother of Christian, Travis, Penn, and Madison

Nolan Devereaux: Owns Tricks and Treats candy shop
Brother of Macy

Oliver Hamilton: Owns Hamilton Realty and the Hummingbird's Nest
Married to Sage Evans, father of Star, twin brother of Seth

Paisley Jones: Works at To Dye For hair salon

Penn Masterson: Graphic novelist
Brother of Murphy, Travis, Christian, and Madison

Regina 'Gina' Ramos: Waitress at the Rusty Spoon
Engaged to Jared Brooks, mother of Samantha, sister of Damien, Erica, Francesca, and Gabriela

Robert Kramer: Owns Robbie's Pizza
Married to Melissa Kramer, father of Dare and Gage, grandfather of Weston, Sean and Hayley

Rory Ferguson: Record producer/rhythm guitarist
Married to Ivy Beck, father of Rhiannon, brother of Thomas and Maureen, best friends with Ian Kagan, friends with Flynn Sheppard and Kellan McGuire

Ryan Moon: Artist and tarot card reader
Friends with Kinleigh Scott, Luna Hastings, and April Finley

Rylee Ford: Barista at Brewed Awakening
Married to Gage Kramer, mother of Hayley, sister of Kelsey, best friends with Macy Devereaux

Sage Evans: Owns the Hummingbird's Nest
Married to Oliver Hamilton, mother of Star, best friends with Ally Lawrence

Seth Hamilton: Owns Hamilton Realty
Married to Ally Lawrence, father of Laurie and Alexander, twin brother of Oliver, ex-wife Marjorie

Tabitha Monaghan: Owns Sugar Rush bakery

Tish Burns: Owns Kramer & Burns Custom, custom fabricator
Friends with Gage Kramer

Travis Masterson:
Father of Carrington, brother of Christian, Penn, Murphy, and Madison

Veronica 'Vee' Dixon: Pastry baker at Brewed Awakening, owns Baby Daddy Wanted
Married to Murphy Masterson, mother of Brayden and twins Theodore and Elijah, friends with Macy Devereaux

Vincent Scott: partner in Wainwright Publishing Industries
Cousin of Kinleigh Scott

Zoe Manning: Artist/photographer
Engaged to Ian Kagan, mother of Elvis, sister of Beckett, Hayes, and Justin, cousin of Lila Ronson Shawcross Crandall, friends with Ivy Beck and Maggie Kelly

as of 02/12/2021

CRESCENT COVE

Have My Baby

Claim My Baby

Who's The Daddy

Pit Stop: Baby

Baby Daddy Wanted

Rockstar Baby

Daddy in Disguise

My Ex's Baby

Daddy Undercover

Wrong Bed Baby

CRESCENT COVE STANDALONES

CEO Daddy

CRESCENT COVE BITES

Fireman Daddy

Mistletoe Baby

For more information about our books visit

www.tarynquinn.com

ALSO BY TARYN QUINN

AFTERNOON DELIGHT

Dirty Distractions

Drawn Deep

DEUCES WILD

Protecting His Rockstar

Guarding His Best Friend's Sister

Shielding His Baby

WILDER ROCK

Rockstar Daddy

Rockstar Lost

HOLIDAY BOOKS

Unwrapped

Holiday Sparks

Filthy Scrooge

Bad Kitty

Saving Kylie

For more information about our books visit

www.tarynquinn.com

ABOUT TARYN QUINN

USA Today bestselling author, *TARYN QUINN*, is the redheaded stepchild of bestselling authors Taryn Elliott & Cari Quinn. We've been writing together for a lifetime—wait, no it's really been only a handful of years, but we have a lot of fun. Sometimes we write stories that don't quite fit into our regular catalog.

* Ultra sexy—check.
* Quirky characters—check.
* Sweet–usually mixed in with the sexy...so, yeah—check.
* RomCom—check.
* Dark and twisted—check.

A little something for everyone.

So, c'mon in. Light some candles, pour a glass of wine...maybe even put on some sexy music.

For more information about us...
tarynquinn.com
tq@tarynquinn.com

QUINN AND ELLIOTT

We also write more serious, longer, and sexier books as Cari Quinn & Taryn Elliott. Our topics include mostly rockstars, but mobsters, MMA, and a little suspense gets tossed in there too.

Rockers' Series Reading Order

Lost in Oblivion

Winchester Falls

Found in Oblivion

Hammered

Rock Revenge

Brooklyn Dawn

OTHER SERIES

The Boss

Tapped Out

Love Required

Boys of Fall

If you'd like more information about us please visit

www.quinnandelliott.com

Made in the USA
Las Vegas, NV
19 July 2021